"You owe me no

Katherine looked over
Tears glistened in her beautiful eyes. "I *chose* to stay
to help you keep your home and shop for Howard's
sake. I'm not sorry."

Then she bent her head and kissed Howard's
cheek. The baby nuzzled at her neck, searching for
something to eat. It was the perfect picture of what
he had longed for, prayed for and lost.

"Now please hold Howard while I warm his bottle."
Trace's stomach knotted as she handed the baby
to him. Howard looked up at him and wiggled his
arms. He took a deep breath and lifted him to his
shoulder. The baby calmed, rested there against his
heart. So small. So helpless.

He looked at Katherine standing by the stove and
his heart lurched. She was so beautiful, so kind and
softhearted, so brave. He jerked his gaze away.

It was growing far too dangerous for him to be here
alone with Katherine and the baby every day.

Award-winning author **Dorothy Clark** lives in rural New York. Dorothy enjoys traveling with her husband throughout the United States doing research and gaining inspiration for future books. Dorothy believes in God, love, family and happy endings, which explains why she feels so at home writing stories for Love Inspired. Dorothy enjoys hearing from her readers and may be contacted at dorothyjclark@hotmail.com.

Books by Dorothy Clark

Love Inspired Historical

Stand-In Brides

His Substitute Wife
Wedded for the Baby

Pinewood Weddings

Wooing the Schoolmarm
Courting Miss Callie
Falling for the Teacher
A Season of the Heart

An Unlikely Love
His Precious Inheritance

Visit the Author Profile page
at Harlequin.com for more titles.

DOROTHY CLARK

Wedded for the Baby

Recycling programs
for this product may
not exist in your area.

® LOVE INSPIRED BOOKS

ISBN-13: 978-0-373-42534-1

Wedded for the Baby

Copyright © 2017 by Dorothy Clark

www.Harlequin.com

Printed in U.S.A.

Who can find a virtuous woman?
For her price is far above rubies.
—*Proverbs* 31:10

To my readers:
Thank you for your faithfulness. I love hearing from you! Your letters are so encouraging. I appreciate your kind words and most of all your prayers.

And Sam. Once again, from my heart—thank you!

"Commit thy works unto the Lord, and thy thoughts shall be established."

Your Word is truth. Thank You, Jesus.

To God be the glory.

Chapter One

Medicine Bow Mountains, Wyoming Territory
November 1868

Katherine Fleming looked away from the sheriff carrying Miss Howard's battered trunk toward the long, black carriage. The train lurched, rolled forward. She blinked the tears from her eyes and jiggled the crying, squirming infant in her arms. Poor baby. Two months old and all alone. Did he sense it? Was that why he was crying so hard?

"Shh…shh…don't be afraid, little one. Everything will be all right. I'll take care of you." Her stomach knotted. How could she keep that promise? She knew nothing of caring for an infant, and there was no one to ask. The last of the other women passengers had left the train here at Laramie. Panic struck. How far was it to Whisper Creek? That had been the destination on Susan Howard's ticket. Was she making a mistake? Would it be better for the baby if she turned him over to the sheriff in spite of her pledge to take him to his new father?

She looked back out the window, torn by indecision. It wasn't a mere pledge she'd made; it was a deathbed promise. Of course, she hadn't known at the time it would be impossible to keep. Miss Howard had begged her, muttered something incoherent about a letter with her last breath. The dying woman had been frantic about what would happen to her child, and so she'd made the promise to give her peace. But she had not found a letter among Miss Howard's sparse possessions. How could she take the baby to a man when she knew nothing about him—not even his name?

She frowned, watched the sheriff shove the trunk into the black carriage. And she didn't know Susan Howard; she'd never met the woman before she'd boarded the train. Surely that freed her from her promise. Oh, what did it matter? She held a helpless little piece of humanity in her arms. She couldn't abandon him. Her stomach churned. The thought of the baby being put in an orphan home made her ill. So many young babies died. She would simply have to do her best for him.

The wheels clacked against the rails. The train picked up speed. Her breath came easier. It was too late to turn the baby over now. He stiffened and let out a wail. She lifted him to her shoulder and patted his back the way his mother had instructed her to do.

"I'm sorry I'm not better at caring for you, little one. But I've had no experience at this sort of thing."

She cooed the words, patted and rubbed the baby's tiny back, feeling completely inadequate.

The infant burped, then fell asleep on her shoulder, his downy hair brushing her cheek, his breath a feathery warmth against her neck. Her heart swelled. She held Susan Howard's son close, allowed herself to pretend for a moment that Richard hadn't disappeared at sea—that they had married as planned and this was their child.

"Almighty God, please let Richard be alive and well. Please bring him home." Her whispered words were automatic. Only the smallest trace of her former faith remained after having repeated the prayer hundreds of times. It had been almost five years since the devastating loss of her lifelong love. It was a long time to hold on to hope. Still, she refused to let go of her last remaining strands of trust that God, in His mercy, would bring Richard home and fill the gaping hole his disappearance had left in her heart.

The passenger car jolted, swayed. She grabbed for the wobbling empty baby bottle and tucked it back into the baby's valise where it would be safe until she could clean it. Her fingertips touched paper. The baby's birth papers? Hope rose that it might be so. It wouldn't help her in her quest for his new father, but at least she would learn the baby's name. She pulled the valise closer, grasped the exposed corner of the paper and pulled it from beneath the baby clothes and diapers. It was a letter. Perhaps the one Susan Howard had been mumbling about. Her pulse sped. She pushed the valise to the end of the seat, slid close to the window and held the letter up to the fingers of sunlight that poked through clean spots in the film of soot.

My Dear Miss Howard,
I received your letter yesterday and am setting pen to paper this evening to tell you I am willing to accept your infant boy and raise him as my own. My acceptance of your infant was the last obstacle in the way of our proposed marriage arrangement. That detail is now settled.

Time is growing short. I am enclosing the train ticket you will need for your journey here to Whisper Creek. I am also enclosing money sufficient to meet any expenses you may incur.

All things necessary to carry out our arrangement will be in place upon your arrival.
With sincere gratitude,
Mr. Trace Warren

Katherine read the letter again, annoyed by the formal tone. A marriage *arrangement*? How emotionless. There was not a single word of warmth or kindness in the missive. How desperate Miss Howard must have been to have agreed to marry this cold man. And now Mr. Warren would be the guardian of this helpless little baby. If he still accepted the child.

She sat bolt upright, staring at the letter. What if he didn't? What if Mr. Warren refused to accept the baby to raise without the mother? Her excuse of keeping the infant to deliver him to his new father would be gone. Would she have to turn the baby over to the authorities? Her stomach flopped. What sort of legal situation had she gotten herself into? Well, there was no help for it now. And she would do the same thing again. Susan Howard had been desperately ill, and it wasn't in her to ignore the distress of a woman too sick to care for her baby. It had been the morally upright thing to do.

She folded the letter, reached down to tuck it back in the valise and spotted faint, shaky writing on the back. She held the letter back up to the window.

My name is Miss Susan Howard. I am ill, and without hope of recovery. I have an infant son, born out of wedlock, whom his father has disavowed, and whom Mr. Trace Warren of Whisper Creek, Wyoming Territory, has accepted to raise as his own child in this letter. I, therefore, give Mr. Trace Warren full custody of my baby, this day, the 19th of November, 1868, and ask only that he care for him with love.

Miss Susan Howard

The letter trembled in her hand. Tears blurred her vision. A sob caught at her throat. That answered her question. The baby was now Mr. Trace Warren's son. She hugged the infant closer, her heart aching for the young mother who had written the note giving her baby into the hands of a stranger. *She* couldn't bear the thought that the helpless baby might be unloved or mistreated. What agony Miss Howard must have suffered when she wrote those words.

She started to put the letter in the valise, decided it was too valuable to take a chance, that it might become lost or damaged, and tucked it in her purse instead. The baby whimpered. She placed her cheek against his soft, silky hair, lifted her free hand and cuddled him closer. "Shh… Don't worry, little one. Everything will be all right…shh…shh…"

The baby quieted, made tiny little sucking noises. She tucked his blanket closer around his little feet, felt the soft booties knitted by his mother. Tears stung her eyes. *I'll keep my promise, Miss Howard. I'll find Mr. Warren, and I'll make sure he will take good care of your baby boy, or—* Her thoughts froze.

She stared out the sooty window and rocked the baby to and fro with the sway of the train, thinking about that small word. *Or.* It had come unbidden from her conscience and her heart. What was she to do about it? Keep the baby? How? She had sold her home. Could she take the baby with her to visit her sister at Fort Bridger? Judith and her husband were still childless after six years of marriage. Perhaps they would want to keep the baby for their own.

Follow that still, small voice inside you, Katherine. The Lord will lead you.

Her pulse steadied. It was the advice her mother always gave when she went to her with a problem. Oh, how much easier this would be if she had the strength of her mother's faith to lean on. Her own faith had become tattered and frail. She sighed, leaned back against the seat, listened to the rhythmic clack of the wheels against the rails and tried to relax. A solution would present itself. At least she now knew the name of the man she was looking for.

* * *

Trace Warren halted the horse, climbed from the runabout and looped the reins over the hitching rail. Two quick blasts of the whistle on the approaching train rent the air. The mare stomped her front hoofs and snorted. He reached out and patted her neck. "It's all right, girl. It's only a noise. Nothing is going to hurt you. Or me."

He glanced at the train, focusing on the passenger car trailing behind the locomotive and tender. Bitterness surged. If he was supposed to have a wife and child, why couldn't it have been his own? Why were they lying in a grave in New York, while he was about to enter a sham of a marriage with a woman he didn't know and a baby he didn't want to care about?

He set his jaw, tugged his jacket into place and climbed the steps to the station platform. At least Miss Howard had agreed that they would live their lives as separate as possible while sharing the same dwelling. Thankfully, he'd built a large house! There would be no reason for accidental meetings.

The beam of light from the locomotive widened, swept over the depot then narrowed again as the engine rolled by and came to a stop. Steam puffed into the air, turning the station oil lamps into momentary blurs. He moved through the quickly dissipating vapor to stand at the bottom of the passenger-car steps and look up at the small platform. The porter opened the door then lit the oil lamp beside it. A young woman holding a swaddled baby and carrying a small valise stepped out onto the platform. His stomach knotted. He squared his shoulders, removed his hat and took a step forward. "Miss Howard?"

The woman started, gazed down at him. Her eyes looked like they were made from the petals of violets—petals picked on a frosty day. She shook her head. "No. I'm not Miss Howard."

"I beg your pardon." He glanced at the man coming out of the door behind her, made a small, polite bow and stepped back to clear their way to the station.

"Wait!" The woman descended, raking an assessing gaze over him. "Are you Mr. Warren?"

He gave a curt nod, his attention focused on the passengers exiting the car behind her—all men. He glanced back at the woman, more than a little put off by her cool tone. Her words clicked into his awareness. "How do you know my name?"

She lifted her hand holding the valise and braced the baby with her arm. "Is there somewhere we can sit down and talk, Mr. Warren? I am not Susan Howard, but I *am* the woman you are seeking."

He stared at her a moment, puzzling over her statement, then looked down at the bundle in her arms and nodded. "There is a bench on the platform out of the wind. If you'll permit me to assist you…" He took the valise, grasped her elbow with his free hand and guided her to the bench against the wall of the depot. "Now, if you would please explain, Miss…"

"Fleming. I am Miss Katherine Fleming from New York."

He touched the brim of his hat, dipped his head.

"Forgive me for being blunt, Miss Fleming, but I don't understand, how—"

"I met Miss Susan Howard on the train. This is her baby." Katherine Fleming took an unsteady breath, looked down at the tiny bundle then raised her gaze to meet his.

"And why do you have Miss Howard's child?" He glanced at the passenger car, irritated by this woman's interference. "Where is Miss Howard?"

"She passed away early this morning, Mr. Warren. They—they took her and her possessions from the train at the Laramie Station."

"She's passed away!" He jerked his gaze back to Katherine Fleming. Suspicion reared. Was this some sort of blackmail scheme? "Perhaps you would be good enough to explain the circumstances, Miss Fleming."

Her shoulders stiffened. "That's why I'm here, Mr. Warren." The baby whimpered. She patted its back and swayed. "When I boarded the train, Miss Howard was very ill. I tended the baby and cared for Miss Howard as best I could, but her condition deteriorated. She—" Pink flowed into Katherine Fleming's cheeks. She took a breath and looked full into his eyes. "When she knew her health was failing, Miss Howard told me the…conditions…of her baby's birth, and that she was on her way to marry you because you had agreed to raise the baby as your own. She begged me to bring her baby to you. I promised to do so." She took another breath and opened the purse dangling from her wrist. "I found this letter in the baby's valise." She held it up to him.

He took the letter, went taut. It was his last letter to Miss Howard.

"There is a note on the back."

Miss Fleming's voice broke. He glanced at her, saw the lamplight reflected by the shimmer of tears in her eyes and turned his letter over.

My name is Miss Susan Howard. I am ill, and without hope of recovery. The words struck the pit of his stomach like a hard-driven fist, froze the air in his lungs. He forced himself to read on, made himself concentrate on the details to calm the pulse pounding through his veins and roaring in his ears. He was the guardian of the child of a woman he'd never met! He folded the letter and slid it in his pocket to gain time to gather his shattered thoughts. Being an ex-doctor, he was accustomed to handling emergencies in a calm, deliberate manner, but this…this was beyond belief! He had a shop to run! What was he to do with an infant without a mother in a town where there was no woman available to hire as a nurse? Was this God's retribution for his turning away from his faith when his wife and unborn child died? Was the agony of his loss coupled with his guilt at being unable to save them not enough punishment?

He shot a venomous look at the darkening sky, forced the stagnant air from his lungs then glanced at Katherine Fleming—*Miss* Katherine Fleming. A wild notion flickered. He grasped on to the idea like a drowning man seizes hold of the flimsiest lifeline. He knew enough about women's clothing to know Miss Fleming's velvet-trimmed gray tweed coat was stylish and well made; the button shoes poking out from beneath the long skirt were the same. And her hat was an expensive one. Clearly, Miss Fleming would not be swayed by the offer of a generous wage. He would have to appeal to her humanity. It was obvious she'd become attached to the infant in her arms.

He glanced down the tracks. The train was still taking on coal and water. But time was of the essence.

"I've kept my promise to Miss Howard, Mr. Warren. So if you will—"

"Please, Miss Fleming, if you would grant me a few minutes more of your time, I need to talk to you. My agreement with Miss Howard—"

"Had nothing to do with me, and is none of my business, sir."

"I believe it is, Miss Fleming—because of the baby you hold." He looked down into her violet eyes, suppressed a tingling reaction to their extraordinary beauty and pressed his case. "My marriage agreement with Miss Howard was a business one. She needed a name for her son and a comfortable home in which to raise him. I need a wife—*any* wife." Those long-lashed, violet eyes widened, then narrowed. He rushed on before she could speak. "You see, I have signed a contract that states that if I am not married within six days from this date, I will lose my apothecary shop, my home and all I have invested in them. I am a widower, Miss Fleming. I am not interested in a personal relationship with any woman. Therefore, Miss Howard was to have been my wife *in name only*." The words brought color flooding into her cheeks. She rose to her feet.

"That's quite enough, Mr. Warren! I am not in the habit of—"

"Nor am I, Miss Fleming! But I have no choice in the matter. If I do not marry within six days, I and the infant you hold in your arms will be *homeless*. And, what is more, without my apothecary shop, I will have no means by which to support the child."

"But surely there is some way—"

He shook his head and looked her straight in the eyes. "There is none. I have told you I am not interested in any form of personal relationship with a woman, Miss Fleming. Therefore, I am asking if you, in your concern for the baby, would be willing to enter into an in-name-only marriage with me." Her gasp told him what she thought of his proposal. He rushed on. "It would be only temporary—until I can think of a way to save my shop and my home and make other arrangements for the baby's care. You see, Whisper Creek is, as yet, only the beginning of a town. There are no women available for me to hire to care for the baby."

Katherine Fleming was clearly shocked. She moved her mouth but no words came forth, only an odd sort of choking sound. He took a breath and laid out the rest of it before her. "There is one thing more. Should you agree to my *business* offer, we will have to act as newlyweds in front of others to keep Mr. Ferndale, the town founder and holder of my contract, from discovering the marriage is not a normal one." His bitterness boiled over into anger.

After two years of grief and loneliness that was the last thing he wanted to do with this far too attractive woman! He harked back to his doctor's training, held his face impassive. "In private, you will have your own well-furnished bedroom with unlimited access to the rest of the house as you choose. The house has every modern convenience. And, of course, I'll pay you a wage for your services as nurse to the baby."

Katherine sank back onto the bench, too stunned to speak...to even think. She stared up at the man in front of her, unable to credit what he had said. *Marry* him? She didn't even *know* him! She tried to answer, to tell Mr. Trace Warren what she thought of his absurd proposition, but couldn't find her voice. All that came out was a sort of choking gasp. What sort of man would even think of such a thing? A selfish one! Mr. Warren had agreed to Miss Howard's condition that he accept the baby as his own in order to fulfill that contract! What a cold, heartless— The baby stirred and began to cry. She looked down at him, so tiny, so helpless, in her arms. Her heart squeezed. If she continued on her journey to visit her sister, what would become of the infant? Who would care for him? Surely not Mr. Warren! He hadn't even *looked* at the baby.

It would be only temporary.

No. The man was insane! His plan ludicrous. She should run for the train as fast as she could! But how could she live with herself if she left a helpless baby to an unknown fate at this callous man's hands? She cuddled the baby close, reached beneath the blanket and brushed her fingertip over his tiny hand. He quieted. Her chest tightened. Her throat constricted. The baby needed her. And she *was* free of all obligations. What should she do?

Follow that still, small voice inside you, Katherine. The Lord will lead you.

Her face drew taut. *Not anymore, Mother.* The familiar pang wrenched her heart. What had she to lose if she agreed to Trace Warren's proposition—a few weeks of idle time? Her chance for a normal life of love and happiness had vanished with Richard almost five years ago. Her life was an empty shell. And if she could help the baby, at least it would give her some purpose.

She caught her breath and looked up at the stranger standing in front of her. "Very well, Mr. Warren. For the baby's sake, I will agree to your proposal according to the conditions you have stated." Had she actually spoken those words aloud? She hastened to qualify her agreement. "*However*, I want those conditions set down in writing *before* any such marriage takes place. And the agreement must also state that you will find a replacement for me as your temporary stand-in bride and nurse to the child as quickly as possible."

"Thank you, Miss Fleming. It shall be as you ask." Tension strained his voice. "Have you trunks on board?"

Her trunks. She hadn't even thought of them. "Yes, three. And my valise."

He gave a curt nod. "Give me a moment to see

to their off-loading, and we will go to my store and take care of that matter of the written arrangement."

"There is one thing more, Mr. Warren."

He halted, looked down at her. "And what is that, Miss Fleming?"

"I have no experience, beyond the last two days, of caring for an infant."

He glanced at the baby she cuddled. "The baby seems satisfied with your care of him, Miss Fleming. And I am a desperate man. My offer stands."

She watched him walk to the conductor, purpose and confidence in his stride. *Her* legs were trembling. Her entire body was trembling. Had she done the right thing? Or had she lost her mind? She rose to her feet and took a tentative step to test the strength of her shaking legs before Trace Warren returned. The baby squirmed, began to cry. "Shh, little one, shh. I've found your new father." *As cold and indifferent as he is.* "Everything will be all right." Would it? Could she be sure of that? She closed her eyes, swallowed hard against the churning in her stomach.

"This way, Miss Fleming."

Her heart lurched. She opened her eyes, stared at the stranger she was about to marry and nodded.

"If I may assist you…" His hand grasped her elbow. She walked beside him down the steps and over to a runabout. She waited, her heart pounding, while he placed the baby's valise on the floor, then grasped her elbow again and helped her take her seat. She shook her long skirt into place and tucked her feet out of sight beneath her hems, then patted the crying baby while Trace Warren loosed the reins and climbed to the seat beside her.

"Is the baby hungry? If so, I will take you to the house, though it is farther away—a little more than a mile out of town. I purchased a few cans of lactated milk in case there was a need. You can feed him while I write out our arrangement."

Lactated milk? She stared at him, taken aback by his knowledge of such a thing. *She* had been unaware of it until she started caring for the baby. "I fed him a bottle just before the train pulled into the station. I don't know why he's so fretful."

"Perhaps he senses the tension of our situation." He clicked to the horse, shook the reins. The buggy lurched forward. "If so, he will quiet as things calm down." He turned his head, and their gazes met. He didn't look nervous. Obviously, it was her. "I will stop at the shop. It's on the way to the church."

The church! She stiffened. The baby wailed. His little body went taut beneath the blankets. She patted his back, forced herself to relax and studied the buildings ahead. There were not many of them. Mountains rose behind them, dark and menacing in the dusky light.

"Here we are. This is my shop."

She looked at the narrow building in front of them, the tasteful sign above the front door centered between two small-paned windows. He climbed down, tossed the reins over a hitching rail and came to her side. "If you need me to, I will hold the baby while you step down."

His voice was brusque, strained. Clearly, Trace

Warren was not eager to hold his new son. But he had to, sooner or later. And, in her opinion, sooner would be better. What her mother called her "German stubborn" rose. She stared at him a moment, then nodded and handed the baby down to him, though she was reluctant to let go of the tiny bundle. At the moment she wasn't sure if she was comforting the baby, or if holding the baby was comforting her. She rose, and Trace Warren cradled the swaddled baby in one arm and held his free hand up to assist her.

She placed her hand in his and stepped down, surprised by the calm, if not loving, way he held the tiny baby. Perhaps everything *would* work out well for Susan Howard's son. Trace released her hand, and the cold night air chilled the place where his long fingers had curved around her palm. He handed her the baby, assisted her up the steps to the porch, then opened the door for her to enter. The warmth of the shop was comforting after the cold. Should she uncover the baby's face? She decided to leave the blanket in place unless he fussed.

Dim light spilled from an oil lamp chandelier hanging over a long, paneled counter. Bottles and crocks, weights and balances stood beside a neat array of mortars and pestles of varying sizes on the polished surface. Mr. Warren moved behind the counter, pulled down the lamp and turned up the wick. Light played over a cabinet with small, neatly labeled drawers sitting on the floor beside multiple shelves holding stoppered jars and bottles that hung on the wall.

"I'll only be a moment, Miss Fleming—Katherine."

He removed his hat, withdrew paper and pen from a drawer and placed it on the counter. "Forgive my familiarity, but as the townspeople have to believe our marriage is a normal one, I think it would be best if we used our given names. Please address me as Trace."

"Very well." Considering the magnitude of what she was doing, that small impropriety was insignificant. She watched him dip the pen and begin writing, and it suddenly all became real. She was going to marry a man she didn't know! Her stomach flopped. She squelched an urge to run out the door and looked around the shop to calm herself. At least he was neat. And he had good manners. And was adept at handling a small baby. Those were all good things.

How could the scratch of a pen on paper be so loud? She lifted the baby to her shoulder and hummed softly to deaden the sound, stole a glance at Trace Warren bending over the paper. The light gleamed on the crests of the waves in his dark blond hair and shadowed his face. What color were his eyes? Surely, she should know the color of his eyes before she married him!

"I believe that covers all of the points of our arrangement."

She jerked when he spoke. He lifted his head and looked at her. *Blue*. His eyes were blue with a gray cast to them. And intelligent, cool and reserved in their expression.

"If you would read this agreement over, Miss— Katherine. I had made arrangements to marry Miss Howard immediately. Pastor Karl is waiting." A muscle at the joint of his jaw twitched. Mr. Warren was not as calm as he appeared. The discovery made her feel better.

He turned the contract so she could read it. She tried her best to concentrate, to remember all that she had insisted be included. It seemed as if everything was there, including his signature and the date. She freed her hand, folded the paper and tucked it in her purse.

Trace donned his hat, trimmed the wick on the chandelier and led Katherine Fleming out of his dark shop. The train whistle blew twice, sending its message of imminent departure into the stillness of the evening. He saw Katherine look toward the station, staring at the beam of light piercing the dark from atop the engine—no doubt wishing she were aboard the train. He wished it, too. But he could not manage without her to care for the baby. His carefully conceived plan had become a trap. He clenched his jaw and locked the door, pocketed the key and adjusted his hat.

"If you don't mind, we'll walk. The church is just there, across the road and down a bit. It's not worth the time to take the buggy."

"Walking is fine. It's a pleasant evening."

Pleasant? He stole a look at her. The word was a mere politeness. Even in the pale moonlight he could see the tension in her face. Admiration pushed through his anger. Katherine Fleming was a very tenderhearted and brave woman to go through with this marriage for the sake of an orphaned baby who had no family connection to her. He led her toward the glow of light spilling from the windows of the church, aware that he should offer her some words of comfort or encouragement, but there were none in him.

"It's very quiet."

Her soft voice blended with the sound of her traveling gown's hem brushing over the hard-packed dirt, the whispering murmur of the waterfall in the distance. Was the slight huskiness in it normal or nervousness? He nodded, forced out a polite reply. "Yes. It takes a little while to get used to the silence when you're accustomed to the rush and noise of city life. Watch the rut." He took her elbow, helped her over the rough spot in the road and then wished he hadn't—she was trembling. "But it's active enough here during the day with all of the building going on. The construction work stops when the sunlight fades and the last train goes through. When that happens, the general store closes and the town, what there is of it, shuts down."

"I see."

Whisper Creek gurgled in the distance. Cold air swept down from the mountains and across the valley. He breathed deep and stared at the glow of light from the church. *Almost there.* His chest tightened. He never would have signed that contract if he'd thought the marriage clause applied to him. He'd been sure his being a widower had made him exempt. But when he'd arrived in Whisper Creek and approached John Ferndale about it, his argument had fallen on deaf ears. The town founder had insisted he either fulfill the marriage clause or turn his new shop and home over to him. And now here he was—trapped in a marriage he wanted no part of.

Pain stabbed his heart. Bitterness soured his stomach. It was even worse than he'd expected it to be when he'd devised the marriage-in-name-only scheme. Katherine Fleming was nothing like his wife in appearance—quite the opposite. But having her walking beside him brought back the memories of his life with Charlotte he'd struggled to bury over the last two years—even the small ones, like the rustle of a woman's skirts. And the baby! He'd thought enough time had passed that he could block any emotion, stop any feeling, but he was wrong—so wrong.

A vision of his tiny unborn son he'd fought so hard to save after Charlotte died trying to give birth filled his mind. He bit back a groan, fought the wave of guilt that flooded his heart. All of his knowledge, all of his skill and talent as a doctor, all of his desperate prayers, had not been enough. His tiny son had never taken a breath or opened his eyes. *Charlotte, Charlotte darling, forgive me.*

He sucked cold night air through his clenched teeth, forced his lungs to accept it. It wasn't worth it. No amount of money was worth this agony of guilt and pain. He would go to John Ferndale tomorrow and sign over his shop and house, then leave Whisper Creek on the next train. He would find employment somewhere and— No. That was no longer an option.

He jammed his hand into his suit pocket and fingered the folded letter with the shaky handwriting on the back. *I, therefore, give Mr. Trace Warren full custody of my baby...* There was no way out. He couldn't just walk away. He was trapped by his own cleverness in trying to save his shop and house and build a facsimile of a normal life.

He halted, stared at the church looming out of the darkness before them. "Here we are, Miss Fleming." He squared his shoulders, looked at her standing there holding the baby with the golden light from the window falling on them. He pulled in a breath. "I truly appreciate what you are doing to help the baby. I give you my word, I will find another solution to my problem as quickly as possible."

"Thank you. I shall hold you to our arrangement, Mr. Warren."

"Trace."

There was a small catch of her breath in the silence. "Trace…"

He escorted her across the small stoop, his boots echoing on the wood planks.

The train chugged off down the valley.

He opened the door, tightened his grip on her elbow and they walked into the church.

Chapter Two

The horse's hoofs thudded against the packed dirt. Katherine tucked the blanket close about the baby and listened to the rumble of the buggy wheels, the sound of water rippling over rocks in the creek that flowed alongside the road—anything to keep her from thinking about what she'd done.

A large house with a turret loomed out of the darkness, the white paint glowing in the moonlight. She stared, surprised at the size and style of it. "What a lovely home." She glanced sidewise at Trace, sitting on the seat beside her. "It looks…a bit out of place out here in the wild."

He nodded, urged the horse forward. "That is the Ferndale home. John Ferndale is the town founder." He glanced her way. "He owns this valley. And he wants Whisper Creek to be a village patterned after the towns back east." He faced forward again. "The Ferndales are older, but I believe you will find his wife pleasant."

Mr. Ferndale—the man who held his contract.

Was that a subtle warning? "I'm sure I will." Cold air swept across the road, chilled her face and neck and sent a shiver down her spine despite the snug velvet collar on her gray tweed coat.

"We're almost there."

The buggy rocked over a rut. She tightened her hold on the baby, braced herself with her feet and peered into the growing darkness. A short distance ahead, the dark form of a building stood in front of the towering pines at the foot of the mountains that embraced the valley. Judging by the shape, it had to be some sort of outbuilding. "Is that your stable?"

"No. That is my house."

She squinted to bring the lines of the building into sharper focus against the trees and made out what looked like a porch wrapped around the strange building. She stared at the yellow blurs that took the form of windows as they neared. It was…different. She looked over at Trace Warren.

"It's an octagonal house."

"I've never seen such a house." She faced front again, studied it as they approached. "It's odd—but very attractive."

"And most efficient. A few years ago I made a hou— I had occasion to pay a visit to a man who owned one. It was an exceptionally hot day in August, and the man's house was pleasantly cool. I decided then and there, if the opportunity arose, I would build one." He halted the horse.

A small man wearing the hat and tunic of a Chinese laborer stepped out of the shadow of a large tree and gripped the cheek strap of the mare.

"This is Ah Key. He is going with me to the station for your trunks." Trace Warren stepped down from the buggy, grabbed the baby's valise, came around to her side and held up his hand.

She acknowledged Ah Key's polite bow with a smile and a dip of her head then cradled the baby close, placed her hand in Trace's and stepped down. He helped her up the three steps to the wraparound porch and opened the door.

The entrance was triangular with a black-and-white tile floor. A table with an oil lamp and a silver tray stood beside an open doorway in the short wall on the left. The room beyond appeared to be the sitting room. The doorway on her right was dark.

"Would you like to tour the downstairs, Katherine? Or would you rather go upstairs to the baby's bedroom and yours?"

Her need to be alone was stronger than her curiosity. She looked down at the sleeping baby. "I think it would be best if I go upstairs and put the baby to bed."

"Do you need me to carry him up the stairs for you?"

Her arms tightened on the bundle in her arms. "No, thank you. I can manage."

He nodded and motioned her through a doorway into a center hall with a beautiful stairway. "The kitchen is through that doorway straight ahead."

She glanced into the kitchen, then gripped the banister with her free hand and started up the stairs to a landing, turned and climbed to a second landing. The carpet runner was soft beneath her feet and quieted his footsteps behind her, but nothing could dull her awareness of his presence.

"We'll turn right and walk down the hall when we reach the top."

If she reached the top. The trembling in her legs was getting worse. She wanted to turn and run back down the stairs and all the way to the train station. She looked down at the baby and finished climbing the stairs. Pewter wall sconces lit a long hallway.

"That is my bedroom."

She glanced at the closed door and continued walking, turned right into a connecting hall, her heart pounding.

"That door straight ahead opens into your bedroom. This smaller room on the left is for the baby. A dressing room joins them."

He opened the door and she stepped into the baby's room, stopped and stared. "It's beautiful!"

"I tried to prepare as best I could for the infant. I take it from your surprise you were expecting... less." He frowned and set the baby's valise down on the floor.

"I wasn't *expecting* anything, Mr. Warren." She squared her shoulders as best she could and looked at him. "I've only been responsible for this baby since this morning."

He dipped his head in acknowledgment. "You're right. I apologize, Katherine. Please excuse my foolish remark. This unexpected turn of what was already an odd situation has taken me by surprise, as well. Now, if you will excuse me, Ah Key is waiting. Please make yourself comfortable. Should you need anything for the baby before my return, I have a store of supplies for him in the kitchen." He stepped back into the hall and closed the door.

She took a deep, calming breath and looked around. There was a shuttered window with a lit oil lamp on the stand beneath it in the center of the outside wall. Shelves hung on the wall to the window's left, a painted chest beneath them. There was a small heating stove and a large wardrobe at one end, and a wood rocker with a pad on its seat, and a wood and wicker crib at the other. An oval, fringed rug covered most of the polished wood floor.

Mr. Warren had, indeed, prepared for Miss Howard's baby. Her chest constricted. Thankfully, she had accepted his strange offer of marriage. If she hadn't, according to Mr. Warren, this house and all that he had done to give the baby comfort would have been lost. The thought gave her pause—and further purpose. She would have to be very careful not to betray the truth of their in-name-only marriage to the townspeople. Mr. Warren—no, *Trace*—must have a chance to save this lovely home and his apothecary shop. And for the baby's sake, she would do all she could to help him.

The quivering in her legs had stopped. She carried the baby to the crib and tucked him beneath the blue-and-white woven coverlet, rubbed her tired arms while she waited to make sure he stayed asleep. It was odd how empty her arms felt without him. He gave a little wiggle, and his tiny lips moved in and out, making those small sucking sounds.

She smiled, walked over and picked up the valise. The used bottles had to be cleaned. And the soiled diapers she had wrapped in a blanket had to be washed. What should she do with them?

He had mentioned a dressing room. Where… She pursed her lips and looked around. If her bedroom was at the end of the hall, then the dressing room had to be through that door close to where the crib sat. She tiptoed to the door and opened it.

"Oh, my…" Her gaze darted from one object to another outlined by the moonlight flowing through the window in the long wall of the triangular room. There was a bathing tub with two spigots attached at the end, a washstand—again with two spigots attached—and one of those flush-down water closets. A small table sat beside the window.

She jerked around at a bump from the other side of the wall behind her. That would be where her bedroom was located. She put the valise on the table, moved to the connecting door and looked in. Trace Warren was standing on the far side of a large bedroom with one of her trunks at his feet. He glanced her way.

"I wasn't sure if you wanted your trunks here in the bedroom, or in the closet."

"The closet?"

"Through here." He opened the door beside him, lifted an oil lamp from a table and held it high. "Why don't you look and then tell me where you want this."

"All right." She slid her palms down the sides of her coat and crossed the bedroom, the short train of her gown whispering against the Oriental carpet that covered the center of the floor. The golden lamplight spilled over shelves lining a short wall and made long shadows of pegs driven into a board that ran at shoulder height along the other two walls of a roomy triangular closet. She'd never seen anything like it. "In here, please."

He set the lamp on a shelf and grasped the handles on the ends of the trunk, letting out a grunt when he lifted it. He placed it against the wall under the window and straightened. "I'll be right back with your other trunks."

"Before you go…"

He stopped and looked at her.

"I was wondering if there is a washroom? The baby has several soiled diapers and only a few clean ones. I need to—" She stopped at the shake of his head.

"You do not need to do any laundry, Katherine. Simply rinse the waste off the diaper into the water closet in your dressing room and flush it down. There is a bucket with a lid sitting beside a wicker basket under the table. Put the rinsed, soiled diaper in the covered bucket, and the baby's clothes with yours in the basket. A Chinese man and his wife have a laundry at the edge of the woods. They will take yours and the baby's clothes with them when they come for my laundry." He moved toward the door then glanced over his shoulder at her. "Should you need them, there are diapers in the baby's wardrobe."

"I also need to clean the baby's bottles and prepare one for when he next wakes."

He turned back to face her. "You told me you were inexperienced at caring for an infant. Do you rinse the bottles and other parts in boiling water?"

She stared at him. He had a quiet, authoritative way of speaking that made her trust him. "No. Miss Howard said only that the baby's food must be boiled."

"I see." He frowned and scrubbed a hand over the back of his neck. "When I have brought up your other trunks, we will go to the kitchen, and I will show you how to clean and prepare the baby's bottles."

He would show her? It must be that an apothecary knew about such things. She removed her coat and hat, hung them on a peg and followed him back into the bedroom. It was larger and more richly furnished than hers had been at home. Clearly, she had made the right decision in entering the strange, in-name-only marriage to save this home and Mr. Warren's apothecary shop. The baby would be well cared for. And she would enjoy every modern comfort while waiting for Trace Warren to find another woman to take her place.

A temporary stand-in bride! Whoever had heard of such a thing? Judith would be highly amused when she wrote her about this absurd situation. Her sister always found the funny, sunny side of a situation. Unfortunately, she herself had inherited their mother's more serious nature. She sighed and hurried to the dressing room to take care of those soiled diapers before Mr. Warren returned.

The whispering rustle of Katherine's travel outfit was wearing on his nerves. He hadn't heard the soft sounds of a woman moving about since— Trace closed off the memory, frowned and returned to the stove to put a little distance between him and the woman he'd married. "When the baby wakes and wants feeding, you have only to take one of the prepared bottles from the refrigerator, place it in warm water and heat it to a comfortable temperature."

Katherine turned from placing the last filled bottle in the refrigerator and smiled. "Thank you for showing me how to clean and prepare the baby's bottles. As I told you, I haven't any experience in caring for an infant, and I'm so afraid I will do something wrong."

Her smile made dimples in her cheeks. He jerked his gaze from her face then blew out a breath to ease the tightness in his chest. He'd avoided personal contact with all women for two years and now this... *marriage* was forced on him. There had to be some way—

"*Did* I do something wrong?"

"Quite the contrary."

"Then why are you frowning?"

He looked back at her, groped for something acceptable to say. "I'm pondering our situation, trying to think ahead so we will be prepared as best we are able for any questions that may be asked of us. For instance, you always say *baby* or *infant*. What is the child's name?"

She shook her head. "I don't know. Miss Howard only called him 'my precious baby.'" She reached in her pocket, pulled out a slip of paper and handed it to him. "I did find this birth paper when I unpacked his valise, but the place for the baby's name is empty."

Her voice choked. Tears welled into her eyes. He'd

prefer Katherine Fleming didn't have such a soft heart. He shoved the paper in his pocket and pulled the coffeepot Ah Key had ready for tomorrow morning over the fire. "We need to talk, Katherine—to learn a few facts about one another…" He glanced down at her. "For instance, do you like coffee? Or are you a tea drinker?"

"I drink both—black and hot."

He raised his eyebrows, gave her another look.

"That surprises you?"

"It does. You appear to be more the genteel 'tea with cream and sugar' type."

She laughed—a musical, feminine laugh that tore at his heart. He turned away, crossed to the step-back cupboard, picked up cups and saucers and placed them on the table.

"I'm sorry if that disappoints you. I can learn to drink my coffee with cream."

She'd picked up on his reaction, though she'd misjudged the reason for it. He'd have to be more careful. "Not at all. You simply surprised me. In my experience, most women prefer their coffee…diluted. Where did you learn to drink yours black?"

"At my father's knee—literally. When I was a toddler, I used to hold on to his knee and beg for a sip. He always gave it to me—to Mother's displeasure." She moved toward the door to the hallway. "I think I'll go upstairs and see if the baby is all right."

"You left his bedroom door open. We will hear him if he cries."

"I suppose…" She hovered near the door. "I'm not comfortable having him so far away. I've been holding him all day. I didn't want him to feel…lost or lonely."

He set his heart against the sympathy in her voice. "I think the first thing we should settle is a name for the baby. It will certainly seem odd if he doesn't have one by now. Have you any suggestions?"

"Me?" She shook her head, playing with one of the jet-black buttons on the bodice of her gray gown. "That's not my place. He's your child, Mr. Warren."

"Trace." He squelched the desire to flee her presence and pressed ahead with his duty to the child. "It's true the baby is now my ward and responsibility, but he is still a stranger to me. If you have any thoughts on the matter of a name, I would appreciate hearing them."

"Very well." She met his gaze then looked back toward the stairs. "I had decided—were I unable to find you—I would name him Howard. I thought…it would be good to…to have him carry his mother's name."

"You were going to *keep* him?" He stared at her, unable to look away, though her eyes shimmered with tears. He did not want to feel sympathy for this woman. He didn't want to feel *any* emotional connection to her.

"I made Susan Howard a promise."

There was nothing grandiose or posturing in her attitude or voice. It was a simple statement of fact. He couldn't stop the surge of admiration and respect. He nodded then moved back to the stove and pretended to check the coffee. "What you say makes excellent sense. I agree. His name should be—*is*—Howard. I'll write it on the birth paper tonight."

She nodded, still playing with that button, then took a step back into the kitchen. "If I may…what is his middle name to be? Howard Warren sounds incomplete. If you'll forgive me my impertinence, perhaps Trace? It has a nice sound—Howard Trace Warren."

It hit him hard, hearing her attach the child to him like that. He clenched his hands, blew out his breath. "I'll think about it." It was the most polite response he could make. He couldn't agree—not to that. He forced back the memory of his own tiny son—of the vision of the name *Trace Gallager Warren, Junior* carved into the marble headstone beneath the one that read *Charlotte Anne Warren—Wife and mother*. He grabbed a towel, lifted the coffeepot and carried it to the table. If he was still a praying man, he'd pray that baby upstairs would begin to cry for attention right now.

The silence remained undisturbed except by the rustle of Katherine's gown as she moved toward the table. He swallowed back the aching bitterness and pulled out her chair with his free hand. A hint of a floral scent rose from her hair as she took her seat. He moved away, poured their coffee and inhaled deeply to rid himself of the smell of lavender. It took all of his fortitude to take the seat opposite her. *Charlotte*… He refused his wife's name—rejected the image hovering at the edge of his determination to hold it at bay. Guilt made the coffee bitter as gall.

"I believe there are a few facts we should know about one another in case we are asked questions by John Ferndale or his wife. Or any other resident of

Whisper Creek. I'm from New York City. Where are you from, Katherine?"

"Albany, New York."

"And have you close family I should know about?"

"A sister, Judith. She's married to a soldier who is presently stationed at Fort Bridger. I was on my way to visit her when I met Miss Howard on the train." She paused, took a breath. "Our mother passed a few weeks ago after a long illness. Father preceded her by two years."

Two years. 1866. The year his world had collapsed into a meaningless void. He jerked his mind back to the present. "I'm sorry for your loss."

"Thank you." She took a swallow of her coffee, straightened her back and met his gaze. "Have you close family I should know of?"

"No. There's no one…now." He put down his cup and forced out words. "I'm not in the habit of lying, Katherine. But to explain the baby, and still protect Miss Howard's reputation, I told Mr. Ferndale that the young woman I was marrying had taken over the care of an infant when a friend died giving it birth." He stared down at his cup until he got his emotions under control, then looked over at her.

She was staring at him. "That's…uncanny."

"It does seem so."

"What else have you told Mr. Ferndale that I need to know?"

"Very little. I've been deliberately vague with any facts. As Miss Howard and I were not acquainted, I wanted a story that would cover whatever situation I found myself in." He took another swallow of his coffee and plunged in. "If we are asked, this will be our story. We—you and I now—met through a mutual acquaintance—"

"Miss Susan Howard?"

He nodded approval. "An excellent idea. It will explain our choice of that name for the baby. To continue…while we have only come to know each other through our recent correspondence, we were both lonely and decided to marry. A second reason for our union is to give the orphaned baby a family—" he almost choked on the word "—and a comfortable home. That will explain why we know so little about each other outside of the pertinent facts concerning our present lives. For instance, you know that I'm an apothecary, recently come to open a shop here in Whisper Creek in Wyoming Territory."

"It seems as if I should know how you learned of this business opportunity."

"Yes, of course." He steeled himself to talk about the past. "I was…*dissatisfied* with my life, and when I came across a notice in the newspaper about the founding of a new town in Wyoming Territory the idea of moving west was appealing. I went to talk with the agent interviewing men interested in building a business and home in the new town. The opportunity was a good one. I signed the contract and sold my business and home in New York."

"And that's when you and Miss Howard—I'm sorry—when you and *I* began corresponding?"

"No. Our correspondence did not start until my shop and home here were built and I came to Whisper Creek."

"Oh. Then—" She shook her head, took a sip of her coffee.

"Then…"

Her gaze lifted to meet his. "I was only wondering if Mr. Ferndale would wonder why you signed a contract with a marriage clause if you had no intended bride."

"He already knows that I thought my status as a widower made me exempt from that clause. It is because it did not that I began my search for a woman who was willing to enter into an in-name-only-marriage."

"You are an adventurous man."

A desperate one. He took another swallow of coffee to avoid looking at her. "I believe you are the adventurous one, Katherine. Most young women as attractive as you plan to marry, not to travel west on their own."

"I have no intention of marrying."

He looked at her. Her cheeks turned pink. She lifted her head and met his gaze full-on.

"That is a strange thing for me to say to you, but you know what I mean. This…temporary *arrangement* is not a marriage. Anyway…" She raised her hand and brushed a wisp of hair off her cheek. "I cared for my mother through her years of sickness, and when she passed—"

Her voice choked. Tears glistened in her eyes. He looked away, not wanting to witness her grief and sorrow.

"When Mother passed, the house seemed so big and empty I decided to come to Fort Bridger and visit Judith. So I sold the house, packed my personal possessions and boarded the train. It was an act of desperation and cowardice, not bravery and adventure."

"All the same, it takes courage—"

"The baby is crying!" She jerked to her feet, spun toward the hallway door and hurried from the room.

"I'll warm a bottle!" The words burst from him, unbidden. He held his breath, listened, hoped. Perhaps she hadn't heard.

"Thank you!"

Her answer floated down the stairs as her footsteps faded upward. *Fool! Getting involved with them.* He took one of the prepared bottles from the refrigerator, put it in a pan and filled it with hot water then carried the coffeepot and cups and saucers to the sink cupboard and rinsed them. He adjusted the stove draft for the night and walked out the door through the triangular back entrance and onto the porch.

He breathed deep, laced his fingers behind his neck and gazed out into the night. There had to be an answer to this dilemma, a way out of this situation. He could see a glimmer of hope for Katherine's freedom. If he couldn't think of another way, he would simply annul the marriage, accept the loss of his fortune and go to a city back east and find a job. That would free Katherine. But the baby— the baby was a different story. He had given Susan Howard his word to raise the child as his own. The baby would go wherever he went. Unless he could find another way...

* * *

"Slumber on, Baby, dear,
Do not hear thy mother's sigh,
Breath'd for him from far away,
Whilst she sings thy lullaby!"

Katherine rocked and sang softly. She watched the baby's eyes close, his little mouth go slack. She blinked tears from her eyes, slipped the bottle Trace had brought up to her from between his lips and put it on the table. He whimpered and drew his legs up. "Shh, little Howard, shh…" She lifted him to her shoulder, pushed with her toes to keep the rocker moving then patted his tiny back and continued to sing the lullaby.

"Slumber on, o're thy sleep,
Loving eyes will watch with care,
In thy dreams, may thou see,
God's own angels hov'ring here;
Slumber on, may sweet slee—"

The baby burped. A sour smell halted her singing. She looked at Howard resting against her shoulder, stared at the acrid mess running down her bodice. Her stomach clenched. She cradled his head with her hand, shoved with her feet and lurched from the rocker.

Howard wailed flailing his little arms.

"Mr. Warren! *Mr. Warren!*" She raced down the hallway, the train of her long skirt flying out behind her, and almost crashed into Trace Warren as she rounded the corner. He caught her by the upper arms.

"What is it?"

"The baby's sick!" She gulped the words, swallowed back tears.

"Calm yourself, Katherine. You're frightening the infant."

She willed herself to stop shaking, watched as Trace lifted a hand and touched the baby's cheek and forehead. He glanced at her bodice. "He's not ill, Katherine. He only spit up. Babies do that sometimes when they eat too much, or if they have too much air in their stomachs to hold the food down."

"Then it was my fault." Tears stung her eyes.

"It is no one's *fault*. It's a common occurrence when a baby is so young. He will outgrow it." He looked at her. "He would have gone back to sleep if you hadn't pan—if you hadn't frightened him."

"And now?"

He bent down and picked up the paper he'd dropped when he stopped her headlong rush toward him. "If you are calm when you change his gown, he should go back to sleep. I would expect him to sleep four or five hours. Now, if you will excuse me, I've work to do." He dipped his head. "Good night, Katherine."

"Good night. I'm sorry for disturbing your work." She watched him walk down the hall toward his room, annoyed by his cool composure. The man had no feelings! She marched down the intersecting hallway and into the baby's room. How did Trace Warren know so much about babies? She could understand an apothecary knowing about cleaning and preparing bottles—even about feeding infants. But Trace Warren's knowledge seemed deeper than that.

She shrugged off the thought, took a clean nightdress and socks for the baby out of the wardrobe and carried them with her to the table in the dressing room. She removed her dress jacket and the baby's soiled clothes, laughing when he kicked his little legs in the air and waved his arms around as she washed his face and hands. She cooed at him while she changed his diaper and soaker, captured his little arms and pushed them through the sleeves of his clean nightdress. The long socks were big on his tiny feet and chubby legs, but they stayed in place.

She hummed the lullaby and carried him back to his crib, swaying with him in her arms. It was as Trace Warren had said—little Howard fell fast asleep. She kissed his soft, warm cheek, tucked him beneath the covers and hurried to her closet to unpack and change into her own nightclothes.

Trace stared unseeing at the page, disturbed by the quiet. It had been some time since he'd heard any sounds. He laid the book aside, rose from the chair and paced the length of his bedroom, pivoted and started back. He stopped at his slightly opened door, stood straining to hear against the silence. There was no baby crying, no hysterical calls for help. Were they asleep? He fought the urge to walk down the hall and listen at Katherine's bedroom door, turned back into his own bedroom and resumed his pacing.

His training had betrayed him. Katherine's frantic cry for help had brought his doctor skills surging to the fore. He scowled, rubbed the back of his neck, strode to the window and stared out into the night. He was being foolish. The baby was fine. The bottles had been prepared correctly—he'd made certain of that. And the infant's diaper had been put on properly. Katherine had mastered that, though her other mothering skills were wanting. He'd have to help her learn to be comfortable with the baby if the Ferndales were to believe she'd been caring for him since his birth. And before Sunday. They had to go to church. It was expected. Only two days...

His strides lengthened, his slippers thudded against the carpet. It was impossible for him to settle to sleep with the concerns and questions tumbling around in his head. It wasn't supposed to be this way. How could his carefully conceived plan have gone so awry? He had thought he had everything under control. But he had also thought he was in control two years ago. *Charlotte*... His chest tightened. His throat closed.

He stopped pacing, pushed the memories away. The situations were entirely different—except each had involved a woman with whom he was supposed to have shared his life. A woman who had died. Bile surged, burned his throat. He pushed back his shoulders, stretched his chest as far as possible and inhaled, compelling his frozen lungs to function.

Thankfully, Katherine Fleming had been on that train to care for the baby. Incompetent as she was in an infant's care, she had likely saved the baby's life.

Something he, with all of his training and skill, had been unable to do for—

He jerked his thoughts from the past and focused them on the present, refused to acknowledge the future. He would find a way out of this situation. He had to. It brought to the fore all of the things he'd spent the past two years trying to forget.

The silk of her dressing gown whispered softly, and the soles of her matching slippers brushed against the Oriental carpet. Katherine walked to the window and looked out into the night. She'd never before noticed the quiet sounds her movements made. She was accustomed to the hustle and bustle of running the house and caring for her mother. Her bedroom had adjoined her parents' room at the front of the house, and, even late at night, she'd been aware of her mother's every movement and of the occasional carriage passing by. Here there was nothing but silence. It was unsettling.

Shouldn't the baby be moving?

She crossed the room to the cradle she'd found sitting in the corner by the heating stove when she'd taken time to explore her bedroom. The baby was sleeping soundly. Was that all right? She resisted the urge to pick him up and make him move, leaned down and placed her ear close to his face then smiled at the soft little puffs of warm air that touched her skin. He was fine. She straightened and moved back to the window. She mustn't allow herself to grow too fond of the baby. Already the thought that she would have to leave him made her heart catch.

She wrapped her arms about herself and stared out into the darkness, memories long buried rising on a faded sorrow. How different her life would have been if Richard hadn't disappeared. She would have been married five years this December. They'd planned to have a Christmas wedding. And children.

She'd buried that desire deep beneath her grief when she'd learned Richard had gone missing, submerged it beneath her need to care for her parents in their last years. But it had surfaced quickly when she began to care for Susan Howard's baby. She had to be careful.

She sighed and turned her thoughts from the baby. How long would it take Trace Warren to find another bride to take her place? How did a man go about such a thing in a town where there were no women? How had he entered into the arrangement with Miss Howard? They'd been strangers. It must all have been done by the exchange of letters. But how did one start such a correspondence?

She removed her dressing gown and slid beneath the covers then stared up at the swirled plaster ceiling shadowed by the low light of the oil lamp on the bedside table. The warmth of the covers eased the tension from her body. Her thoughts lost their focus, drifted. Trace Warren was taller than Richard…and broader of shoulder. And nice-looking—he was *very* nice-looking…

She yawned, snuggled deeper under the covers. The man was too reserved and aloof to be likeable. Kind, though… He was kind. And polite…

Chapter Three

Katherine pulled the baby bottle from the hot water, shook it and tested the warmth of the liquid on the inside of her wrist the way Trace had shown her. Perfect. "Here you are, Howard." She offered the bottle to the crying infant in her arms. He puckered up and squalled louder. "Shh, little one. Do you want to wake Mr. Warren?"

"Mr. W awake. Light in window."

"Oh!" She jerked her head up and whipped around, stared at the Chinese houseman standing in the kitchen entrance. A coal bucket sat at his feet. "Good morning, Ah Key."

He gave her a small bow, removed his coat and hung it on a peg then lifted the coal bucket. "Missy W, baby, not be cold." He crossed the kitchen to the stairs, the long black braid dangling down his back gleaming in the light from the chandelier.

The baby squalled. She looked down and touched the rubber tip against his mouth again. He stopped crying, gave a little whimper then sucked greedily. She adjusted the dampers on the stove, left the kitchen and carried Howard back upstairs. Ah Key was in the hallway; the coal bucket now held gray ashes. "Thank you, Ah Key."

He dipped his head, halted. "I fix Mr. W breakfast. You eat, too, maybe so?"

She smiled and nodded. "Yes. I will eat breakfast. Thank you."

"One hour." He dipped his head and padded off down the hall.

She glanced at the closed bedroom door beside her, hoping she'd done the right thing by accepting Ah Key's invitation to breakfast with Trace Warren. Surely Trace wouldn't mind. After all, this situation was his idea. And she was hungry! She hugged Howard close and continued down the hallway to his bedroom. If Trace Warren was displeased with her presence at his morning meal, she would make her own breakfast from now on and not eat with him again. The problem settled, she opened the door to the baby's room and stepped inside.

Muted sounds came from behind the end wall on her left. She walked to the wardrobe, listened at the door beside it. Water splashed and gurgled, objects clacked against a shelf, someone moved. *Trace*. His dressing room must adjoin the baby's room on this end, as hers did on the other. She eyed the door— no lock. What if he entered? She touched her hair tumbling down her back, glanced down at her dressing gown. She would prefer to meet the cool, polite Mr. Warren when she was groomed and dressed for the day.

She slipped open the wardrobe door, snatched out a diaper, gripped the baby and his bottle tight and ran on tiptoe through the dressing room and into her bedroom. The baby whimpered. She jiggled him, tossed the diaper onto her bed, sank into the rocker and pushed with her feet. "I'm sorry, Howard. Someday you will understand about these things." Her pulse slowed. She smiled down at the baby, set his bottle on the nightstand, then lifted him to her shoulder and patted his back. He wiggled, burped and relaxed. A glow of satisfaction warmed her. She was learning to be a mother.

That thought was a sobering one. She would have to give Howard to another woman soon. Best if she kept that in mind. She snuggled him back into the curve of her arm and gave him back his bottle, pondering which gown she would wear today to keep from thinking about how wonderful it felt to hold him.

She would wear one of her simple dresses. Nothing made of silk or satin. It seemed as if the softer touch of cotton would be more comfortable against Howard's baby skin. She burped him a last time, placed him in his cradle and glanced at the clock on the wall. She had to hurry—it wouldn't do to be late for her first meal with Trace. An unusual name. Would he give it to the baby? He hadn't seemed to like the idea last night.

She hurried to the closet, chose a red cotton dress and hurried to the dressing room to wash and prepare for the day. Trace Warren was a confusing combination of aloof coolness and competent thoughtfulness. Thankfully, she didn't have to try to understand him. She would be gone soon.

* * *

"Good morning."

Trace turned, stared and was instantly tongue-tied by the sight of Katherine standing in the doorway. The golden light of the chandelier fell on her beautiful fine-boned features and gleamed from her dark hair.

"I hope I'm not imposing on your privacy… Trace." Pink edged along her cheekbones. A shadow darkened her violet eyes. "I wasn't certain what your wishes were when Ah Key asked me to breakfast with you." The blush faded. She straightened her shoulders. "I will be happy to eat later should you—"

He shook his head, cleared his throat. "Not at all. I'm pleased to have you join me." *Liar.* Having her share his breakfast was the last thing he wanted. How many lies would he have to tell in the name of civility? He stepped to the table, pulled out the chair at the opposite end from where he sat. "There is still much we have to discuss."

She started forward, paused and looked over her shoulder into the kitchen. "Will I be able to hear Howard from here if he cries?"

"I believe so. If not, Ah Key will tell us he's awake and wanting attention."

She stood there a moment, then nodded and moved toward him, the long skirt of her red gown whispering softly across the floor. The germ of an idea flickered. The scent of lavender rose to tease his nostrils as she took her seat, and the thought was lost. He moved away from her chair and strode to the other end of the table, motioning toward the side-by-side windows as he took his own seat. "I was admiring the shifting light of dawn on the mountains. Seeing the rising rays glisten on the snowcaps and sparkle on the rugged stone is a sight I'm certain I will never tire of."

"Do you like it here in Wyoming Territory?"

"I do."

"Eat now." Ah Key entered the dining room carrying a tray with several dishes on it, placed them on the table and walked out.

He looked at Katherine's shocked expression. "Ah Key's serving style leaves a lot to be desired. But he's a good cook." She shifted her gaze to him. The beauty of her eyes took his breath. He looked down at the food.

"Did Ah Key come to Whisper Creek with you?"

"No." He spooned some rice porridge in a bowl, placed food from the other dishes on a plate and handed them down the table to her. "I went to the Union Pacific work site and asked if any of the laborers who knew how to cook spoke English. Ah Key does both, though his repertoire in each is limited."

She laughed, that beautiful, musical, feminine laugh that had the force of a punch to his gut. He turned the subject. "Are you familiar with Chinese breakfast fare?"

"No. I've never had the opportunity to try it."

She sounded a little doubtful. He smiled encouragement. "It's really quite good. This—" he pointed to the bowl "—as you might guess, is rice porridge. And this—" he touched his fork to the small white bundle on his plate "—is baozi, a steamed meat and vegetable dumpling. And these—" he indicated some small, flat fried squares "—are turnip cakes." He picked up his knife and cut off a bite, tried to recapture that inkling of an idea.

She bowed her head and folded her hands, murmured words beneath her breath.

All trace of the impression fled. His face drew taut. He put down his fork and waited politely for her to finish asking a blessing on the meal. It was as much of a concession to praying as he was willing to make. Prayers were worthless. When she finished, he reached for the coffeepot and filled their cups. "Did you find your bedroom comfortable, Katherine? Is there anything you need?"

"No, nothing at all. The room is lovely." She tasted a small bite of turnip cake, smiled and cut off another piece. "You're right—this is quite good."

He nodded, cut into one of his dumplings. "I think, perhaps, we should know a few more facts about one another. I'm twenty-eight years old, and an only child."

She put down her fork and picked up her coffee cup. "What made you choose to be an apothecary?"

Guilt. He held back his scowl. "I sort of…drifted into it." It was an evasive answer, and he could tell she knew it. Curiosity flared in her eyes. Tiny pinpricks of light flickered in their dark violet depths. He jerked his gaze down to his plate.

"Since good manners dictate that you should not ask—I'm twenty-three years old. And I was a spinster…until last evening." Her voice floated down the table, soft, a tiny bit husky, pleasant to his ears.

"I will be twenty-four in December." He glanced up. She smiled and nodded. "Yes, I was a Christmas baby."

Her smile faded. She busied herself with her food. Clearly, he was not the only one who was being evasive. Something else had happened to her at Christmas... something she didn't want to talk about. "My birth month is October." She looked at him, a question in her eyes. "The fifth day to be exact. My mother always said my birthday ushered in the winter season because there was a blizzard the day I was born."

"So at the end of September there is only a week of autumn weather left to enjoy?"

The dimples in her cheeks appeared with her smile. "I didn't say Mother's prognostication was true." He heard movement, looked toward the kitchen.

"Baby, he crying."

"Oh! Thank you, Ah Key."

He looked back across the table. She was already out of her chair and on the way to the door. "Katherine."

She spun about. "Yes?"

"There's no need to rush. It doesn't hurt the infant to cry a bit. In fact, it's good for his lungs."

"I just don't want him to miss his mother—to feel alone."

Tears shimmered in her eyes. He pulled in a breath, turned his thoughts to a clinical explanation as refuge against any softening of his own heart. "He's too young to remember her. Infants cry because they are hungry or because they are soiled and wet and uncomfortable. He doesn't know what 'alone' is. However, babies learn very quickly that crying gains them attention."

"If that is true—if babies cry for attention—then babies must know they are 'alone,' even if they don't understand what 'alone' is. And this isn't simply a baby—this is *Howard*. So, if you will excuse me, I will go and tend him." Her skirts billowed out around her, swishing across the carpet as she left the room.

She was angry, and he didn't blame her. He'd sounded cold and clinical and uncaring—just as he'd intended. All the same, her anger stirred his conscience, riled his guilt and spoiled his appetite. A baby deserved love and tender care. It wasn't the infant's fault he couldn't bear the sight or sound of him. He rose and walked out into the back entrance, grabbed his coat and hat and shrugged it on as he crossed the porch. Dawn was just a promise at the top of the mountains, but it was bright enough he didn't need a lantern.

The blast of a train whistle echoed down the valley. The seven-ten would be here in a few minutes. He was running late. He'd be hard pressed to get the store ready to open before the train arrived. He frowned, trotted down the steps and loped toward town.

Katherine laid Howard in his cradle then hurried to the window beside the writing desk and opened the shutters. Sunshine poured in. She forgot her purpose, stood in the cheery light and marveled at the snow-capped mountain behind the house. The rugged granite soared upward to where white patches of snow filled its gullies and hollows. A feathery gray mist rose from the icy top to form clouds in the vast blue blanket of sky overhead. The beauty of the scene brought a wish that she was able to capture the sight in oils on canvas. At last she understood what Judith had meant when she wrote home saying the mountains in New York were mere hills when compared to the towering mountain ranges in the West.

Laughter bubbled up at the thought of her sister. How astounded Judith would be when she learned what had happened. Reminded of her task, she sat at the desk and dipped the pen in the ink bottle.

My dearest sister,

You are no doubt surprised to receive this letter when you were expecting me to arrive on your doorstep. Obviously, my plans have changed.

Oh, Judith, I have so much to tell you, I don't know where to begin. You had best sit down and take a deep breath, my dear sister. I'm married! Well, not truly so. It is strictly a business arrangement for the sake of a little two-month-old baby boy. There is, of course, no intimacy involved.

My husband (oh, how strange it is to write those words!) is Mr. Trace Warren, an apothecary whose shop and home is in Whisper Creek, a new town recently founded here in Wyoming Territory. I met Mr. Warren last evening when I delivered the baby to him. He is an intelligent, kind and polite man, but cold and reserved enough to make you shiver like a New York winter's day—though there is something compelling about his eyes.

But I am getting ahead of my story. I shall start at the beginning. When I boarded the train to come west, there was a young woman with an infant seated at the back of the passenger car. She appeared to be very ill, and, as the other passengers seemed to want to stay their distance from her, (I presume they were afraid of catching her illness) I took the seat across the aisle and, seeing her distress, offered to hold her baby so she could rest. Yes, I know— I could "hear" Mother saying, "Katherine, you are too softhearted for your own good," but the poor woman needed help. She was too weak to tend to herself, let alone her infant. And no one was paying her any mind, Judith! I couldn't simply ignore her need. Or the baby's crying.

Howard whimpered. She wiped the nib of the pen and hurried to the cradle, her long skirts whispering over the rug with her quick steps. Howard was fast asleep, his stubby little blond eyelashes resting on his chubby pink cheeks. Tears stung her eyes. Was he dreaming of his mother? No. Trace said he was too young. *She* was the one who remembered Susan Howard's pain at leaving her infant when she passed from this world. Her chest tightened at the memory. She resisted the urge to pick Howard up and cuddle him, went back to the desk, picked up the pen and continued her letter to Judith.

* * *

"Have you something that will help a scratchy throat?"

"Indeed I do, madam." Trace took a bottle off the shelf on the wall behind him and held it out to the elderly woman. "This will ease your discomfort. Take one spoonful every four hours and sip water in between the doses to keep your throat well lubricated. Or, if you prefer, I have Smith Brothers cough drops you may use for that purpose."

"May I take the elixir and then use the cough drops in between the doses?" The woman placed a plump hand on her ample chest and gave him an expression of long-suffering. "Mind you, I have a fragile constitution."

He had seen women of her sort when he was a practicing doctor—most of them perfectly healthy, but lonely and wanting attention. He arranged his features in a grave expression and put a cautionary note in his voice. "It will be fine to use both. But don't have more than one cough drop in between the doses. You don't want to overmedicate your throat."

She smiled and nodded, obviously pleased by his admonition. "I'll take a bottle of the elixir and a dozen of the cough drops, thank you. And I'll be careful to do as you say." The woman sighed, slipped the bottle into her purse, dropped a coin onto the counter then adjusted the wool wrap covering her round shoulders. "And thank you for your concern. When one appears healthy, it is difficult to make others understand you have a debilitating malaise."

"Indeed." He opened one of the Smith Brothers

cough drop envelopes and scooped in a dozen of the round drops from the large glass jar. "Here you are, madam." He handed her the envelope and her change. "Now, don't forget—one cough drop only between doses of the elixir."

The woman beamed. "I'll remember." She stuffed the envelope of cough drops into her reticule, put the change into her coin purse and left the store.

The bell on the door jingled a merry goodbye.

He turned his attention to a man who had stepped up to the counter. "May I help you, sir?"

"I'm in need of some sort of tonic for my wife and daughter. They have a distressing stomach ailment, and are unable to hold down any food or drink."

His doctor's training surged to the fore. "Have they a fever, or aches or pains, or any other symptoms beyond vomiting?"

The man frowned and tugged at his ear. "Not that I'm aware of. They haven't complained of anything but their stomachs."

"I see." He studied the man's discomposure. Obviously, he hadn't been paying much attention to his family's sickness. "And how long have your wife and daughter been ill? When did this ailment begin?"

The man's face brightened. "Two days ago. Shortly after we boarded the train."

"And does the sickness come over them in waves?"

The man gave an enthusiastic nod. "That's what my wife said."

"Then I believe your wife and daughter are suffering from motion sickness."

"What's that?"

"A stomach illness caused by the rocking of the train. It's quite common, and will have no dangerous effects as long as they are treated and can take nourishment to prevent any dehydration from occurring." He walked to the refrigerator at the end of the counter, took out two bottles and placed them in a bag. "This tonic should take care of the problem. When you return to the train, immediately give your wife and daughter each two spoonsful then wait until ten minutes pass and give them both another two spoonsful. After that they may take a spoonful whenever they begin to feel queasy in their stomach. How much longer will you be riding the train?"

"Four days."

"The tonic will not last that long. You will also need some of my stomach drops." He filled two small tins and put them in the bag with the tonic. "The drops are a bit sour, but to receive the full benefit they must be sucked, not chewed or swallowed."

"I'll see to it. What do I owe you?"

"Two dollars will cover everything." The train whistle blasted its warning of pending departure.

The man pulled the coins from his pocket, tossed them on the counter and grabbed the bag. "Thank you for your help, sir. My wife and daughter have suffered exceedingly and will be most grateful to find relief."

"I'm glad to have been of service, sir. Now, you'd best hurry back or you will not have time to administer the first dose before the train leaves the station. Remember, two spoonsful immediately, another two spoonsful after ten minutes have passed and then as needed!" His called words followed the man out the door. He dropped the coins in the cash box and slipped it beneath the counter, grabbed his dusting rag and straightened. The bell jingled.

"That fellow's in a hurry. He almost knocked me off the steps." Blake Latherop strolled into the shop and set the boxes of lemons and ginger roots he carried on the counter. "I'll tell you, Trace, it's downright dangerous to be anywhere on the porches or the station road when a train blasts its warning of departure."

"The man's family is ill." He returned Blake's smile, squeezed one of the ginger roots and sniffed a lemon for freshness. "Thanks for bringing these over. I was hoping they had come in on the train. I'm out of my stomach elixir."

"Your other order came in on the train, too. The crates are sitting at the station. I'm going to pick them up now. I just stopped in to see when you want them delivered. I'm sure your bride is anxious to have them." Blake held out his hand. "May I offer Audrey's and my congratulations on your marriage? Audrey is thrilled to have another new bride in town."

"Thank you. I'll pass your felicitations on to Katherine." He ignored the knot forming in his stomach and shook Blake's hand. "As for the delivery…" The knot twisted tighter at the thought of having to go home. "I have to make the stomach tonic right now. And roll some headache pills…"

"What about after dinner, between the afternoon trains?"

Dinner. There was no escaping that. His stomach roiled. He took another sniff of the lemon and wished he had a bottle of his medicine handy. "That will be fine, Blake. And I'll come over to your store after I've finished my work and settle my account for the month. Now, if you'll excuse me, I have to get started on the tonic. There may be a passenger on the next train who has motion sickness." He picked up the boxes and turned toward his back room, away from Blake's studied look. Did his friend suspect something was wrong? He blew out a breath at the sound of Blake moving toward the door, stopped walking and listened for the click of the latch. The bell jingled, signaling his departure.

Blake was gone. He set the boxes on his work table, turned to the sink and filled a dishpan with cold water to soak the fresh ginger roots clean. *Dinner.* An image of Katherine sitting across the table from him at breakfast popped into his head. His face tightened. Katherine Fleming was a beautiful young woman. And, though he still was not interested in having any sort of relationship with her or any woman, if he was honest, her beauty made things more…difficult. He was, after all, a young, healthy man. Sharing another meal with her was a test of his resolve he did not look forward to. Thankfully, he had his work to concentrate on meanwhile—once he got the image of her out of his head!

Katherine put the knitted coat and hat from the wardrobe on Howard and wrapped him in a blanket. The outfit was a little large, but she wanted to take the baby outside, and if Wyoming weather was anything like New York's it would be cool. Not that it could be any cooler than Trace Warren had been at dinner.

She fastened her everyday cape around her and carried Howard down the stairs and out onto the porch. Trace was faultlessly polite, even thoughtful, but...distant. Dinner had been completely impersonal. They had exchanged more factual information, and then he had left the minute his meal was finished. He had said he had work to do, but she had the distinct feeling he had wanted to escape her company. Irritation quickened her steps to the railing. She had agreed to enter into this in-name-only marriage to help the baby, and she was well aware that it was a simple business arrangement, but it wouldn't hurt the man to smile.

"Stop it this instant, Katherine Jeanne Fleming! You're only feeling sorry for yourself. You agreed to this ridiculous *marriage*—make the best of it. The poor man is probably feeling as uncomfortable and constrained as you."

Howard squirmed and let out a whimper. She looked down at his sweet face snuggled against her neck and smiled. "I'm scolding myself, not you, Howard. You are far too adorable to ever scold." She shifted his weight in her arms and gazed out at the towering walls of granite that enclosed the vast valley watered by Whisper Creek and divided by the silver rails of the Union Pacific Railroad. "My, but this valley is beautiful! And just look at those mountains, Howard! Perhaps when you are grown you will climb them. But for now we'll stroll around the porch and investigate your new home together."

She pulled the blanket high around his neck and started forward, stopping when a horse snorted. Muted voices came from the other side of the house. Had Trace brought a friend home? She stopped walking and listened. Should she intrude? The sound of a woman's voice decided her. She patted and smoothed her hair as best she could with her free hand, cuddled the baby close and hurried along one of the angles that formed the deep wraparound porch.

Trace and another young man were lifting a crate from a small wagon. Her attention went immediately to the slender, young woman climbing another set of porch steps. The woman had beautiful, curly red hair. And there was a covered plate in her hands. Their gazes met—so did their smiles.

"Ah, Katherine dearest, you're just in time to meet one of Whisper Creek's businessmen and his wife."

Dearest? She jerked her gaze to Trace. He looked at her over the top of the crate, a warning in his eyes. "I'm not exactly in a position to make a formal introduction." He shifted his hold on the crate, felt behind him with his foot and backed up the steps. "This is Mr. Blake Latherop and his wife, Audrey. Blake owns the general store. Blake, Audrey, this is my wife, Katherine."

The young man dipped his head. "A pleasure to meet you, Mrs. Warren." He lifted his end of the crate higher and followed Trace up the steps.

"And you, Mr. Latherop…" She glanced back at the young woman. "And you, Mrs. Latherop…"

Should she invite them in for tea? Or leave that to Trace? It wasn't her house. She smiled to cover her uncertainty.

"Please excuse my unexpected visit, Mrs. Warren, but Blake had these crates to deliver to your husband, and I couldn't resist coming along to welcome you to Whisper Creek." Audrey Latherop lifted the plate she held. "I know you have a cook, but I thought you might enjoy a few cinnamon rolls."

"How thoughtful of you. Thank you, Mrs. Latherop." Katherine glanced around. There was a small table with two accompanying chairs sitting against the house wall. "Would you care to sit down?"

"Thank you, but we have to get back to the store. I'll just set the rolls on the table as you have your hands full. And please, call me Audrey." The young woman's gaze lowered and her expression softened. "I heard you had a baby."

"Yes. This is Howard." She lowered the baby from her shoulder.

Audrey stepped closer, smiled and touched the tiny hand clutching the edge of the blanket. "So you're the one we've been ordering all of this baby furniture for, young man."

Howard blinked and went back to sleep.

"He's beautiful, Mrs. Warren."

"Katherine, please." There was a thunk as the men set the crate they carried on the porch next to another larger one.

Audrey nodded, glanced toward the men. "I was just telling your wife you have a beautiful son, Mr. Warren."

Wife. That sounded so strange. She looked at Trace to see how he would respond, stiffened when he stepped to her side and put his arm around her waist. His hand held her immobile when she instinctively started to pull away.

"We couldn't agree more, could we, dear?"

He looked at her. His arm tightened. A reminder? She smiled up at him.

"Do you need help opening these crates, Trace?"

"No. I can do it." Trace smiled, brushed some dust from his coat. "I may not look it now, Blake, but I grew up on a farm. I'm no stranger to a hammer."

A farm? She looked up at him, struggling to keep the surprise from showing on her face. He should have told her that.

"Then we'll be going back to the store. Ready, Audrey?"

A spurt of envy rose at the way Blake Latherop looked at his wife. She squelched it. Being a spinster was her choice. She had her memories—and her fading hope. She fixed a smile on her face. "It was lovely to meet both of you. Thank you so much for the cinnamon rolls, Audrey. It is very kind of you." She bit off the invitation to come again hovering on her lips, stood like a statue with Trace's arm around her and returned Audrey's wave. It wasn't her place to entertain.

The moment the wagon was turned and headed toward town, Trace moved away from her. She watched him head for the steps and her ire rose. They may be strangers—*married strangers*—but he needn't ignore her. She deserved better treatment than that. "You should have told me you were raised on a farm."

He paused, looked over his shoulder at her. "Yes. We lived on Long Island. I'm sorry I forgot to mention that."

"Are there any more surprises in store for me?"

"Most likely. As I'm sure there will be for me. Now, if you'll excuse me, I need to get my hammer."

She stared after him, shocked by the change in his expression. His face had simply…closed—like a shutter on a window. Trace Warren was hiding something from his past. But then, she had her secrets, also. And what did it matter? This strange alliance would soon be over. She sighed and glanced at the sizable crates. Her curiosity stirred, but she ignored it. Whatever the crates held had nothing to do with her. But those cinnamon rolls did. She needed to take them inside. She glanced at a door a short distance from the table, walked over and peeked inside. It was another triangular entrance, this one with pegs holding a man's raincoat with boots on the floor beneath it. A sound drew her attention. She looked through a door on her right and spotted Ah Key cleaning vegetables at a table. She'd found a back entrance into the kitchen.

She turned to get the rolls and jumped at a sharp screech. Trace, his coat and tie removed, his collar open and shirtsleeves rolled up, was prying at the largest crate. His bared forearms strained against the opposing pressure. His sleeves rippled over the muscles in his upper arms and shoulders. Effort had his brow furrowed. The end of the board splintered and came free. He grabbed hold of the loose end, braced his foot against the crate and yanked, tossed the board aside and looked her way. "I think you'll like what's in these crates—if I ever get them open." He ran his fingers through his hair then jammed the claws of the hammer beneath the end of another slat and pried.

She took his words as an invitation and sat at the table, resting the baby on her lap and watching him work. He looked so different in his shirtsleeves with his tie off and his hair mussed—almost pleasant. And handsome. Trace Warren was a *very* handsome man.

"That's got it! I can lift it out now."

She jolted from her contemplations, watched him bend over an end of the opened crate and tug. There was a scraping sound, and a curved arm and portion of a straight spindle back and solid wood seat above legs attached to rockers appeared. "A rocking bench?"

"For on the porch." He glanced over his shoulder. "It's something called a nanny bench. At least it will be as soon as I get it out of there and find the other piece." He hung the end of the bench over the crate and strode into the house, coming back with Ah Key in tow and stopping by her chair. "Where would you like the bench, Katherine? Here by the kitchen entrance? Or by the front entrance?"

Why was he asking her opinion? What he did was not her concern. She took a quick glance around.

Because of the octagonal shape of the house, she could see in three directions—down the valley at the front of the house, down the road toward the Ferndale home and the town at the side, and toward the towering pines and wall of mountain at the rear. The gurgle of Whisper Creek flowing by was a pleasant, soothing sound. "It's lovely here."

He nodded and walked to the crate. "Grab that end, Ah Key."

She held her silence as the men carried the bench to the other side of the kitchen door and placed it along the wall. Trace pushed the back, watched the bench rock back and forth for a moment. "There you are, Katherine. A place where you can sit and rock the baby if you're of a mind to." A frown creased his forehead. "Though I suppose there will be little of that until the days start warming up again."

In spring, when I will be gone. She closed off that thought. "The baby likes rocking."

"It's a soothing motion." He walked back to the crate and leaned inside.

"Like mother walk." Ah Key patted his stomach and went inside.

She looked at the still rocking bench and wished Trace had invited her to try it out.

He grunted and straightened, a piece of wood that resembled two rails held together by spindle posts at the ends in his hands. It was painted the same dark green as the rocker bench.

Her curiosity got the better of her manners. "What is that?"

"It's the piece that makes this a nanny bench." He

fitted the rounded bottom ends of the spindle posts into two holes at one end of the front edge of the bench seat and pushed down. The ends of the posts slid through the holes and came out on the bottom side of the seat.

"Why, it makes a crib out of that end of the bench!"

"A clever idea. A woman can rock a baby and have her hands free to read a book or do piece work or something at the same time." He tried to wiggle the short piece of railing he'd attached. It held firm. "I guess that's safe enough. Why don't you give it a try, so I can see how it works."

"All right." She walked to the dark green bench and smiled. "Look, Howard, your papa bought you a porch rocker." She sat and laid the baby beside her on the seat behind the safety rail. A gentle push with the tips of her toes against the porch floor set the rocker in motion.

"The Latherops seem very nice."

Trace nodded, glanced at Katherine sitting on the porch bench and looked away. The soft expression on her face as she cooed to the baby touched an answering chord inside him, and he couldn't afford that. "Blake is a very good businessman. He's managed to find me every item I've ordered for the house or the shop."

"And for the baby, as well?"

"Yes." He held back a scowl and fastened the last iron wheel to the wicker baby carriage he'd taken out of the second crate. He reached up and grasped the handle, rolled the carriage back and forth, testing for steadiness and making certain the pins that held the wheels on stayed in place. He stood and braced himself to do what had to be done. "I believe the carriage is ready to be tested now, Katherine. Once around the porch should be enough."

"All right." Her dimples flashed with her smile. She looked down at the baby in her arms. "Do you want to go for a ride in your new carriage, Howard?" She rose, kissed the baby's cheek and placed him in the carriage. He started to whimper. "The carriage is beautiful, Trace." Her gaze met his. "Do you want to push him?"

His stomach knotted. He looked away, shook his head. "No, I have to watch the way the different parts are working. I want to be certain the carriage is safe."

"Very well." She grasped the turned wood handle and pushed the carriage forward. He moved off to the side and fixed his gaze on the wheels and undercarriage. The iron wheels rolled smoothly over the porch floor, the sound blending with the rustle of Katherine's gown and his own footsteps. The baby stopped crying and waved his little arms in the air. "Look, Trace, he likes it."

He nodded, glanced out at the rutted dirt road. "You won't be able to walk him on the road at present. It's too rough. But they intend to cover it with scree in the spring. It will be packed smooth then. Of course, you will still have to watch for the rattlesnakes."

"Rattlesnakes!" She jerked to a halt and stared out at the surrounding fields. "Do they live in the grass? Will they hibernate through the winter?"

"I don't know. I've not been here long enough to become familiar with their habits. I'm only telling you so you won't walk to town by yourself."

"You needn't worry. I won't get off of this porch! Snakes!" She shuddered.

A smile tugged at his lips.

The baby started to fuss.

She leaned forward over the handle and pulled the blanket back over him. "Hush, little one. I won't let anything hurt you."

The baby kicked and wiggled at the sound of her voice. His smile died aborning. The infant was already recognizing Katherine. Guilt pounced. He had to work out a plan to end this phony family situation before the child and Katherine became too attached. But how to do so and still save his shop and home had him confounded. He'd considered simply giving it all to John Ferndale, but he couldn't walk away from his home and means of livelihood now. He had a child to provide for. Still, there had to be a way. Too bad the baby wasn't old enough for a boarding school.

His chest tightened. He glanced at Katherine when she started walking again and knew instinctively that she would never approve of that idea. He didn't, either. A prayer for guidance formed. He scowled and banished it from his thoughts. He hadn't prayed for two years. He wouldn't start now. He would continue to handle his own affairs. Not that the results were as he expected.

He watched Katherine pushing the carriage and smiling down at the baby, and the expression on her face made his heart ache. He jammed his hands into his pockets and stared out at the surrounding fields. Whatever he was going to do, he'd best figure it out soon.

Chapter Four

"Katherine…"

"We have company, Howard. Yes, we do…" She lifted the baby from her lap to her shoulder, rose from the rocker and went to answer Trace's knock. "Yes?"

"I'm sorry to intrude, Katherine, but I wanted to remind you that tomorrow is Sunday. We'll be expected to attend church."

The look in his eyes said he'd rather chew on the nails he'd pulled from the crates earlier. She filed the information away to ponder later and nodded. "All right. What time shall I be ready?"

"The service will begin at ten o'clock." He glanced down at the baby. "It occurred to me that, with your limited experience in caring for an infant, you may not know how to bathe one." His eyes clouded, turned more gray than blue. The small muscle in front of his ear twitched. "He's old enough for a proper bath now. It would be good if you gave him one this evening when you won't be hurried making your own preparations for church. I've come to instruct you in the proper way to do so, if you would care for my help."

"Indeed I would." She tried to keep a rising panic from showing. "I was about to change him into his nightclothes, give him a bottle and put him to bed."

"Then this is the perfect time. If you will permit me, I will join you in your dressing room." That muscle in his jaw twitched again.

"Yes, of course."

"I'll get the nightclothes from his wardrobe."

She watched Trace enter the baby's room, turned and hurried through her bedroom to the dressing room, hugging Howard close and hoping he would not be frightened. "Do babies like to be bathed?"

"Most do." Trace opened the corner cupboard, pulled out a small tin tub that hung from a nail in the back wall and placed it on the table below the window by the washstand. He removed his coat and rolled his shirtsleeves above his elbows. Her thoughts jumped to the feel of his arm about her waist, holding her close to him. Her pulse skipped. His gaze fastened on her, his face impassive—rather like a teacher's when instructing a student.

"The first thing is to make certain the water is the right temperature—too hot will burn a baby's tender skin, too cold will make them take a chill." He picked up a pitcher, filled it halfway with hot water and then added the cold. "Test the water with your elbow. Do not use your hand as it is too accustomed to more pronounced hot or cold." He stuck his elbow in the water. "This is the temperature you want. Put the baby down so you can feel it."

She laid Howard on the table, unbuttoned her cuff, pushed up her sleeve and dipped her elbow in the water.

Trace emptied the pitcher into the small tub and repeated the process until it was half-full. "Next, put a washcloth in the bottom of the tub to keep the baby from slipping on the wet tin. Have the soap and two towels ready to hand. When everything is in place, undress the baby."

She undressed Howard, her movements now quick and sure.

"Now, lay his head on your elbow, hold his leg in your hand and lower him into the water."

She shook her head and backed away. "I would rather watch you bathe him this first time. I might hurt him."

"Nonsense, Katherine. Simply—"

"No, Trace. I'll watch." She crossed her arms. That muscle in front of his ear jumped. He was not pleased with her refusal.

"Very well." He lifted Howard and cradled him in one arm. "Talking in a calm voice helps a baby to feel safe." He slid the baby in the water as he'd described. "Now release him, holding his head above the water."

Howard wiggled, kicked his legs and waved his arms. Water splashed, dotting the front of Trace's shirt.

"He likes it!" She laughed as the baby's movements became stronger.

"Yes. Now, quickly, while the water is warm, wet your free hand and soap him all over—including his hair—everywhere but his face. Slowly lift and turn him over your arm to do his back and rump. Turn him back over and rinse him thoroughly. Throw a towel over your shoulder with your free hand...thus. Lift him to your shoulder and wrap the towel around him. When he is dry, dress him."

He handed Howard to her, wrung out the washcloth, poured the bathwater into the washstand and dried and hung the tub back in its place while the water gurgled down the drain.

The lesson was over. She studied Trace's face. It wasn't impassive now. "Thank you for showing me how to bathe Howard."

He looked away and rolled down his sleeves. "He will probably sleep a little longer than he usually does. Bathing relaxes a baby. Good evening, Katherine." He gave her a curt nod and left the dressing room.

She stared after him, quite certain that Trace Warren would be very displeased if he knew the tenderness his face revealed while he was bathing the baby. It was completely at odds with the dispassionate tone of his voice. Why? She pushed the question to the back of her mind to contemplate later and dressed Howard for bed.

He should not have bathed that baby! Trace scrubbed at his forearms to erase the memory of the infant resting there...so small, so innocent, so *trusting*. His face tightened. It was no use. Soap and water didn't work. He could still feel that light pressure, the little wiggles and squirms. And he would never get to sleep until he blocked out that memory.

Coffee. He'd go make coffee. That would do it! He grabbed his shirt off the chair where he'd tossed it, buttoned it on and hurried out of his dressing room. There was no sound from Katherine's room. She had probably retired early because of church tomorrow.

A knot twisted in his stomach. His steps slowed. At the very least he would have to pretend to be happy with his new family tomorrow. He jammed the tail of his shirt into his belt, stormed to the stove and reached for the draft. The stove was hot. He frowned and opened the door on the firebox. Coals winked red, flared into flame at the sudden draft.

"I had to fix Howard's bottles for tomorrow."

Katherine's soft, slightly husky voice floated the length of the kitchen. He pivoted, stared. She stood by the refrigerator, moonlight from the window washing her lovely, delicate features with silver.

He stared, unable to tear his gaze from her.

She smiled and lifted her hand. "I made coffee while I waited for his bottles to boil. Would you care for some?"

The aroma rising from the pot on the stove hit him, bringing moisture flowing back into his dry mouth. He nodded, cleared his throat. "That's why I came downstairs—to make coffee. I often have a cup out on the porch when I can't sleep." The instant the words were out, he wished them back. She began to speak then turned and took a cup off the cupboard shelf.

"What a lovely custom."

It wasn't what she'd started to say. *Fool. Why didn't you just tell her this situation was tying you in knots?* He thought that over while he watched her pour his coffee. Perhaps honesty would be best. At least it would clear away the tension vibrating between them. He tugged his lips into a wry smile. "I don't know about lovely…but it calms the nerves." He took hold of the cup of steaming hot coffee she held out to him. "Why don't you join me?" She glanced up, and her beauty hit him full force. *Another mistake. Why don't you guard your tongue, Warren!* Tiny bits of golden light flickered in the depths of her violet eyes. Her full lips curved.

"Wouldn't that defeat your purpose?"

Her dry tone restored his ability to breathe. She smiled, and he knew she had deliberately saved him embarrassment with her flash of humor.

He tugged his lips into another grin. "There's one sure way to find out." He dipped his head and waved toward the door. "After you, madam." He grabbed his jacket and coat off the hooks and followed her through the entrance onto the porch. "This will keep you warm." He draped his wool coat over her shoulders, shrugged into his jacket and walked over to the railing, leaving the table for her use. It was easier to maintain his emotional equilibrium if he didn't look at her.

Moonlight silvered the face of the mountains. Water chuckled over the rocks that lined the banks of Whisper Creek. It was quiet and peaceful—except for the roiling emotions in his chest. He blew across the coffee and took a cautious swallow, thankful for the deep shadow on the porch. Fabric rustled, wood whispered against wood. She had shunned the table for the rocker bench.

"It's lovely out here at night. But I don't know if I will ever become accustomed to the quiet—though I'm certain there is a good deal more activity around my sister's home at Fort Bridger."

That last bit sounded like a warning. As if she wanted him to know she didn't expect to stay in Whisper Creek for long. Well, he would do his best to accommodate her. He leaned his shoulder against a post and nodded. "I expect there is. A fort is a busy place. Especially with these Indian uprisings."

"Indian uprisings!" The whisper of the rocker against the porch stopped. "*What* Indian uprisings?"

He turned and looked at her. She was clutching her cup in her lap and staring up at him. "Didn't your sister warn you the Indians have been attacking the miners and their suppliers this summer? It seems as if her husband would be ordered out on patrol to keep the Indian raids in check. The skirmishes are in that area, around South Pass. They attacked some freighters on the Sweetwater River only a few weeks ago."

She shook her head, looked down at her cup. "I haven't heard from Judith since I wrote her in September telling her I was coming to visit. I told her not to bother to answer as I was selling the house and wasn't sure of my schedule."

There was apprehension in her voice. He could have kicked himself for causing her to worry. "I'm sure your sister and her husband are fine, Katherine. There have been no rumors of attacks on Fort Bridger."

She nodded, rose and set her cup on the railing. She gathered the edges of his coat, held them closed at the base of her throat and stared out into the night. "How different it is here in the wild." She glanced over at him. "Is that why there are wood shutters on all of the windows in the house? Because of the Indians?"

"It was suggested to me as a precaution." He gave her a reassuring smile. "You're safe here, Katherine. I'm a careful man."

"And a kind one. Thank you for trying to make me feel better."

"Did it work?"

"A little." She smiled and the tension left her face.

He took another swallow of coffee and watched her pick up her cup and retreat to the bench. "Time will take care of your unease."

"I suppose." She sipped her coffee, clutched her cup in one hand, his coat edges in the other, then set the rocker into motion and gave him a smile that brought her dimples out of hiding. "I prefer to be a moving target. How can you simply stand there drinking your coffee?" Her gaze shifted from him to the dark beyond the railing. "Don't you ever wonder who or what may be watching you from the shadows of the trees?"

"Only if I hear the hoot of an owl or the howl of a wolf or some other animal."

"Or an Indian war cry?"

There was a teasing note in her voice. He quashed

the desire to answer her humor with his own—that was more dangerous to his safety than any Indian attack. He took another swallow of coffee, glanced at her over the brim of his cup and made his voice merely polite. "You have a vivid imagination."

"So I've been told." She looked at him a moment, then rose and took a firmer hold on his coat. "I had better go and check on Howard. But first…if you would refresh my mind, Trace. I'm afraid I was so nervous at the wedding ceremony, I have forgotten your pastor's name."

Her voice matched his politeness. She had understood his silent message. "It's Karl, Pastor Konrad Karl. His wife's name is Ivy. And—I don't believe I mentioned that they have children—three of them… a boy and two girls." His throat tightened. He stared down at his hand clenched on his empty cup. Those children were another reason he hated going to church. It was hard to ignore them sitting on the front pew with their boundless energy barely contained. But his attendance was expected by John Ferndale.

"Thank you. I'll remember." Her skirt rustled, brushing against the painted planks of the porch floor. The door opened. "Good evening, Trace."

"Good evening." He resisted the urge to turn and look at her once more before she went inside. The click of the latch put an end to the temptation. He stayed there, leaning against the porch post while the silence settled around him. He tried to convince himself the quiet was peaceful. But he couldn't believe the lie. It wasn't peace he felt. It was loneliness. The terrible loneliness he'd suppressed since

Charlotte's death had boiled to the surface that first night when he'd stood at the bottom of the Union Pacific passenger-car steps and looked up into Katherine's eyes.

A carriage and a wagon stood beside the church. Katherine drew in a breath and glanced over at Trace. "Did I take too long with the baby? Did I make us late?"

He halted the horse beside the wagon and shook his head. "No. I come at this time every Sunday. I like to arrive just before the service begins." He threaded the reins through the loop at the top of the cast-iron tethering block, climbed down and set the heavy weight on the ground. "Don't forget we have to act as husband and wife." He lifted the baby's valise from off the buggy floor and held out his hand to help her down.

His face was taut, his voice strained. Did he think she would fail him? "I won't forget. I've been reminding myself all morning. Little Howard's future depends on our...charade."

His brows lowered. "It's hardly that. The marriage is legal, Katherine. And real enough—as far as it goes."

"Of course. I didn't mean to imply otherwise. *Charade* was a poor word choice." She restrained the urge to wrap her fingers around the warmth of his hand, to cling to its strength. She shook out the long skirt of her brown checked dress and tugged the jacket into place over the lace-trimmed ecru bodice. It was not her best or most attractive gown, but the soft wool would be comfortable against Howard's tender baby skin. And the dress was warm against the chilly morning.

Trace clasped her elbow and turned toward the front of the church. She shivered, held her ground. He stopped and looked down at her. "Is there something wrong? Do you want me to carry the baby?"

"No..." She stared at the narrow trodden path through the grass. "I was thinking of what you said about rattlesnakes..." Another shiver shook her. "I'm sorry, Trace, but a snake wrapped around my leg when I was a child picking berries with my mother. And it kept trying to climb higher. She—she had to pull the snake off..." She shuddered, struggled to control the fear. "I'm *terrified* of snakes."

"Wait here." He walked the path, kicking down the grass on his left and right, pivoted at the end and returned to grasp her arm. "The way is clear." His deep voice washed over her, calm, reassuring.

How thoughtful and kind! She nodded and walked beside him toward the church. "Thank you for doing that." She sighed and studied the ground. "I know it's foolish of me to allow a childhood experience to make me so fearful. But I can't seem to master the fear."

"There's no need to apologize, Katherine. Sometimes things happen to us that leave...scars inside." He assisted her up the steps to the porch and opened the door. A low murmur of voices floated out of the sanctuary. Warm air caressed her chilled face and hands.

"It's nice and warm in here. I won't need the extra

blanket on the baby." Her whispered words earned a curt nod in response.

"There's no shortage of fuel in Whisper Creek. Both wood and coal are abundant in these mountains. Ready?"

She took a breath and nodded, felt the slight pressure of his hand at the small of her back and walked beside him down the center aisle. She lifted her head and glanced around, pushing away the memory of the last time they had walked down this aisle to become an in-name-only family.

Two men seated on the back bench glanced up, smiled and dipped their heads in greeting, then resumed their low-voiced conversation. Trace stopped at the empty wood bench behind the one the Latherops occupied and stood aside. She returned the Latherops' welcoming smiles, slipped into the narrow space and sat, wondering if Audrey Latherop would be as friendly if she knew the truth about her temporary marriage to Trace Warren. And what of the pastor and his wife? They had children. What would they think of what she had done? Her stomach churned. What had she been *thinking* getting involved in this phony marriage! And coming to *church* and pretending to be a family!

She skimmed her gaze over the older, fashionably dressed couple sitting on the bench in front of the Latherops and swallowed hard, fighting back the bile burning its way into her throat. They looked wise…discerning.

Trace placed the valise on the bench beside her and took his seat. "Are you all right?"

She glanced over at him, swallowed again at his probing gaze. "Yes." She indicated the older couple with a small nod. "The Ferndales?"

"Yes." He lowered his mouth toward her ear and whispered back. "Relax. Forget about us... Think of the baby."

She looked down. The tightness in her chest eased.

"Good. Just keep looking at the baby and breathe slowly."

Footsteps interrupted him. She looked forward.

Pastor Karl entered from a side room. "Greetings, everyone. It's good to see you all here this morning." He beamed a wide smile their way. "I'd like to extend a special welcome to our new family in Whisper Creek—Mr. and Mrs. Warren and their baby boy."

Trace covered her hand with his, squeezed. Heads turned; smiles were aimed in their direction. Trace smiled and dipped his head. She curved her lips, prayed her forced smile looked natural.

"If you will please stand, we shall begin with a hymn." The pastor motioned to where his wife sat on the first bench with their three children. Ivy Karl stood and faced the congregation. Her lovely voice floated through the room.

"'Rescue the perishing, care for the dying, Jesus is merciful, Jesus will save.'"

Katherine removed the extra blanket from around Howard, folded and tucked it into the valise and rose to stand beside Trace. He stood silent and rigid, the small muscle just in front of his earlobe pulsing. There was something wrong. Was he angry with her for some reason? She shifted her gaze to Ivy Karl lest he feel her staring. Howard squirmed and lifted his head, dropped it back to her shoulder. She cuddled him close, listening to the next verse.

"'Down in the human heart, crushed by the tempter, feelings lie buried that grace can restore. Touched by a loving heart, wakened by kindness, chords that are broken will vibrate once more.'"

The words touched the ache in her heart, stirred her loneliness for Richard and exposed her dead dream. Tears filmed her eyes. If only the Lord *could* restore her hope for tomorrow, her dream for love and a happy life that had died with Richard's disappearance. But her once-strong faith had died a bit more with each of the hundreds of unanswered pleas for Richard's return she'd prayed over the years. She was devoid of hope.

She blinked her vision clear, glanced at Trace and wondered what caused the tension she could feel pulsing through him. It took her mind from her own unhappiness and strain to study his profile, to watch that small throbbing muscle. She lowered her gaze to the baby sleeping in her arms. Should she give him to Trace to hold? Would that give him comfort as it did her? No. He never offered to hold the infant unless it was to assist her. But then, most men weren't as naturally comfortable holding an infant as women were. But—if that were true—what of the tenderness she had seen on Trace's face last night when she'd forced him to bathe Howard? The thought took hold, clung.

The singing stopped. She sat and cradled Howard in her arms, plumbing her memory for every instance where Trace was with the baby. He had never held Howard by choice—there was always a reason. And he never held him a moment longer than the situation required. Her heart sank. If Trace didn't want to be around the helpless infant, what would happen to Howard when Trace found another woman to take her place as wife and mother, and she left to get on with her life? She had thought when she saw the baby's room with all of the beautiful baby furniture that Trace truly wanted the child—but he didn't. Yet, what of his tenderness with Howard? Perhaps he simply needed more time with the baby. Perhaps she was doing them both a disservice by spending all of her time with Howard.

She stole a sidelong glance at Trace from under her eyelashes. His jaw muscle had stopped twitching. She looked down at the baby, tugged at her lower lip with her teeth. Should she? Trace was too polite to refuse to help her. She leaned close, tipped her head back to look at him.

He glanced over at her movement, lowered his head. "Do you need something?"

She nodded and lifted the baby over to him. "Would you hold Howard please? My arm is getting tired." His face closed. It was as if he had shuttered and locked away all emotion.

"Yes, of course."

He took the baby from her, settled him in the crook of his arm and stared straight ahead. She could have *pinched* him. Anything to take that frozen look from his face.

"Amen."

She'd missed the opening prayer! A fine way to act during her first attendance at a church service in Whisper Creek. She jerked her gaze to Pastor Karl, hoping he hadn't noticed her inattention.

"This morning, I am going to deviate a bit from my habitual procedure of taking my text from the Bible, and instead base my sermon on the hymn we sang to open the service."

There was a rustle of fabric as the congregation stirred in their seats. She ignored the urge to look around to see if they disapproved and kept her attention focused on Pastor Karl.

"The hymn has been running over and over again through my mind the last couple of days. I've found myself singing it and humming it at odd times. I have no explanation for that—it's certainly not a common occurrence. And since you've all heard me sing you will understand why that's so." He chuckled.

The pastor's self-deprecating humor charmed her. Movement drew her eye. The baby had awakened and was waving his arms through the air. His hand batted against Trace's tie, and his tiny fingers closed into a fist on the smooth silk. His erratic movements yanked the tie out of Trace's vest, tugged the end toward his small mouth. Trace freed the tie from Howard's little fist and tucked it back into place. The baby curled his tiny hand around Trace's little finger. A sharp intake of breath drew her gaze upward, and she saw the flash of pain in Trace's eyes. *What—*

"It is the third verse of the hymn that has so gripped me. Listen to those lines again. 'Down in the human heart, crushed by the tempter, feelings lie buried that grace can restore...'"

She looked back at the pastor, startled to find him looking in their direction, compassion warming his eyes. His gaze moved on and he continued to speak.

"As I was singing the hymn yesterday, it suddenly occurred to me that I was in that very condition. That I have had wounded, hurtful *feelings* buried deep in my heart for years. The grief of my mother's death, the pain of a good friend's unexpected betrayal for personal gain. I'd buried the pain of those things deep inside. And I'll venture to say that most of you have done the same thing at one time or another. It's a very *human* thing to do." Pastor Karl paused, rubbed his hand over his chin. "The problem is, when we do that, the pain we bury doesn't go away—it festers. Ignoring it doesn't work. Sooner or later, something happens that reminds us of the incident that caused us the pain and it flares up and we struggle to bury it again."

She stared at the pastor, her attention riveted by the sincerity in his voice. What he said was true. The pain she'd buried almost five years ago was still with her. She still struggled to overcome it. To—

"Well, there's a better way!"

She jumped, startled by the sharp crack of Pastor Karl's palm slapping against the podium. She glanced at Howard. He was still clinging to Trace's little finger and staring up at him.

"Listen, people! Listen to the words of the hymn! *'Feelings lie buried that grace can restore!'*" He leaned forward. "I have a confession to make. When my mother died, pain wasn't the only feeling I buried in my heart. I buried anger at God there, too. And it was the same when my good friend betrayed me. Why did God let those things happen?"

There was the creak of wood as people stirred on the benches.

Pastor Karl straightened, swept his arms out to his sides. "Did He? What does the hymn say, 'crushed by the *tempter*...' Why do we blame God for the bad things that happen to us? He warned us that we would have tribulation here on Earth. But He also told us that He would help us through the hard times. How foolish to carry pain and anger in our hearts when God's grace can restore the buried feelings, the broken hearts, the devastated emotions. 'Touched by a loving heart, wakened by kindness, chords that are broken will vibrate once more.' Only the Lord can do that. He is the only one who can make us whole again. But not if we *blame Him* for our pain. Turn to Him, confess your anger and ask Him to heal you. He will. Now let us bow our heads for the closing prayer."

"Oh, how precious he is! Just look at those pink chubby cheeks..."

"Thank you, Mrs. Ferndale." Katherine's heart swelled with pride. She looked at Trace to see if he had heard the compliment. The smile on his face looked natural, except for a certain tightness around the corners of his lips and eyes. It was a small thing she wouldn't even notice, if he wasn't standing so close to her. She took a delicate sniff.

Trace looked down, a question in his eyes.

Heat crawled into her cheeks. She couldn't very well explain to Trace in front of the Ferndales that the pleasant garden scent clinging to him reminded her of her father. It smelled like the Pears shaving stick her father had used after he was bedridden and no longer able to visit his barber. She looked down and pulled her handkerchief from her purse dangling from her wrist then dabbed at her nose.

Howard let out a squall.

"I think your little one is hungry, Mrs. Warren."

"And tired." Trace slipped his arm around her waist. "Shall we take him home, Katherine?"

His slight squeeze told her he wanted her to comply...not that she needed the encouragement. She was ready to go home and leave the feeling of being on tenterhooks behind. "Yes. It's time for him to sleep." She reached for the baby.

Mrs. Ferndale yielded her hold on Howard. "I know you're still settling in and becoming a family—and that it's difficult to socialize with an infant to care for, Mrs. Warren. But please bring your sweet baby and come for a visit soon. I am looking forward to getting acquainted with you, and I love babies!"

"Thank you for your kind invitation, Mrs. Ferndale. I will look forward to calling on you after we are settled as a family." A family that would never be. She was only a stand-in bride and mother. She ignored the pang the thought brought, covered her temporary baby with the blanket Trace handed her and walked out of the church beside her pretend husband.

Chapter Five

The mare tossed her head and stopped in answer to Ah Key's tug on the reins. "I leave buggy with Mr. W. Tell him you come home with him to eat. One hour. You not forget."

Katherine rose, hugged Howard close with one arm and stepped down from the buggy to hide her amusement. No matter the time of day Ah Key always said they would eat in one hour. "I won't forget. I will come home with Trace."

"One hour!"

Ah Key shook the reins and drove off, the rumble of the buggy wheels mingling with the jingle of the bell on the door of Blake Latherop's general store. After almost a week spent alone with the baby, it was lovely to come to town. She turned and climbed the steps, smiled at the family that came out onto the porch, the father carrying a toddler and a paper bag, the mother herding two small children, each sucking on a peppermint stick.

She hurried by them to enter the door a soldier

was holding open for her, her smile deepening at the look of pure joy on the toddler's sticky face. One day Howard would— Her smile died. She would not be here to see him taste his first peppermint stick. Or for all of the other "firsts" he would experience before then. Those pleasures would belong to the woman Trace chose to replace her.

She shoved the sobering thoughts away, determined to hold on to her anticipation of visiting Whisper Creek's one and only general store and seeing Audrey Latherop again. She moved aside to clear the path to the door and stopped to look around. The store was awash with blue uniforms. Her breath caught. Could her brother-in-law be here? She swept her gaze over the soldiers looking for Robert's kind face. Warmth crept into her cheeks—most of the soldiers had stopped what they were doing and were staring at her. A hush fell. She dropped her gaze, lifted Howard to her shoulder and pulled back the blanket she'd draped loosely over his face to protect him from the cold morning air. There was a general stir as the soldiers went back to their shopping.

An older woman headed for the door, chuckled and stopped beside her. "What a clever way to turn away those soldiers' interest, my dear."

The warmth in her cheeks increased. "Thank you."

The woman nodded and touched Howard's cheek. "You have a beautiful baby. I'm on my way to my daughter's. She's going to present me with my first grandchild in a few weeks."

"Oh, how wonderful! You must be very excited."

"Yes, I am." The woman coughed, shoved her hand into the purse dangling from her thin wrist, pulled out a handkerchief and dabbed her mouth. "Pardon me, but I can't seem to control this tickle in my throat. It's from the coal dust of the train, I suppose." She tucked the handkerchief away again then brushed her finger over Howard's tiny fist. "I came in thinking some hard candy would help, but the proprietor said there is a new apothecary shop next door so I'm going there. Goodbye, my dear. I wish you and your adorable baby well." The woman hurried out the door.

Two soldiers tipped their hats her way and went outside carrying paper bags. Another left pulling at a plug of chewing tobacco.

She cradled Howard back in her arm then glanced toward the counter. Audrey was busy, and would be busy for quite a while judging from the line of soldiers in front of the counter. She looked toward a clear area on her left and smiled. Bolts of fabric and baskets of notions rested on a long table. No wonder there were no soldiers swarming over that area. But it was exactly what she needed. She wanted to replace the trim at the neck of her silk velvet gown. The lace there now was stiff and scratchy, and she wanted Howard to be comfortable if he rested his soft baby cheek against her. But she also wanted to look her best while she was Trace's stand-in bride. Her feminine pride would permit no less.

She fingered through the baskets of ribbons and laces and braids searching for something acceptable that would still look pretty. *Oh, my!* She stared down at a filmy silk trim that flowed from light gray to dark gray in a three-inch span. The colors were so delicate and the blending so subtle, the filmy trim looked like the mists that rose over the ice-capped mountain that surrounded the valley. It would look beautiful against her gown's dark mulberry color. And a thin black velvet ribbon would make a perfect accent bow at the point of the V neckline.

She pulled the cone of silk trim from the basket, set it on the table and began to hunt through the next basket for the ribbon. And she needed some soft white lace…

The muted blast of a whistle vibrated through the store.

"The train leaves in five minutes, gentlemen. You'd best hurry and make your purchases. May I help you, Private?" Blake Latherop's words spurred a rush of activity.

Throats cleared. Boots shuffled against the floor. She glanced up. A soldier stepped to the counter and pointed.

"I'll have two packages of that Virginia Belle chewing tobacco, a tin of Gold Leaf and a box of Lucifers."

The older soldier standing in line behind the private thumped him on the shoulder. "You're too young for that Virginia Belle chaw, Dawson."

"Ah, leave him be, Thomas. He only wants it fer the picture."

The growled words came from a gray-bearded sergeant with laugh wrinkles around his eyes.

Hoots and guffaws erupted from the other soldiers.

"I'd a sight rather look at that picture of a pretty woman than some old grizzled sergeant!"

"Good one, Dawson!" The hoots grew louder.

"Well, maybe I can arrange fer you to be lookin' at some young brave holdin' a bow with his nocked arrow pointin' straight at you instead of that picture or me."

"That's what I joined up for, Sarge." The young private laughed, slapped a coin on the counter and strode for the door. He spotted her watching and dipped his head to her in a polite nod. "Don't pay us no mind, ma'am. A man tends to forget his manners out here."

The door banged open, the bell jingling wildly.

She started and spun around to face it.

A soldier held the door open and roared, "Two minutes, men! Hit the road running!"

Howard squalled. She jiggled and patted him, cooed soothing words and watched the soldiers still in the store run for the door, their boots pounding on the floor. The planks quivered beneath her feet.

The soldier looked her way. "Sorry I woke your young'un, ma'am." He touched his cap's brim and raced after the others. The door banged close with a jangle of the bell.

Silence fell.

"Gracious…" It came out a sort of stunned whisper.

Audrey laughed and came toward her, the brush of her long skirts against the floor loud in the silence. "That's exactly how I felt the first time I experienced that furious rush of the soldiers to beat the train's departure. Now I'm used to it. But, if you want to shop at your leisure, it's best to come in between trains. Did you find anything you want? Or were you just looking?" Audrey bent and slipped her finger under Howard's hand; her thumb rubbed across his tiny back. "Hello, Howard. .did those noisy old soldiers frighten you?"

The baby looked up at Audrey. his blond-fringed blue eyes wide, his tiny lips trembling.

"Ahh… You are so sweet…" Audrey's gaze lifted to meet hers. "May I hold him, Katherine? Blake will help you with anything you need."

"Of course." She handed Audrey the baby and glanced up at Blake. Her throat tightened at the look on his face as he gazed at his wife. Jealousy pricked her heart. Oh, how she wished things had been different. That Richard had returned to her and Howard was their son—that she would never have to give him up. She swallowed back the foolish yearning, picked up the notions she wanted and walked to the counter.

"That's a lovely trim, Katherine. It's so filmy it's almost as if it isn't there at all." Audrey smiled down at Howard. "But I'll bet this one will find it."

She glanced at Audrey and smiled. "I'm sure he will. And probably tug and chew on it!" She laughed, caught and kissed one of Howard's tiny hands he was waving in the air. "He's getting quite good at grasping what he wants."

"And he'll get better at it." Blake drew his ledger close and picked up his pen. "Pretty soon you'll be pulling all sorts of things from his hand—"

"Ouch!"

"Including your hair."

Not I. Another woman. She joined Blake and Audrey's laughter and reached to free one of Audrey's red curls from Howard's tiny fist. Tears filmed her eyes. She dipped her head to hide them and cleared a lump from her throat. "I want three feet of the black ribbon and the entire rolls of the silk trim and the white lace." She blinked her eyes clear, pulled a coin from her purse and held it out to Blake. "Will this be enough for everything?"

"You don't want me to put it on Trace's account?"

"What?" She stared across the counter at Blake. She hadn't even thought— *Foolish woman!* Of course Trace would have an account here! Now what should she do? She weighed her choices, smiled and shook her head. "Not this time, Blake. I didn't tell Trace I would—"

"Put it on my account, Blake."

Trace! She turned toward the door, watched Trace close it and walk toward them. He looked at her and smiled. Her pulse sped. Gracious, but he was a handsome man!

"I'm sorry, Katherine. When you told me you were coming shopping, I should have told you to put any purchases on my account." He slipped his arm around her waist then looked at Blake and smiled. "I guess we forget about discussing the mundane things of our life when we're together. We've been too involved with learning all there is to know about one another." His arm tightened on her waist and he smiled down at her. "Right, dearest?"

She gazed up at him, unsettled by his closeness, the strength of his arm around her. She reminded herself it was only an act and fought the urge to lean against him, to rest her head on his shoulder. It had been so long since anyone had taken care of her... *Stop it!* She cleared her throat and smiled. "Yes. It's so wonderful learning—"

"Oh! *Oh! Take the baby!*" Audrey gasped and leaned against the counter.

She reached for Howard, but Trace was quicker. He grabbed the baby, thrust him into her outstretched arms, turned back and grabbed hold of Audrey's shoulders.

Blake ran to his wife, slid his arm around her and supported her. "Audrey, what is it? What's wrong?"

"I don't kn-know, Blake. I— Oohh!" Audrey bent forward, crossing her arms over her abdomen.

"Is it the baby?"

"I don't— Oohh!" She looked up at Blake, her face drained of color. "Oh, Blake, our baby..."

Blake stroked Audrey's red curls. "Shh, my love. All that matters is that you be all right."

"Audrey, I may be able to help you." Trace's quiet voice broke through Audrey's moan.

Help her? Katherine jerked her gaze to Trace. He had his fingers wrapped around Audrey's wrist and was staring at the watch he'd pulled from his vest pocket.

"I know you're in pain, but you need to answer my questions. You're with child?"

Trace's voice was calm, authoritative. The way it was when he was instructing her about caring for the baby. She watched him, drawn by his confident command of the situation.

"Y-yes." Audrey gasped the word.

"How far along are you?"

"T-two m-months."

"Is it a sharp pain or a cramp?"

"Cr-cramp. Is—is something wrong with my baby?" Audrey leaned against Blake's arm, tears rolling down her cheeks.

Katherine hugged Howard and looked back at Trace. Her heart squeezed at the pain in his eyes. She watched him tuck his watch away and place a hand on Audrey's upper arm.

"I don't know, but it won't help if you are upset. I want you to breathe slowly and try to relax, Audrey. Let the cramp ease." Trace's calm, soothing voice belied the tension in his face.

She looked back at Audrey, saw some of the rigid stiffness leave her shoulders. Her own breath came easier.

"Has it stopped?" Trace's voice almost demanded that it had.

"Yes." Audrey slowly straightened. She wiped the tears from her face with shaking hands. "Thank you for your help, Trace. Now, if you will all please pardon me, I need to go upstairs and—"

"No. No walking. Blake, you need to carry her." Trace's voice was firm. "She must not walk or climb stairs or do any work at all. These next few weeks are a dangerous time for your baby. Audrey must go to bed and *stay* there. It's important that she not get out of bed for any reason."

"But—I can't do that!" Audrey choked out the words.

"You can and you will, Audrey." Blake's voice brooked no argument. He scooped Audrey into his arms and headed toward the back of the store.

"But, Blake, there's no one to help—"

"I'll do it." They all stared at her. She jiggled Howard and squared her shoulders.

"Oh, Katherine, it's sweet of you to offer, but you have the baby—" Audrey's voice broke. She buried her face against Blake's shoulder.

"I'll bring Howard with me." She locked gazes with Trace and wished she knew him well enough to read what he was thinking at her declaration. Because that was what it was. She would not be dissuaded from caring for Audrey—not after what Trace said about it being a dangerous time for the baby.

"We will discuss that possibility after Blake carries Audrey upstairs. She needs to be in bed."

She looked at the taut muscle along Trace's jaw and nodded. At least he hadn't said no.

Trace stepped out onto the porch, crossed to the top of the steps and stared into the darkness. The air was heavy with the promise of rain. A blue-white brilliance flickered and flashed across the night sky at the top of the mountains, and the grumble of thunder vibrated in his chest. The storm was moving fast. It would be over the valley in a few minutes.

He lifted his cup and took a swallow of the hot coffee in an effort to loosen the knots in his stomach that had plagued him all afternoon and evening. He had sent Audrey Latherop to bed and told her to stay there until after the third month of her pregnancy had passed. It was all any doctor could do in the face of a threat of miscarriage. And he was no longer a doctor. Audrey and her baby were not his responsibility. Still, the morning's events haunted him. Had he missed anything? Was there more he could have done for them without revealing his past? He'd told Blake to come for him, that he might be able to help if there was any change.

If Audrey started bleeding…

The knots in his stomach twisted tighter. He lowered his gaze and watched Katherine's shadow moving through the golden light that fell from her bedroom windows to spread over the ground. She was packing the baby's valise—preparing what she would need to take with her tomorrow. He frowned, rubbed his free hand over the taut muscles at the back of his neck. She had been surprised when he had agreed that she should care for Audrey. They had all seemed surprised. But it was the perfect way for him to stay abreast of the news of Audrey's condition and pass along any advice he might be able to offer without getting personally involved. And, in a way, it was like a reprieve from his situation.

Katherine would not be spending her days in his home and that would ease the emotional turmoil he'd suffered since her arrival with the infant. The hours she and the baby would be at the Latherops, he already spent at his apothecary shop—but he would not have to eat his afternoon meal with her sitting across the table from him, talking about the baby. And her evenings would be taken up with the needed preparations for the next day. And there was another benefit. It would give him time to come up with a plan to replace her in a way that would be explainable to Mr. Ferndale. And this time there would be no error. The woman would be older and less…attractive.

The wind rose, plucked at his coat and pants. Raindrops splashed on the ground and spattered on the steps. He moved farther back on the porch and watched the storm come. Rain pounded on the roof, splattered against the railing and wet the floor. Lightning streaked to the ground and made towering shadows of the nearby pines. Thunder shook the planks beneath his feet and rattled the windowpanes. But it was nothing compared to the tempest inside him. The muscle in his jaw twitched. His fingers tightened around his cup. Another baby had been thrust into his life. An unborn one. Like his son. Would this one also die before it could live because he wasn't skilled enough to save it?

Pain took his breath. He glared up at the black storm-filled sky. "Haven't You punished me *enough*? You took my wife and child. What else do You want from me? Stop bringing helpless infants into my life!"

Lightning flickered, thunder grumbled and then there was only the sound of the falling rain.

He threw the rest of his coffee out onto the grass, spun on his heel and went into the house.

Chapter Six

Breakfast was over. Trace stood and watched Katherine leave the dining room to go upstairs and get the baby. His liberation had begun. He tossed his napkin onto the table and walked to the kitchen, his step lighter than it had been since Katherine and the baby had arrived.

"Ah Key, I need you to go and hitch up the buggy. Mrs. Latherop is ill, and Mrs. Warren will be spending her days with her until her condition improves. It will be your job to drive Mrs. Warren to town and then go and bring her back every day."

The houseman emptied the shovel of coal he held into the stove's firebox, straightened and brushed his hands together. His long black braid swung back and forth in refusal. "I no have time to cook and clean house and hitch and drive horses all day. Have much work to do. You go town. You take Missy W to town, bring Missy W back. I clean up breakfast dishes, make good dinner. Be ready one hour!" The houseman grabbed a dishpan and headed for the dining room.

Trace stared after Ah Key, stunned by his refusal, irritated because the houseman's argument made good sense. Of course people would expect *him* to drive Katherine and the baby to town when they learned of her offer to care for Audrey Latherop. He should have thought of that instead of focusing on his freedom from having to eat his afternoon meal with her. He plunked down on the bench in the kitchen entrance, yanked on his boots and coat, lit a lantern and headed for the stable.

The tops of the mountains to the east were rimmed by the golden promise of a rising sun. He frowned, pulled up his collar against the predawn chill and quickened his pace. He needed to open the shop before the first train arrived, and hitching a horse to a buggy was not something he was practiced at—though he soon would be. His frown deepened to a scowl. He opened the double doors, stepped out of the dim early-morning light into the deeper darkness of the stable and hung the lantern on a hook screwed into a beam.

A low whicker came from the stall. The smell of hay and dust rose from the litter disturbed by his boots. He slipped the bridle on the dapple gray mare, opened her stall and snubbed her to the hitching post. She stood quietly while he harnessed her. He smiled and patted her neck, pleased by his quick progress. "Good girl, Shadow. Now let's get you hitched to the carriage." He loosed her snubbing, gathered the reins in his left hand, grabbed her cheek strap with his right and pushed. "Back, girl, back."

The mare stamped her hoof and tossed her head. He grabbed for the cheek strap that had slipped from his grasp and the mare danced sideways.

"Whoa, Shadow! Whoa…" He tugged on the reins, drew the mare's head close, took a firmer grip on the strap and pushed harder. "Now back! Back, girl!" The mare snorted and yanked against the restraint of the reins, trying to pull away.

"Forget tell you no push. Horse stubborn."

He spun around and looked at his houseman standing in the open doorway. Ah Key hurried over to him and held out his hand. "Take apple, put by nose, move apple, horse follow. All good."

He took the apple and held it by the mare's muzzle. Her nostrils flared. She dipped her head to take a bite and he pushed the apple toward the buggy as Ah Key suggested. The mare stepped back. Slowly, step by step he backed her between the shafts. "Good girl, Shadow." He gave the mare the apple, patted her neck and listened to her contented munching while he finished harnessing her to the runabout. He led her outside, closed the stable doors and then continued on toward the house, vowing to never again enter the stable without an apple at hand.

The mare's hoofs thudded against the damp dirt of the path and the buggy rumbled along behind her, yellow circles of light from the side lamps glowing in the dark. He led Shadow into the wide curve that followed the octagon shape of the house, looked up and frowned. Katherine stood at the top of the porch steps with the baby in her arms and the valise at her feet. The sight of her waiting there took his breath. His reaction to her stole his composure. He tossed the reins over the railing, picked up the valise and turned back to stow it on the buggy floor. The soft whisper of Katherine's long skirts slipping from step to step as she descended intensified his awareness of her. "There was no need for you to wait out on the porch in the cold. I would have come inside for you."

"I didn't want to make you late in opening your shop. Will you hold Howard while I get in, please?"

His gut tightened. He cradled the swaddled baby in his arm and handed her into the buggy, stood waiting while she arranged her skirts and then tugged at the sleeves of her wool coat and adjusted its velvet collar. Howard squirmed and twisted, and the flap of the blanket protecting the baby's face from the morning chill fell away. His chest constricted. He replaced the flap of blanket, trying his best not to see the baby looking up at him. *What is taking her so long?* He held his tongue while Katherine reached down and moved the valise a little closer to her feet then straightened and smoothed out the wide velvet band around the bottom of her coat.

"I'm ready now." She smiled and held out her arms.

He returned the baby to her, snatched the reins from the railing and climbed to his seat. His arm brushed against hers. He scowled and snapped the reins to start Shadow moving. The thought of making this trip to and from town morning and evening of every day until Audrey Latherop's third month of pregnancy was over made him wish he'd bought a carriage instead of the small, cozy runabout.

"It looks as if it will be a nice day. I thought perhaps the storm from last night would continue."

"Once a storm passes over the mountains to the east, it's gone." He frowned at his curt reply. Katherine didn't deserve such treatment. She may be the cause of his discomfort, but it wasn't her fault. She didn't know the effect her presence had on him. He softened his response. "At least, I've never known a storm to return. The height of the mountains probably prevents it."

"I suppose so."

The wheel in front of him fell into a deep rut and the runabout lurched.

"Oh!"

Katherine fell against him, struggled to right herself, the task made difficult by the baby in her arms. He turned slightly, helped her sit erect then turned back, trying to ignore the catch in his lungs from the feel of her against him.

"Thank you." She gave him a grateful smile.

He nodded and concentrated his attention on his driving, trying to spot any deep ruts or holes in the road ahead—he wanted no more such incidents. The lamps were useless against the thick gray mist that rose from Whisper Creek to hover over the road. The gurgling sound of the stream rushing over its rocky bed made a soft accompaniment to the clop of Shadow's hoofs and the rumble of the wheels.

"You made it very clear yesterday that Audrey

was not to get out of bed for any reason. Is she permitted to recline against propped up pillows to eat?"

Oh, no! He wasn't going to have the responsibility for Audrey's and her baby's life or death thrust on him! He glanced over at Katherine. She was looking at him, waiting for his answer. The muscle along his jaw twitched. "A gentle incline on pillows will be all right—as long as she doesn't push herself up or strain to rest against them. Have Blake lift her into the reclining position."

"All right. I'll make certain she doesn't try to move herself."

He could feel her studying him. He kept his gaze focused on the road. They were almost there…

"You're very knowledgeable about Audrey's… condition."

She'd left the "why?" unspoken, but it was clear he had to quell her curiosity or face probing questions at some time in the future. He clenched the reins and phrased his answer carefully. "I had several doctor assoc—friends back home. They use to talk to me about their cases." *Asking for my advice, but no more. Never again.* The lamps in Blake's store were lit. He halted the mare.

Blake opened the door and hurried out to the carriage. "Good morning, Trace, Katherine."

"Good morning, Blake." He tried not to ask, but his training and doctor's instincts were too strong. He couched his inquiry in the form of a politeness. "I hope you and your wife had a good night."

"Yes, very." A frown creased Blake's forehead. "Audrey feels so well she's sure it would be all right to get up and do some simple tasks. I told her I'd ask what you thought."

He nodded, tried to act normal while the bile churned in his stomach and burned into his throat. It was always the same. Once the pain stopped the women felt they should get back to their wifely duties. "That would not be wise. Any slight strain could bring on another cramping episode." *And the death of your baby.* "It may happen anyway." *There's no way to stop it. I tried, Charlotte. I did all I knew and more.* His hands fisted on his knees. He held himself from urging the mare into a run to get away from Blake and the talk of Audrey's condition.

"I'm sure she will be more content with Katherine here."

"I'll do my best to make that so." Katherine placed her hand in Blake's offered one, stepped down and looked back up at him. "I'll see you this evening."

He nodded and handed Blake the baby's valise. "I will be here to pick you up as soon as I've closed the shop and hitched the carriage."

"Let me help you with the hitching, Trace. It's the least I can do to repay your kindness in letting your bride spend her days here caring for Audrey. Where will the carriage be?"

"At the church. I'll let Shadow graze in the pen out back." The tension across his shoulders eased at the change of subject. "And thanks for the offer. I haven't much experience with horses and I can use the help. Oh—and bring an apple."

He drove off, chiding himself for not giving Katherine a warmer farewell, but it was all he could do to look at her holding the baby in her arms. He would do better when he greeted her tonight.

A long blast of a whistle echoed down the valley, announcing the first train of the day. It would be arriving in a few minutes. He turned the mare and drove to the church to unhitch.

"I feel terrible having you go to all of this trouble for me, Katherine."

"I'm only happy that I'm here to help, Audrey. Mrs. Ferndale seems nice enough, but she looks a bit…pampered. And the pastor's wife has her hands full with her family.' She gave a small laugh and laid Howard on the bed beside Audrey to remove his hat and coat. "It's not as if there is an abundance of women in Whisper Creek."

"That's certainly true. It's a little daunting to think of birthing a baby with no midwife or doctor in town to help. If something goes wrong…" Audrey touched the blond fuzz on Howard's head then looked up at her. Tears shimmered in her hazel eyes. "I don't know what I would do if you weren't here, Katherine." Audrey's voice broke. "You have such a good heart to offer to do all of this work for me when you don't even know me."

Follow that still, small voice inside you, Katherine. The Lord will lead you. Her breath caught. Had the Lord orchestrated all that had happened so she would be here to help Audrey in her time of need, as well as helping Trace and little Howard?

"And Trace—how generous of him to sacrifice his time with you so you can be here with me."

I think Trace is relieved to be free of my presence. The thought hurt. She smiled and placed Howard's little hat and coat in the valise sitting on the chest at the end of the bed beside her folded coat. "Only at dinner, Audrey. Trace is at the shop all day."

"I forgot about that. Still, it's very kind of him. Katherine?"

"Yes."

"Blake padded a small crate with a blanket and put it in the kitchen for your baby to sleep in. But… would you mind terribly if he slept here on the bed beside me?"

She looked at Audrey's hand touching Howard's tiny one. "Only if you promise you won't try to lift him if he cries."

"I promise."

She smiled, covered Howard with his blanket and straightened. "It's early. Are you hungry or—"

"No. Blake gave me one of the cinnamon rolls left from the other day." Audrey's lips curved. "He's not much of a cook."

"Well, I think I can manage to do a little better than a roll for dinner and supper. Not that your cinnamon rolls aren't delicious! We enjoyed them." She took Howard's bottles from the valise to put in the refrigerator. "Have you anything in mind for dinner, or shall I improvise with what I find in the kitchen?"

"There is cabbage salad, and cold roasted beef and bread you could use for sandwiches for dinner. I hadn't planned anything for supper. If you can't find something you need in the kitchen, you've only to ask Blake. He will bring it to you from the store.

Oh—there is a clean apron in the long drawer in the worktable. And be careful when you turn on the cold water. It flows with a great deal of force."

"All right. Now you rest." She leaned down and kissed Howard's soft cheek. "I'll be back to check on both of you in a short while."

"I'll have a dozen of those Smith Brothers cough lozenges please."

"Yes, madam." Trace opened one of the Smith Brothers envelopes and counted the lozenges into it. "Will there be anything else?"

"I've been feeling very tired and listless these last few days. Have you anything to make me feel stronger?"

"I have several health-restoring products, madam. Or perhaps Weld's Strengthening Bitters might help."

"I'll try the bitters."

"A good choice, madam." Trace turned to the shelf behind him and took down a bottle of the bitters and put it in a bag with the cough drops. He studied the woman's face. She looked pale and drawn. "May I suggest you concentrate on eating good strengthening soups and drink plenty of liquids for the next few days? Lemonade would be a good choice. And get plenty of rest."

The woman smiled and nodded. "Thank you, young man. I'll do as you suggest. Though it may be a bit difficult aboard the train."

A tough-looking bowlegged cavalry lieutenant held the door open for the woman then stepped up to the counter and scanned the shelves.

"May I help you, Lieutenant?"

The cavalryman glanced toward a couple who had followed him into the shop and lowered his voice. "Do you have any Dr. Beach's Pile remedy?"

Trace nodded, pulled a tin off the shelf and held it out so the lieutenant could see the label: Dr. Beach's Pile Electuary—for hemorrhoids and piles—an internal and international medicine. "Is this what you are wanting?"

The lieutenant looked at the woman approaching the counter and his face flushed. "I'll take two of them. And some of his Black Salve, too."

He placed the items in a paper bag and slid it across the counter. "That will be eighty-seven cents, Lieutenant." He accepted the coins and turned to the couple. The man was coughing. The woman was dabbing at her nose with a handkerchief. Her face was flushed, her eyes glassy. His fingers twitched to feel her forehead and confirm his suspicion that she had a fever.

"My wife and I are both feeling poorly, sir. We seem to have succumbed to the colds that are spreading around back home in Chicago. Have you any medications that might help us regain our health?"

"I have several that might help you." He pulled bottles off the shelves behind him and set them on the counter as he called out the names. "There is Blandiff's Vegetable Antidote for Ague... Armistead's Ague Tonic... Dr. Swett's Health Restorative..."

The man frowned. "I don't think those are necessary for a cold, sir. I would like to see a remedy for a cough."

"Very well." He turned to select several cold and cough tonics from his inventory, but his suspicion wouldn't let him remain silent. "However, I must say, sir, that in my opinion, your wife's illness is more than a cold. She appears to have a fever."

"I told you I felt overly warm, William." The woman picked up the octagon-shaped, aqua glass bottle. "Is this vegetable antidote good?"

"I have had good reports of it, madam, but I have not had occasion to use it personally."

The man coughed, cleared his throat. "All right, Marie. If you feel the need for it, we'll take a bottle of that. And one of this cough remedy. And I'll have two dozen of the Smith Brothers cough candies."

"Very good, sir." He put the bottles in a paper bag, filled two Smith Brothers envelopes with the drops from the glass jar and tucked them in beside it. "Will there be anything else?"

"Have you any Dr. Tobey's Headache Pills?"

He glanced at the woman. "I do, madam. But as you say you have a fever, if I may—" he pulled a box of his own pills from off the shelf and set it on the counter "—these pills are formulated to reduce fever and ease the head pain caused by it."

The woman opened the box and peered inside, took a sniff. "I believe I smell mint. What are the pills made of?"

"They are a scientific blend of feverfew, willow bark, peppermint and—"

"I'll take them."

"A wise choice." He put the box in the bag. "You'll find the pills work better and your illness will improve faster if you drink a lot of water. Adding a spoonful of apple-cider vinegar to the water will make it work even better." He made change for the five-dollar bill the man handed him. "It will also help your illness to eat a lot of good strengthening soup—chicken soup is the most beneficial."

"Thank you for your helpful advice. Have you any apple-cider vinegar?"

The double blast of the train whistle echoed through the shop, muted but clear.

"There's no time to buy it now, Marie. We have to get back to the train." The man escorted his wife out the door.

Trace frowned and watched the couple walking back to the station amid a sea of blue cavalry uniforms. For the last few days, almost every train from the east brought people to his shop seeking medicinal help for colds. But that woman had more than a cold…

Chapter Seven

She'd lost her appetite. Katherine tossed her half-eaten sandwich into the scrap basket and went to stir the soup she was making for the Latherops' supper. It was easier not to hear the low murmur of voices coming from Blake and Audrey's bedroom if she stayed at the far end of the kitchen. She had cleared Audrey's bedside table and placed Blake's dishes there so they could be together while they ate. And though they had graciously asked her to join them for the afternoon meal, she had declined. The way Blake looked at Audrey stirred memories and dreams and longings that were best left buried.

She hummed softly to further deaden the sound of their voices, laid the spoon on a saucer on the work-table and looked out the window over the coal box. There was the sound of hammering coming from the hotel. She focused her attention on the building. It was attractive, three stories high, with a pagoda at the top. Had Mr. Todd, the man who was in charge of all of the building being done in Whisper Creek, designed it? Or had Mr. Stevenson, the owner? When Trace had introduced her to the two businessmen at church last Sunday, Mr. Stevenson had impressed her as a man who was used to being in charge. Like Trace. No. Not like Trace. She'd never met a man like Trace Warren. He was…unique. And so was his choice of a house.

She crossed her arms over her chest and thought about the octagonal house to keep from thinking about its owner. The house was beautiful. And very spacious and convenient. She would have to write and tell Judith all about the unusual structure. And include a sketch so that she would believe it. She smiled, imagining her sister's reply.

The whistle announcing the arrival of a train bounced off the mountainsides and echoed down the valley. She ran hot water into the dishpan, added the soap and waited to hear Blake hurrying down the stairs to the store. She had already learned his daily routine was centered around the trains' arrivals and planned her actions accordingly. All she had to do was listen for the whistles. She grabbed a tray and headed for the Latherops' bedroom to gather their dirty dishes.

A quick glance told her Blake had removed the extra pillows from behind Audrey as instructed. And that he had kissed her. In spite of her worry over their baby, there was a happy glow in Audrey's eyes. She squelched a tingle of envy and gathered the dishes onto the tray.

"Thank you for fixing dinner for us, Katherine. It was very good."

"It was also *your* cooking." She curved her lips into a smile.

"Not the pudding. And it was delicious."

"I'm glad you liked it. There's enough left for you to have some with your supper."

Howard whimpered. She moved to the bed and looked down at him. He was squirming and kicking his legs beneath his blanket. Her heart squeezed. "He's getting ready to cry. He's probably wet, and it's time for his feeding." She glanced over at Audrey. "I'll go heat his bottle and be right back. Don't try to pick him up!"

"I won't. I'll just talk to him."

She hurried to the kitchen, put a bottle in a pan of hot water and washed the dishes while she waited for it to warm. Howard's whimpers grew louder. He let out a squall. She grabbed the bottle from the water, tested it and hurried back to the bedroom.

"Shh, shh, little one. I'm right here. Everything is all right. Shh…shh…" She cooed the words as she changed his diaper, taking delight when he calmed at her touch. She cuddled him close, picked up the bottle and went to sit in the rocker to feed him. "Here you are, Howard…" She offered him the bottle. He fastened his little mouth on it and sucked greedily. She smiled, leaned back in the rocker and pushed with her feet to start it moving.

"You are so good with Howard, Katherine. Anyone would think you are his natural mother." Audrey's face flushed. "I'm sorry. I hope I didn't offend you by mentioning your…situation. Trace told us you had taken Howard for your own when his mother died."

"I'm not offended, Audrey. I'm flattered by what you said. I've had no…previous experience with caring for infants or in being a wife. But I'm learning." *That should cover any mistake.* "But I guess every bride—" *how odd to call myself that!* "—has to learn to be a wife. And every mother, natural or otherwise, has to learn to be comfortable caring for their first baby."

"Unless they were born into a household with younger brothers and sisters they helped raise."

"True." She hadn't thought about Audrey having a family. She glanced toward the bed. "Have you any siblings? Any sisters who will want to come and care for you? I didn't mean to intrude on your family when I offered."

A shadow of sadness slipped across Audrey's face. Her hands twitched and smoothed a wrinkle from the blanket. "I have one sister. But Linda decided she wanted be an actress in California. I—I haven't heard from her since she left a few months ago. I don't know how to reach her." Audrey's hands stilled, resting on the blanket. "But she wouldn't want to come. And she definitely would not want to care for me. Linda's talents do not extend to mundane things like caring for a house or a sister. She's very beautiful…"

"Then beauty runs in your family."

"What a kind thing to say!" A smile chased the shadow from Audrey's face. "What about you, Katherine? Have you any siblings?"

She nodded and lifted Howard to her shoulder to burp him, the action second nature to her now. "I also have one sister. Judith is married to a soldier stationed at Fort Bridger." She fussed with one of Howard's booties, lest she say too much and give away her true situation with Trace Warren.

"That's not far from here. A lot of soldiers on their way to the different forts come into the store when the trains stop to take on coal and water. I've heard several of them mention that Fort Bridger is their posting."

She tensed. Her chest tightened. "Do the soldiers talk about the Indian attacks in that area?"

"No. The soldiers mostly joke with each other while they shop. But news reaches us from other sources—the train conductors and engineers and railroad workmen. People like that. I heard there were several attacks near Fort Kearny and Fort Reno in October. And also at Crazy Woman Creek. I'm sure we would hear if there were any serious attacks by Indians at Fort Bridger."

Her stomach clenched. *Judith, are you all right?* "What do you mean by *serious attacks*?"

"Sometimes the Indians just attack and then ride away rather than engage in a battle. They often do that to wagon trains or the railroad."

The railroad! A vision of the railroad station at the end of the short road popped into her head.

"A *serious* attack is when someone is wounded or…worse." Audrey's gaze fastened on hers. "I'm sorry, Katherine. I hope I haven't frightened you."

"No. I've been frightened for my sister and her

husband ever since I learned of the Indian attacks in the area. And now, of course, for Howard. And Trace." She clutched the baby tight against her.

"I was frightened, too. But Blake says Mr. Ferndale made some sort of private treaty with the Indians and we are safe as long as we stay in the valley."

"I see." Howard burped. She lowered him to her lap and resumed feeding him, struggling to control her trembling. He sucked contentedly while she rocked him. "I've written to Judith, telling her of my…arrival in Whisper Creek. Trace posted the letter for me. But where do I go to receive her answering letter?" *Please, Lord, let me receive an answer!* "I haven't noticed any post office in Whisper Creek."

"We get our mail at the train depot for the present. But we are hoping that will soon change. Blake has petitioned the Postal Department to have the Whisper Creek Post Office here in the store. He will be the postmaster." Pride glowed in Audrey's eyes.

"That will be more convenient than walking to the train station." *And safer.*

"Yes. When Blake receives the appointment, he's going to have Mr. Todd make a cubicle in the storage room for the safe and sorting table, then cut a window with a shelf in the back wall of the store and fasten rows of boxes beside it. That way Blake will be able to keep all of the mail separate from the store activity. Not that there will be much mail at the start. But Whisper Creek will grow. It already has." A smile curved Audrey's lips. "I have you for a friend now."

But not for long. Guilt smote her. She set the bottle

aside on the table and lifted Howard to her shoulder again to hide her emotions. "How are you feeling since you ate dinner?"

"I feel fine. In fact, I feel so well that I'm ashamed to be lying here in this bed when I should be up and about doing my own work instead of stealing your time from your husband."

"Trace is at his shop. And Ah Key does the cooking and cleaning. Howard is my only responsibility, and he is here with me." She rose and walked to the bed. "He's asleep again. I'll put him here beside you while I go and stir the soup I've made for your supper."

"It smells wonderful."

"Good. How does chocolate cake sound for dessert tomorrow?"

"Delicious! It's one of Blake's favorites. He'll love you forever."

She covered Howard with his blanket and forced a smile. "From the way he looks at you, I'm quite certain that place in Blake's heart is already occupied." She moved to the nightstand and picked up the glass sitting there. "I'll bring you some fresh water. Is there anything else you would like?"

"No, nothing."

She nodded and headed for the kitchen.

"Katherine?"

"Yes?" She turned and looked back at Audrey.

"Trace seemed very sure about my condition and what to do about it yesterday. And I'm very grateful for his help..."

There was more Audrey wanted to say. She stood in the doorway and waited.

Audrey plucked at a piece of fuzz on the blanket. "But I feel so well this morning I'm not sure I need to stay in bed. But I don't want to hurt my baby." Audrey looked up and fastened her gaze on her. "How does Trace know what I should do?"

She smiled, relieved that she could answer Audrey's question honestly. "I asked Trace about that last night. He said he had doctor friends back in New York that used to discuss their cases with him."

"Oh, well…that makes sense."

"Yes. Is there anything else?"

Audrey smiled and nodded. "I have a basket of knitting in the sitting room. If you wouldn't mind bringing it to me, I'll just lie here and knit soakers and booties for my baby while I watch Howard sleep."

"That's an excellent idea. I'll be right back with your basket." She hurried down the hall toward the sitting room, trying not to think about Indians and half-truths and the day she would have to walk away from Howard forever.

Trace held the reins loosely and let the mare pick the path out of the darkness. The circles of light from the side lamps were more comfort than help. The golden beams skimmed along over the ground, shaking and dipping with each lurch of the runabout. Katherine's shoulder rubbed against his arm with every motion, setting his nerves jangling. At least

YOUR PARTICIPATION IS REQUESTED!

Dear Reader,

Since you are a lover of our books – we would like to get to know you!

Inside you will find a short Reader's Survey. Sharing your answers with us will help our editorial staff understand who you are and what activities you enjoy.

To thank you for your participation, we would like to send you up to 4 books and 2 gifts – **ABSOLUTELY FREE!**

Enjoy your gifts with our appreciation,

Pam Powers

**SEE INSIDE
FOR READER'S
SURVEY**

Get up to 4 Free Books!

Romance ◆ **Historical**

We'll send you 2 Free Books from each series you choose plus 2 Free Gifts!

Try **Love Inspired® Romance Larger-Print** books featuring Christian characters facing modern-day challenges.

Try **Love Inspired® Historical** novels featuring Christian characters confronting challenges in vivid historical periods.

Or **TRY BOTH!**

YOUR READER'S SURVEY
"THANK YOU" FREE GIFTS INCLUDE:

▶ 2 lovely surprise gifts   ▶ Up to 4 FREE books

PLEASE FILL IN THE CIRCLES COMPLETELY TO RESPOND

1) What type of fiction books do you enjoy reading? (Check all that apply)
   - ○ Suspense/Thrillers   ○ Action/Adventure   ○ Modern-day Romances
   - ○ Historical Romance   ○ Humor   ○ Paranormal Romance

2) What attracted you most to the last fiction book you purchased on impulse?
   - ○ The Title   ○ The Cover   ○ The Author   ○ The Story

3) What is usually the greatest influencer when you plan to buy a book?
   - ○ Advertising   ○ Referral   ○ Book Review

4) How often do you access the internet?
   - ○ Daily   ○ Weekly   ○ Monthly   ○ Rarely or never

YES! I have completed the Reader's Survey. Please send me
2 FREE books and 2 FREE gifts (gifts are worth about $10 retail)
from each series selected below. I understand that I am under no
obligation to purchase any books, as explained on the back of
this card.

Select the series you prefer (check one or both):

❑ **Love Inspired® Romance Larger-Print** (122/322 IDL GMRL)

❑ **Love Inspired® Historical** (102/302 IDL GMRL)

❑ **Try Both** (122/322/102/302 IDL GLYY)

FIRST NAME	LAST NAME

ADDRESS

APT.#	CITY

STATE/PROV.	ZIP/POSTAL CODE

HLI-817-SCT17

▲ If offer card is missing write to: Reader Service, P.O. Box 1341, Buffalo, NY 14240-8531 or visit www.ReaderService.com ▲

BUSINESS REPLY MAIL

FIRST-CLASS MAIL   PERMIT NO. 717   BUFFALO, NY

POSTAGE WILL BE PAID BY ADDRESSEE

READER SERVICE

PO BOX 1341

BUFFALO NY 14240-8571

NO POSTAGE
NECESSARY
IF MAILED
IN THE
UNITED STATES

the baby didn't cry with the occasional unavoidable jolt. It was easier when he was silent.

"Audrey wondered about your knowledge of what to do for her condition."

He glanced sideways. The light of the lamps was reflected in tiny flashes of gold in Katherine's violet eyes, shimmered on the fullness of her bottom lip. He jerked his gaze back to the road.

"I told her what you said to me—about having doctor friends in New York who discussed their cases with you." She lifted her hand and tugged her collar up around her cheeks. "I hope that was all right."

"Yes, of course." It had to be that way in order to keep his past hidden. But he didn't like dealing in half-truths.

"While I was caring for her today, I felt a little… dishonest in letting her think I would be here to care for her until she is able to be on her feet again. I kept thinking about the plan you are developing in order to replace me." He watched her smooth a wrinkle from Howard's blanket, thought of how soft and small her hand felt in his. "How soon might that be?"

Concern shot through him. If she told Audrey the truth… He glanced her way again, caught her gaze on him and held it. "The truth is, Katherine, I haven't been able to think of a plan that will work yet. And I think it's too soon—because of the baby. I know I promised you it wouldn't be long, but I have to be careful. I don't want Mr. Ferndale to think I'm trying to trick him and risk him getting angry with me. I'm on very shaky legal ground. And if he takes my shop, I'm left without a means of livelihood. I'll have no way to provide for the child."

"I see." She snuggled her chin closer to the baby resting against her neck and shoulder. "Then it's certain I will be here long enough to care for Audrey?"

Was that her concern? The length of time? He hastened to apologize. "Yes. I'm sorry for the delay, Katherine. But I based my promise on my experience. Finding a woman willing to enter into an in-name-only marriage in exchange for a comfortable home and abundant provision was easy. But now I have the baby to think of. I have to devise a plan that will enable me to be certain the woman I select will treat the baby well." He felt her stiffen beside him. Her arm tightened around the baby—an instinctive, protective, *maternal* reaction. Guilt surged. He didn't want to hurt Katherine, but there was no way he could avoid it. The longer she cared for the baby, the more attached she would become to him. And the baby to her. And the harder it would become for him to maintain his…disinterest. *Disinterest, ha!* He almost snorted.

He guided the mare into the carriage way and stared at the house that loomed against the darkness, its windows glowing with welcoming light. The house he had intended to live in *alone.* And now look at what had happened! *"Oh, what a tangled web we weave when first we practise to deceive!"*

She should be angry or disgusted or upset… *something*! Katherine paced about her bedroom, her long dark hair dancing against her back and shoulders, her silk dressing gown flowing out behind her. Trace Warren had broken his word to her! She should *not* feel relieved. But she did. How could she not? The truth stopped her cold.

She moved to the cradle and stood looking down at Howard. He was growing. She could see and feel the difference in him even in these few days. He would be too big for his cradle soon. And she would be here to move him into his crib in his own bedroom. She frowned and tucked the blanket more closely about him. She liked having Howard close where she could hear his soft little sucking sounds and the whisper of his arms and legs brushing against the blanket. What would she do when she had to leave him? Tears stung her eyes.

She turned her thoughts away from that inevitable day, sat at the desk and took out writing supplies to begin her letter to Judith. Her sister would be very likely to come looking for her if she didn't tell her she would be delayed. And she did not want Judith on the train. She wanted her to stay safe in Fort Bridger. The fear she'd been holding at bay swelled. She arranged the paper, picked up the pen and moved it toward the ink bottle, then stopped.

She glanced at the window she'd shuttered tight. Was Trace on the porch, drinking a cup of coffee? A sudden need for his company pulled her to her feet. Her silk dressing gown rustled softly. She looked down, frowned and hurried to her closet to change into her warmer quilted cotton dressing gown. A ribbon tied at the nape of her neck brought her loose hair under control. She glanced down at her fur-trimmed slippers, decided they would be warm enough if she tucked her feet beneath her on the bench and grabbed her green wool everyday cape off its hook. Howard was sleeping soundly. She swirled the cape around her shoulders and fastened it, tugged up the hood to hide her hair and hurried from her room.

She smelled the coffee when she was halfway down the stairs and quickened her steps. The kitchen was empty, but the coffeepot was hot. Was he out on the porch? Or had he chosen to drink his coffee elsewhere because of the cold? She poured a cup and stepped into the back entrance, looked out the window.

He was leaning against the post at the top of the steps. Her stomach fluttered. She pressed her hand against it and frowned. She was more nervous than she had realized about the uncertainty of her welcome. Trace had made it clear he preferred solitude to her company. She glanced back toward the kitchen then steeled herself to face Trace's cool demeanor. He was too polite to refuse her company, and she needed someone to talk to—to be with until this fear eased along with the vague dissatisfaction that had hovered over her all day. She took a deep breath, opened the door and stepped out onto the porch. "May I join you while you drink your coffee?"

The light from the oil lamp beside the door fell on his face when he turned. Their gazes met. Her breath caught, froze in her lungs—not from the cold air, but from the look in his eyes. A look that was hastily replaced by one of cool civility. "If you care to brave the cold."

"I'm from Albany, remember? I'm no stranger to cold weather."

He nodded and turned back to look out into the darkness.

So much for any welcome. She wasn't even sure she'd seen that warmth in his eyes when he first turned and looked at her. It was most likely a trick of the lighting or her imagination. Even so, she was staying. She needed his company tonight, reluctant or not. Her "German stubborn" drove her to the porch bench. She curled up on it, tucked her feet beneath the hem of her quilted dressing gown and covered them with the bottom of her cape. "I hope rattlesnakes don't like the cold weather." *Or Indians.* She shivered, refusing to look out and search the darkness.

"I asked one of the soldiers that came into the shop about the snakes. He said they hibernate all winter."

She stared at him, touched that he had thought to inquire about the snakes. "Thank you for asking, Trace."

He shrugged his shoulders and nodded. "It's good to know."

She looked down at her cup, wrapped both hands around its warmth and changed the subject to something without danger attached to it. "Howard was very good today. I let him sleep on the bed beside Audrey. Is that all right?"

"It's fine, as long as she doesn't lift him."

His tone said clearly he was not interested in hearing about her day. Or about Howard. Well, she'd known that before she came downstairs. At least he wasn't completely ignoring her. She took a sip of the

hot black coffee and studied him. The thick blond
waves at the top of his head gleamed in the lamplight.
The collar of his brown jacket was pulled up high
on his neck, and the heavy wool fabric fitted snug
across his broad shoulders. He looked strong and
capable leaning there against the post and drinking
coffee. But there was something in his posture—a
sort of *rigidity*. What had happened to Trace Warren? What had made him this way?

*I am a widower, Miss Fleming. I am not inter-
ested in any personal relationship with any woman.*

Her breath caught. *His wife's death.* She should
have thought of that before. Her heart had broken
when Richard disappeared, and she had withdrawn
from society. It had been the need to care for her
mother and father that had brought her out of isola-
tion. Perhaps having to care for Howard would be a
blessing for Trace.

Whisper Creek gurgled by in the stillness. An
owl screeched somewhere in the towering pines at
the foot of the mountains. Trace remained silent and
still as a statue. She stared at his back, wanting to
ask about his wife, to tell him she understood the
pain of the loss of the one you loved. But that would
be presumptuous of her. She was only a temporary
part of his life.

She uncurled from her perch on the bench and
went into the kitchen, rinsed her cup and returned
to her room.

Trace set his jaw and held his stance, staring out
into the night. The sound of Katherine's long skirts

brushing against the porch floor rasped along his nerves. She was going back inside. He gripped the post beside him, his fingernails scraping against the wood. He dare not turn and ask her to stay. It would open the way to possibilities he wanted no part of. Katherine Fleming could be the end of him.

"Down in the human heart, crushed by the tempter, feelings lie buried that grace can restore. Touched by a loving heart, wakened by kindness, chords that are broken will vibrate once more."

Not his. He wouldn't have it! He would crush every stirring Katherine roused in him. He knew better than to let her into his heart.

Chapter Eight

"Thanks for helping me unhitch, Blake." Trace turned Shadow into the pen behind the parsonage and gave his friend a wry smile. "One thing is certain. I'll never be a cowboy."

Blake laughed and draped the bridle over the fence post. "I'm with you there, Trace. I think you have to be born to it to handle cows and ride horses the way a cowboy does. I watched the men who drove cattle through this valley to feed the railroad work crews before the trains were running any farther than Whisper Creek, and I'd never attempt to do that. But I have learned to shoot a pistol well enough to hit what I'm aiming at most of the time."

Trace fastened the gate and they walked out to the road, headed for the lights shining in Blake's store windows. "A pistol, not a rifle? What are you planning on shooting?"

"Any rattlesnake that tries to take up residence in the stable or under the loading dock."

"Hmm, that makes sense."

"Or any Indians that might decide to attack."

Trace glanced sideways. "Do you think that's likely?"

"I don't know. We've not been bothered here in the valley, but the Indian attacks against the railroad are worrying. And there have been warriors on the hills watching us a few times."

Trace's gut tightened. He stopped walking and looked at Blake. "I didn't know that." Had he inadvertently put Katherine and the baby in peril by trying to save his shop and home?

"I've seen them. So far they've just gone away. But if those miners around South Pass keep breaking the Laramie Treaty, who knows what will happen? I can't protect the store, but I've added bars to the doors of the storage room so I can take a stand there and keep any attackers from going upstairs. There's only one small window in that room and I've strong shutters on that. I intend to keep Audrey safe if any Indians should attack. Especially if she has a baby."

Where could he make a stand in his house? Where would Katherine and the baby be safe? His breath hitched. This was the answer he was looking for! Ferndale couldn't object to him sending Katherine and the baby away to a place of safety. And meanwhile he could replace Katherine with an older, unattractive woman willing to care for the baby who was looking for a man to provide a home for her. Perfect! His lips lifted in a wry smile. It could work! He'd plan it out tonight and have everything ready for when news of a nearby attack came their way. He started up the steps to his shop, turned and looked down at Blake. "Maybe you'd better order one of those pistols for me. And a rifle, too. Just in case."

"I'll order them this morning." Blake stopped walking and looked up at him. "*Will* Audrey have a baby, Trace? You seemed to know quite a bit about her condition the other day. Are Audrey and the baby going to be all right?"

He stiffened, froze at the top of the steps, his key pressed into his palm. He couldn't send Katherine and the baby away. Not until Audrey had passed her third month and no longer needed continual bed rest. If he did and she lost her baby it would be his fault. His stomach twisted into a burning knot. He ran his thumb over the key and shook his head. "I can't say, Blake. I was only sharing information I've heard over the years from some doctors who were friends of mine. Audrey's life and your baby's life are in God's hands."

"I know. I've been praying."

So did I. Bitterness rose. He crossed the porch and fitted the key in the lock.

"Oh, I almost forgot!"

He stifled the anger and turned back. Blake stood holding to the newel post and looking up at him.

"Audrey and I were talking about your kindness in sacrificing your time with your bride and new son so that Katherine can care for Audrey. And we want you to come and have dinner with Katherine."

He stared at the smile on his friend's face. Obviously, this was meant to be a wonderful surprise. He fought back the inappropriate "no" forming on his tongue and groped for an acceptable excuse.

"We know it won't be the same as eating the noon meal in your home together, but it will give you two back the time we are stealing from you. And it makes more sense than you hitching up the runabout to go home every day."

Ah. He had his excuse! "Well, that's very kind of you, Blake. But I intend to walk—the way I did before Katherine came." He moved to open his door.

"Even so…"

He stiffened, waited.

"I'm sure you'd rather eat dinner with your bride than sit alone at your dining table. And Audrey told me I was not to allow you to refuse."

This couldn't be happening! Still, once again Blake had handed him his excuse. He forced his lips into a smile. "Thank Audrey for me, Blake, but Ah Key will have dinner ready for me."

"We thought of that. Ah Cheng comes for the laundry this morning. Audrey will have him tell Ah Key you will not be home for dinner."

"Well, then…" He groped but came up empty. He'd run out of excuses. The trap clicked closed. He forced a pleased tone into his voice. "It seems you have thought of everything. Thank you. I will see you this afternoon."

He unlocked the door, stepped inside and turned up the wick on the oil lamp on the shelf. The whistle announcing the arrival of first morning train reverberated through the cold, still air in the shop. He hung the open sign in the window then tossed coal on the live embers in the stove. A quick twist of his wrist adjusted the dampers for maximum heat—but nothing could warm the cold place in his heart. He pulled down the chandelier over the counter and lit the lamps to chase away the darkness. As if anything ever could.

He stalked to the back room and removed his coat and hat, hung them on the hook and added coal to the small stove. He grabbed a few bottles of assorted cough elixirs to sit on the counter, put them in place and grabbed pen and paper to make out an order for more. It was selling fast, and his stock was already severely depleted. He'd go to the depot and place the order when he went to the Latherops—

It makes more sense than you hitching up the runabout to go home every day.

He froze, his fingers clenched on the pen. *Every day?* Surely Blake didn't mean— No. It couldn't be. He'd been distracted and hadn't heard clearly. He was remembering wrong. He blew out a breath, relaxed his grip and finished writing the order.

The bell on the door jingled.

He slid the order ledger under the counter, looked at the man and woman entering and smiled a welcome.

"Good morning! I'm here!" Katherine called out to alert Audrey to her presence, climbed the stairs and walked to the bedroom. "Mmm, it feels nice and cozy in here." She smiled down at Audrey. "It's getting really chilly outside."

"That's what Blake said." Tears glistened in Audrey's eyes. "I'm sorry, Katherine. It's my fault you and the baby have to be out in the cold."

"Poof, this is nothing! It's probably *freezing* in Albany. My coat is warm. And this little man is so bundled up it's impossible for the cold air to touch him. Isn't it, Howard?" She uncovered the baby, kissed his cheek and laid him on the bed beside Audrey. "It's odd to not know what to expect of the weather. Does Wyoming have mild winters or blizzards?" *Will I be here or at Fort Bridger?* She removed Howard's knitted hat and coat and pulled up his long booty socks. "Will you be bundled up tight all winter, little one— or warm enough in cotton flannel gowns?" She tickled him as she cooed the words, and he waved his little arms and kicked his feet.

"He's so adorable, Katherine. And to think that Blake and I will soon have a baby son or daughter..." Audrey lifted her hands and wiped tears from her cheeks. "I'm sorry. I'm doing a lot of crying lately. I try to be brave, Katherine, but I'm so afraid something will go wrong and I'll lose the baby..."

As I will lose mine. There is more than one way to lose a baby. The thought ripped at her heart. Her eyes filmed with tears. She blinked them clear, covered Howard with his blanket and turned her back under the guise of removing her coat and hat. "Now, just let me put these bottles in the refrigerator, and I'll get to work while Howard sleeps." She pulled the bottles from the baby's valise and started for the kitchen. "Is there anything you need me to do for you? Are you hungry?"

"No, nothing, thank you. Blake is wonderful about helping me to wash and prepare for the day. And he made us oatmeal for breakfast. He said to apologize to you for him. He didn't have time to do the dishes before he went to help Trace unhitch. And he will need to open the store when he returns."

"Well, gracious, there's no need for him to apologize for a few dirty dishes. It's kind of him to help Trace." She went to put the bottles away, heard Blake run up the stairs and into the bedroom and busied herself looking at the supplies in the pantry.

Blake's steps pounded down the stairs. She went back to the bedroom, tried not to envy the glow on Audrey's face. "I saw some canned salmon in the pantry, Audrey. Do you and Blake like salmon loaf? I thought I'd make one for your dinner."

"Yes, we do. Very much. Does Trace like it?"

"Trace? I have no idea." She pressed her lips together at the slip of tongue and hastened to cover her bald statement of fact. "Ah Key does all of the cooking at…home, and I've not been here long enough to discover Trace's likes and dislikes of food."

"You're about to."

She blinked, stared at Audrey's gleeful smile. "I beg your pardon?"

"Make enough salmon loaf for four, Katherine. Trace will be joining you for dinner today!"

"Wh-what?"

Audrey clasped her hands and grinned. "You should see your face, Katherine! You look perfectly *astounded*."

"I *am* astounded." She couldn't very well deny it. "Trace didn't tell—"

"He didn't *know*. Blake and I planned it as a surprise for you two." Audrey's voice turned thick with tears. "We both feel so guilty for taking your time away from each other we decided to have Trace come and eat his afternoon meal here with you."

"And he *agreed*?" An image of him standing on the porch with his back turned toward her popped into her head.

"Why, yes, why wouldn't he?"

Why, indeed? "Well, he's…so busy at the shop."

"Yes. But he has to eat, Katherine. And every newly married man wants to spend time with his bride."

Not Trace Warren. I'm not his bride. "But Ah Key—"

"That's been taken care of. When Ah Cheng goes to collect your laundry he will take him a message to not prepare a dinner meal from today until I am able to be up and about and doing my own work!" Audrey's voice rose in a crescendo of joy.

"Until—" She stopped the expression of shock trembling on her lips and clapped her hands against her cheeks. "Well, that's quite a surprise." She tugged her lips into a smile. "I don't know what to say except— I'd better get to work preparing that salmon loaf." She laughed along with Audrey, wiped her palms down the sides of her long skirt and hurried back to the kitchen, her thoughts tumbling one after another.

Trace was coming for dinner. How had Blake and Audrey convinced him? She glanced down at the white pleated bodice and plain gray skirt she wore and wished she had chosen one of her prettier gowns—not that it would make any difference to Trace. It was only that it would make her feel more…

comfortable. *Liar. You want to see something other than that cool reserve on his face when he looks at you.*

She grabbed an apron, slipped the strap over her head and pulled the ties taut around her small waist to make a bow at her back. Trace tried to hide it under a cover of extreme politeness, but it was apparent he could barely tolerate sharing a meal with her in the large dining room at home. Of course he *had* to pretend he was eager to spend time with her in front of others. Poor man. He was trapped.

She ran hot water into the dishpan, added soap and washed and rinsed the breakfast dishes, then scrubbed at the oatmeal pan. However would Trace manage here? She glanced at the eating table situated against the end wall just inside the kitchen doorway. The Latherops' bedroom door was only a few steps away down the hall, and she could easily hear Blake and Audrey talking together. And though she tried hard not to hear what they were saying, their loving tone was very clear.

And then there was Howard. She brought him into the kitchen with her when he was fussy, and also while Blake and Audrey were together throughout the day. And they would expect Trace to be delighted to spend time with his new son.

She rinsed the scrubbed pan and slid her gaze to the blanket-padded crate resting on the seats of two of the table chairs Blake had positioned facing each other. Trace would not be able to ignore Howard as he did at home. The thought gave her pause. She stared at the improvised crib beside the kitchen table and a smile touched her lips. Perhaps this would work out well after all.

Now, what should she have with the salmon loaf?

Trace followed Blake into the storage room, his shoulders tense, his steps reluctant. "Most of my patrons the last few days have been ill with coughs or sore throats, but quite a few of them look to have a fever. Of course it's only natural that those who are feeling ill would come to me. But I've been wondering if you have noticed much sickness among your patrons?"

Blake stopped, waved his hand to the left. "You can hang your hat and coat on one of those hooks." His eyes narrowed. "Come to think of it, I have. It seems like most of them are coughing or sneezing."

"I thought as much." He shrugged out of his coat, hung it on a hook then tugged his suit coat back in place. "I've ordered a dozen bottles of Gilbert & Parsons Hygienic medical alcohol. I'm going to use it to wipe down my counter and clean my hands between trains and before I leave the shop. I suggest you do the same."

"Why?"

"To protect yourself and Audrey from the illness." *Just do it, Blake. Don't make me explain.*

"I don't understand. How would the alcohol keep us from getting sick?"

He looked at Blake, willing him to agree to the precaution. "I don't fully understand, either. But I heard a lec—I heard about a doctor named Semmelwies who discovered a…*connection* between childbed fever and the unclean hands of those who delivered the women's babies. When a few of my coll—doctor friends began cleaning their hands and instruments with alcohol, the spread of illness among their patients decreased significantly. I've been using alcohol to protect myself against disease ever since."

"I see." Blake stared at him. "Well, if it will keep Audrey from getting sick, I'll do it. I'll make out an order for the alcohol this afternoon. But—"

No more medical questions! "What is that?" Trace indicated a large wooden box in the far corner to change the subject.

"I hired one of Mitch's men to build a large coal box here in the storage room. I want to be prepared for a blizzard or whatever might happen."

"That's a good idea, Blake. I think I'll do the same. My place is farther from the station, and if we get deep drifts, the wagon would have a hard time getting through."

"True." Blake started up the stairs, eagerness in his steps.

He set his face in a pleasant expression and followed.

"Good afternoon, Katherine. How's my wife?"

"I'm fine, Blake." Audrey's voice floated out into the hallway. "Impatient to see you, but fine."

"I'm coming, my love! I'll see you after dinner, Trace." Blake hurried down the short hall on the left, entered a room and closed the door.

He took a breath and slid his gaze to Katherine. "Well, I—"

She held a finger to her mouth, shook her head and

motioned for him to come. He bit back a question as to her odd behavior and followed her to the far end of the Latherops' kitchen. She stopped in front of a worktable and turned to face him.

"I'm sorry, Trace, but I couldn't let you say anything in the hallway. The house is small and conversations are easily overheard—even soft-spoken ones. And, well, they would expect—" pink spread across her cheekbones "—you know." She made a helpless little gesture.

Yes, he knew. And the thought was far too appealing. "I see. Thank you for the warning." He took refuge in teasing her. "Do you think we've whispered long enough that they will think our loving greeting is over? Something smells good in here! And I'm hungry."

"I think enough time has passed so that we can eat." She laughed and motioned him toward the table. "I made a salmon loaf. I hope you like it."

"I do. And I haven't had any since I came to Whisper Creek." He turned, spotted the baby in the makeshift crib, paused and then continued on toward the table. At least the infant was sleeping. He held a chair for Katherine, trying not to smell the floral scent clinging to her hair. Or to notice the way the lamplight gleamed on its dark waves when she bowed her head to ask God's blessing on the meal. He closed his eyes to resist the temptation to look at her. When he opened them again, a small lock of wavy hair had fallen forward onto her smooth forehead. His fingers twitched to brush it back, to feel the softness of her skin. He picked up the knife on the plate and sliced off two servings of the salmon loaf.

"I'm not familiar with your likes or dislikes, so I made simple fare." Katherine's voice was pitched low, its slight huskiness more pronounced. "There's mashed potatoes and buttered green beans and applesauce. I left it chunky and added a bit of cinnamon." She brushed back the lock of hair. "And rolls. And butter and jam."

A soft murmur came from the Latherops' bedroom. He clenched his jaw and lifted his gaze from his plate to look at her. The table was small, and she was so close, he could see tiny flecks of reflected light in her violet eyes. He had only to reach out his hand to touch her... "I'm sorry I've gotten you into this uncomfortable position, Katherine. I never meant for you to be embarrassed or—"

The baby let out a squall. Katherine rose and bent over the crate then lifted Howard into her arms. "You owe me no apology, Trace. I *chose* to stay to help you keep your home and shop for Howard's sake. I'm not sorry." She looked over at him and met his gaze. Tears glistened in her beautiful eyes. "I may be hurt by my choice, but I'll never be sorry." Her whisper was fierce. She bent her head and kissed Howard's cheek. The baby nuzzled at her neck, searching for something to eat. It was the perfect picture of what he had longed for, prayed for and lost.

His chest tightened; his stomach knotted. He looked down at his plate, picked up his fork and forced himself to take a bite of salmon loaf.

"Trace..."

He braced himself and looked up.

"Please hold Howard while I warm his bottle."

She handed the baby to him, took a bottle from the refrigerator and set it in a pan of hot water.

The baby looked up at him and wiggled his arms. His little mouth puckered and his eyes squeezed shut. He let out a whimper and then another. His little fists beat at the air. It was clear he was getting ready to express his discontent in no uncertain terms. Trace took a deep breath and lifted Howard to his shoulder, patted his tiny back. The baby stopped wiggling and rested there against his heart. So small. So helpless.

He looked at Katherine standing by the stove, holding a towel while she waited for the bottle to warm. Her lips curved in the suggestion of a smile. His heart lurched. She was so beautiful, so kind and softhearted, so brave to take on the care of an infant of a woman she didn't even know. Katherine Fleming was an amazing young woman.

He jerked his gaze away and stared down at his plate. He had to think of an acceptable excuse to leave as soon as the baby's bottle was ready. And a reason why he could not come again. It was far too dangerous for him to be here alone with Katherine every day. The baby squirmed, nuzzled at his neck and shoulder, whimpered.

There was a soft rustle. Katherine's long gray skirt appeared at the edge of his vision. Awareness of her sizzled along his nerves. He groped for an excuse to leave but could think of nothing.

"I'm sorry. I just realized I forgot to pour our coffee. I'll get it now." She set the baby's bottle on the table. "Would you please start feeding Howard before he begins to cry? I don't like him to disturb the Latherops' meal." Her skirts flared out as she turned back toward the stove.

He swallowed his protest, clenched his jaw and shifted the infant to the crook of his arm. The baby's lips closed on the offered bottle; his tiny fingers brushed his hand and clung, their touch as light as a feather. Pain ripped through him. The pain of a broken heart vibrating to life again. It was his greatest fear coming true.

Chapter Nine

Trace took another small swallow of his coffee, looked down at the cold brew and frowned. It wasn't as good as the coffee Katherine had made at the Latherops' that afternoon. He'd been nursing the strong, bitter brew along, listening for sounds from the kitchen and waiting for Katherine to join him. He might as well admit it. He'd already stood there staring at the light from her bedroom windows for so long the cold had penetrated his jacket. He'd be shivering in another few minutes. And for what? So he could talk to her about helping Audrey now that she'd done it for two days? A flimsy excuse. The truth was he'd grown to like her coming out on the porch to share a cup of evening coffee with him. Even if he did hide the fact from her.

He rolled the growing stiffness from his shoulders and pulled his collar up higher in the back, glanced down at the pool of light on the ground. It was plain foolish to stand there waiting for her. He needed to erase the images of her serving his meal and caring for the baby that had filled his mind since this afternoon—not add to them. The memory of her standing in the Latherops' kitchen wearing an apron with her cheeks pink and a welcoming smile on her face still jolted him to his toes. She'd only been pretending to be a loving wife, of course. But the love glowing in her eyes when she tended the baby was real—and heart-rending. His frown deepened. He'd never meant to cause her hurt. And now…now it was inevitable. Guilt as dark as the night swept through him.

The light disappeared, returned. He watched her shadow pass through the glow from her bedroom window then pass through it again going the other direction. She was pacing. Why? The baby should be asleep by now. Was there something wrong?

A dozen possibilities flooded his mind. He scowled at the sudden catch in his pulse and threw the dregs of his cold coffee over the railing. He was becoming too involved with Katherine and the baby. His agreement was to provide for them—not to allow them to intrude into his life. It would serve him better to stop thinking about this afternoon and try to think of a plausible excuse to not join them at the Latherops' for dinner every day. But it was the sensible thing to do. And so was going inside out of the cold.

He strode into the entrance, hung his jacket on a peg and went to the kitchen to rinse his cup. He glanced at the coffeepot and reached to dump the contents down the drain, stopped and instead shoved the pot to the back of the stove and closed down the dampers for the night. It would stay hot for a little while—just in case she came downstairs.

The muscle in front of his ear twitched. He walked to the doorway, cast a glance at the stairs, paused then moved on. He needed a distraction—something to get those images out of his head so he could sleep. He strode into the parlor to get a book, hesitating in front of the piano. He'd had the Steinway shipped even though he hadn't played it in two years. The piano, his grandmother's china dishes and his father's watch were all he had kept of his former possessions. They were the only things he owned with memories attached to them. His chest tightened.

He pivoted away from the piano and walked to the bookshelves, selected *The Pioneers* by James Fenimore Cooper and turned to go upstairs, but something wouldn't let him leave. He turned back to the piano and stared at the gleaming wood, the matching stool he had sat on while he took his lessons.

No, no, Trace darling. Don't play from your head, play from your heart!

How many times had his mother said that to him? He could almost feel her hands resting on his shoulders as she encouraged him to use all of his natural talent. She'd called it his *gift*. He placed the book on top of the piano and sat down, compelled by memories too strong for him to withstand. He opened the cover and ran his fingers over the keys. He was too out of practice to play anything that required precise timing and intricate fingering. He closed his eyes and let his fingers drift over the keys, find chords and fill in the melody of his mother's favorite popular song. His throat filled with the words.

"'Tis the last rose of summer, left blooming alone... All her lovely companions are faded and gone...'"

What was wrong with Howard? Why wouldn't he settle down to sleep? Katherine patted the baby's back and tried to stay calm. Trace had told her that first night in the carriage that a baby could sense it if you were upset or anxious, and that it made them fussy. But how did she rid herself of this hollow ache she'd been carrying around the last couple of days? Witnessing the love between Audrey and Blake had stirred longings she had thought buried and gone. And now—after today with Trace—

She swallowed hard, tried to reject the memories from this afternoon. It had been a pretend situation. But acting the part of a wife and mother had made her buried hunger for love and marriage and a family spring to life. And the sight of Trace feeding the baby—

She caught her breath, blinked her eyes. Howard wiggled, whimpered. "I'm sorry, little one. Shh, shh..." She put him in his cradle and covered him, rocked him until he calmed then went to the window and looked outside.

Was Trace out on the porch? She glanced toward her closet, pressed her lips together and sat down at the desk. She would not join Trace for coffee again. She was allowing herself to become too close to Howard and Trace. She ignored the lure of her cloak hanging in the closet and took out paper and pen and ink.

My dearest sister,
Have you recovered from the surprising news in my first letter? I hope so, for I have more to share. But first, I must tell you that I am fine. Trace's house is exceptionally comfortable with beautiful furniture and accoutrements. It is built in the shape of an octagon! Oh, Judith, I can hear your laugh of disbelief, but it's quite true! I will draw a sketch of the placement of the rooms at the end of this letter so you can see how lovely it is. Outside, a porch wraps around the entire house. I put Howard (the baby I told you of) in his new carriage and walked him around the entire length of it. It was quite a long walk!

Judith, why did you never tell me about the *rattlesnakes* here in Wyoming Territory? You know I am terrified of any sort of snake, but a rattlesnake! I assure you, I do not get off the porch or walk anywhere by myself. Trace takes me to town every day so I may tend Audrey. And that is the news I have to share.

There will be a further delay in my coming to visit. There is a young, newly married couple here in Whisper Creek who needs my help. Mr. Latherop is the owner of the town's one and only general store, and I happened to be there shopping for some new dress trim when his wife, Audrey, suffered a severe attack of cramps. It seems she is with child, and is in danger of losing the baby if she does not stay in bed. I offered to take care of her until the danger to the baby passes. That will be almost a month. I will be staying here for at least that long.

I know… I can hear you sighing and saying, "Katherine, what have you gotten yourself into now?" But truly, Judith, there is no one else here in Whisper Creek to care for Audrey. If I don't do so, she could lose her baby!

I will come to visit you as soon as possible, although I am a bit apprehensive of riding the train to Fort Bridger. I understand there are Indian attacks occurring around the fort and upon the trains, also. Please do *not* come to see me. I do not want you in danger riding on the train.

I am busy at the Latherop home all day. I make their meals and do simple cleaning. And now Trace is joining me there for dinner every day. It's quite…cozy…is the most descriptive word that comes to mind. It's enjoyable cooking for people again. I miss taking care of Mother and Father. I suppose that is not surprising as doing so was the center of my life for five years. Perhaps I should look into becoming a nurse when I return home.

Little Howard is growing so

What was that? She stopped writing and listened. The faint sound of a piano being played floated on the silence. She glanced over at Howard. He was fast asleep. She wiped the pen and walked over to open the door. The music grew louder. Trace was a musician! The man was full of surprises. She stepped out into the hallway, drawn by the sound of him playing and singing.

"'Beautiful dreamer, out on the sea, mermaids are chaunting the wild lorilie… Over the streamlet, vapors are borne…'"

She clutched the staircase banister, torn between wanting to hear Trace play and the desire to go back into her bedroom and close the door on the lyrics of the song. He had a nice voice, deep and full. She hesitated then took a breath and slipped down the stairs. The song would be over soon.

"'Beautiful dreamer, beam on my heart, e'en as the morn on the streamlet and sea… Then will all clouds of sorrow depart…'"

Her breath caught at the words. Tears stung her eyes. It was a lie. The sorrow of Richard's disappearance at sea had never left her. But Richard would never return. She'd accepted that now. There was no hope. This horrible emptiness would be a part of her forever.

"'Beautiful dreamer, wake unto me… Beautiful dreamer, wake unto me.'"

If only he could. She followed the music to the parlor and stopped outside the doorway as the melody ended. Her gaze slid over the beautiful settee and chairs in front of the fireplace, moved to the marble-topped table with its silver candelabra and tea service gleaming in the moonlight streaming through the double windows. She waited there, ready to leave if he was finished playing. She heard movement to her left, and he began another song.

She inched forward, her eyes filling at the melancholy ache in Trace's voice as he sang the words.

"'Oh tell me how from love to fly—its dangers how to shun... To guard the heart, to shield the eye... Or I must be undone...'"

His head was lifted. His eyes were closed. The moonlight edged the blond waves on his head with silver, flashed on his fingers as they moved in and out of the beams, coaxing a haunting lament from the keys. She lifted her hand to the base of her throat and pressed her fingertips against the lump forming there. How much Trace must have loved his wife. How lonely he must be without her.

"'For thy impression on my mind... No time, nor power can move... And vain, alas, the task I find... To look and not to love... To look and not to love...'"

She wiped tears from her cheeks, whispered the last verse along with him.

"'Could absence my sad heart uphold... I'd hence and mourn my lot—but mem'ry will not be controll'd. Thou ne'er cans't be forgot... Thou ne'er cans't be forgot...'"

Oh, Richard, why did you have to go to sea? The ending notes quivered on the air, faded into silence. She started to slip out of the doorway but froze when Trace closed the cover over the keys and turned in her direction. Her heart lurched. She looked at his eyes, but the moonlight was behind him, and she could not read their expression.

"Good evening, Katherine."

His *voice*... There was something underlying the cool politeness with which he always addressed her. "Good evening." She grasped hold of a button, twisted the smooth metal in her fingers. "Please forgive me for intruding. I heard the music and couldn't resist coming to listen. You sing and play very well."

"Thank you."

He rose and came toward her. Her pulse sped. She inched backward, suddenly nervous in his presence. This was a Trace she did not know.

"My mother was an accomplished musician. She taught me to play. I like to think I inherited some of her talent as well as her skill."

His gaze caught and held hers. *Leave! Go to your room! Now!* The look in his eyes held her rooted to the spot.

"I left the coffee on the stove. It should still be hot. Would you care for a cup? I have something I want to discuss with you."

Had she done something wrong today? Was he displeased with her? She was back on safe ground. She took a shaky breath. "All right. As long as it won't take too long." She stepped into the hallway, intensely aware of him moving to walk beside her. She brushed her palms against her skirt and hurried her steps. "Howard was fussy tonight. He didn't want to go to sleep." She preceded him through the doorway and all but ran to the stove to put space between them.

She dampened her fingertip, touched it to the coffeepot and drew it back. "It's still hot." She grabbed a folded towel to protect her hand.

"Here are the cups." He set them on the worktable. "Does Howard have a fever?"

He had big hands with long fingers. Her mind flashed to how strong and warm they were when he handed her into or out of the buggy. How safe she felt at his touch. "I can't tell, but I don't think so. His forehead isn't hot. And his cheeks are always rosy." Like hers were at the moment, judging from the warmth in them. She poured. The coffee splashed. "Ouch!" She dropped the coffeepot onto the table and grabbed at her other hand with the towel. "Clumsy of me…"

"Did you burn yourself?" He clasped her wrist and led her to the sink. "Let me wash off that coffee so I can see…" He lifted the towel, then held her hand and wrist under a flow of cold water. "Now come closer to the light." He slipped his free arm around her waist, turned her back around and lifted her hand toward the oil lamp over the worktable. Heat from his hand and arm and shoulder spread through her, warmer and more dangerous by far than the coffee burn on her hand. He leaned forward, his face so close that even in the dimmed light she could see a tiny scar at the edge of his cheekbone where the bristles of his shaved beard began. Her pulse raced.

He turned his head and their gazes met—held. His fingers twitched, his grasp tightened. "Katherine…"

Her heart beat like a wild thing. She fought for breath to speak, for strength to look away. "I—I'm fine. I— Is that Howard crying?"

"I don't hear anything."

She did. In his voice. No. She had to be imagining it. She slipped her hand from his, grabbed the coffeepot and finished pouring their coffee. He studied her a moment, then picked up his cup and moved to lean against the cupboard. She looked down at her coffee and wished she took sugar or cream so she would have something to do. She picked up the towel he'd dropped on the worktable and began to refold it.

"He could be reacting to the change."

"What?" She looked up. He was watching her hands. Could he see them trembling? She pushed the towel aside.

"Howard." His gaze lifted to meet hers. "It could be he's only restless from having spent all day away from home. It's too early for him to be teething."

Her heart skipped. It was the first time Trace had used Howard's name. And he'd said *home*. Trace was accepting the baby! He would take good care of Howard. She smiled and nodded, her throat too thick to speak.

"I wanted to ask you how you feel about caring for Audrey Latherop now that you've spent two days doing so, Katherine. I don't want you to overly tire yourself. You have Howard to care for, and he will become more work every day. Babies change rapidly at his age. If it's too much work for you, I will help Blake find—"

"No, please—I truly enjoy caring for Audrey. I've missed caring for my mother and father." She looked down and swirled the coffee in her cup. "Tending to my parents gave purpose to my days. And now I have Howard—" *For a little while.* Her voice broke.

She paused for control, blinked her eyes clear and looked up. "I was writing to my sister, before I heard you playing, and I told her that I'm considering becoming a nurse when—" The words lodged in her throat. She swallowed hard and made a helpless little gesture. "When all of this is over."

His quick intake of air drew her gaze. The muscle at his jaw was throbbing. The look in his eyes so intense she had to look away. "A nurse?"

"Yes." She lifted her chin and squared her shoulders. "I know that nurses are looked down upon by some. But I like taking care of people who are unable to care for themselves." Her chin went a notch higher. "Why shouldn't I do so? I believe it is a suitable occupation for a spinster."

"Why, indeed? I think it's…admirable. But I find it hard to believe a woman as…caring…as you are will spend her life alone."

She would spend her life alone. The words hit her hard. Empty years flashed before her. She fought back a rush of tears and forced another smile. "Not all of my life. Right now I have a baby who needs me. At least for a little while." She made herself swallow some coffee; it helped with the lump in her throat. And it was a perfect excuse not to look at him. She didn't want the sheen of tears in her eyes to give the lie to her cheerful tone of voice. "And now, if you will excuse me, I'd better get back upstairs and check on him."

He watched her go, the ache in his heart agonizing, the emptiness of his arms unbearable. He had come so *close*. So close to holding her…kissing her. If she hadn't pulled her hand away… The muscle at his jaw twitched; his fingers tightened around the cup. He had to get Katherine out of his house, out of his *life*, before she destroyed him!

He set the cup down and stormed out into the entrance to get his hat and coat. He needed some fresh air to clear his mind—to bring him to his senses! There had to be a way! There had to!

Chapter Ten

Trace blotted and folded the paper, put it into an envelope, added the direction and placed it with the others ready to take to the station upon leaving the shop. His stomach knotted. It was almost time to leave for dinner at the Latherops'.

He jerked his mind from thoughts of the torture of Katherine sitting beside him at the small table. It had been over a week now and every day it became more agonizing to spend that time alone with her. Sitting there pretending to feel nothing when in truth—in truth *nothing*!

He let out a growl and picked up the pen to write out another order. He was running low on the supplies he needed to compound his fever and headache pills. Many of the people riding the trains from the east were ill. And he had noticed Asa Marsh coughing and sneezing when he went to the station to pick up his mail yesterday. If the stationmaster took the flu—

The jingle of the bell on his shop door stopped his

dire thoughts. He splashed some alcohol on his hands and stepped out of the back room. John Ferndale was leaning over the counter, peering at the bottles on the shelves behind it. "Good afternoon, Mr. Ferndale. Is there something you need?"

"Good afternoon, Trace. Dora sent me for some of your headache pills. And a restorative."

Trace stiffened, studied John Ferndale for signs of illness. "If you tell me what complaints Mrs. Ferndale is suffering, I can better choose the correct medication."

The portly man opened a tin and popped a peppermint candy in his mouth. "She says she has a headache and a fever. And she's tired. She wants something to give her some strength."

"Has she any physical discomfort?"

"Says she aches all over."

Headache, fever and aches, fatigue... Trace silently clicked off the list of symptoms. The thing he'd been fearing had happened. The flu, manifested by the symptoms exhibited by the people on the trains, had come to Whisper Creek. "I believe these products will give her the most relief." He placed a bottle of Blandiff's Vegetable Antidote for Ague in a bag and added a box of his own fever and headache pills. "Please tell Mrs. Ferndale the pills will work better and her illness will improve faster if she drinks a lot of water. Tell her to add three spoonsful of apple-cider vinegar to each glass. It is especially effective to stop any stomach upset." He handed John Ferndale his change and pushed the bag toward him. "It will also strengthen her to eat a lot of soup—chicken soup is the most beneficial."

"I'll tell her. But she's not been eating much." The older man dropped his change into a small leather purse and picked up the bag. "We are fortunate to have you in Whisper Creek, Trace. You're the closest thing to a doctor we've got. I've tried to interest several doctors in coming to our village but they're more interested in going where there are more people. I can't fault them for wanting to make a decent living, but we need medical help here. If anything serious happens, the nearest doctor is miles away at one of the forts. Which one is a guess. The few doctors they have make the rounds."

He cleared his throat of a lump of guilt. "I guess that's right. But I'll do whatever I can to help." *Except be a doctor again.*

"Well that's more than any of the rest of us can do." John Ferndale switched the bag to one hand, opened the door with his other and stepped outside, the bell jingling behind him.

Coward. The accusation rang in his head. He set his jaw, wiped down the counter with alcohol then strode to the back room, took off his apothecary apron, picked up the pile of orders and shoved them in his suit pocket. Walking to the station and back to mail them would brace him for his dinner with Katherine and the baby.

He donned his hat and coat, glanced at the fever and headache pills he'd compounded earlier, stuffed a tin of them in his pocket with the orders and stepped outside. Cold air bit at his face and hands. He locked the door, yanked his leather gloves from his coat pocket and pulled them on. His long strides ate up the short distance to the depot.

"Good afternoon, Asa. I have some orders to mail." A grunt was his answer. He eyed the red wool scarf the stationmaster had wrapped around his neck, noted the sheen of perspiration on the man's forehead and the squinted eyes in his pale face. "You have a headache?"

"Clear to my t-toes." The words were gruff, scratchy. "Be b-back…"

He nodded, watched Asa slide off the stool and shuffle over to answer the clicking telegraph machine on the table. Someone, probably Asa himself, had pulled one of the platform benches inside by the heating stove and thrown a striped blanket on it for a makeshift bed. Steam billowed into a cloud above the coffeepot sitting on the heating stove. He looked back at Asa—the man was shivering so hard he was struggling to write down the message coming through.

He stared at the stationmaster's hands. All of those letters and telegraph messages Asa was handling… It would be a wonder if anyone in Whisper Creek escaped getting the flu. But there was nothing he could do about it. The man would never be able to wash his hands with alcohol in between touching each letter or message. He frowned, pulled the orders from his pocket, put them on the shelf with the money for postage and placed the tin of pills on top of them.

Asa shuffled his way back and picked up the tin. "What's th-this?"

Guilt assuagers. "Pills to help reduce your fever and headache. Take two of them now, then take two with your meals and at bedtime. I'll send Ah Key with some soup for your supper tonight. Meantime, it will help those chills if you'd wrap that blanket around your shoulders. And close one of these shutters when no one is here. Leave the other one open for fresh air."

"Y-you s-sound like a d-doc."

He stiffened, shook his head. "I make the medicine. I know how sick people need to use it. The rest is common sense. Good day." He turned from the window and hurried off the platform onto the road. There would be little time for dinner if—

"Mr. Warren! *Mr. Warren!*"

Trace jerked his gaze toward the call. Minna Karl was sobbing and running toward him, her eyes wide with fear. He knelt to the child's height, catching her when she stumbled into his arms, gasping for air. "What is it, Minna? What's wrong?"

"Ed—Eddie won't get up!" The child flung her arms about his neck, sobbing against his shoulder.

"Eddie?" He pulled her arms from around him and set her back to look at her. "Calm down, Minna. Tell me what is wrong."

"You've got to h-help him! Mama says come qu-quick!" The child grabbed his hand and pulled.

Self-preservation warred with his instinct to help those in need. Hadn't he suffered enough? "No,

Minna, I—" The words choked him. He lunged to his feet. "Show me where."

He ran with her down the road and onto a narrow path that led to the copse of trees out back of the church. He could see a patch of blue between the lower branches of a towering pine. Minna veered around the tree and jolted to a stop in a small clearing. Ivy Karl was kneeling on the ground leaning over her son and patting his hand, her toddler daughter beside her. There was a broken branch on the ground on the other side of the boy.

He looked up into the tree, spotted the place about halfway up where the branch had broken, and sucked in a breath. It was high—too high. Cold knots formed in his stomach. He shoved the branch aside and knelt on the ground beside the small boy, reached under his coat sleeve for his pulse and ran a quick assessing glance over him. Eddie's right arm was twisted at an odd angle. It would need setting. And there was a nasty gash visible through the torn pants on his left thigh that would need stitches, as would the cut on his forehead. His heartbeat was a little slow but strong—

"Thank you for coming, Mr. Warren... I— Konrad's gone to call on those cowboys he heard about, and I didn't know who else—" Ivy Karl's voice broke. "I—I can't w-wake Eddie. Is he...is he..."

He moved his fingers gently up and down the boy's neck and blew out the breath he'd been holding. There was no misalignment or break or odd movement he could feel. He looked up at Eddie's frightened mother and put as much reassurance in his voice as he could muster. "He's only unconscious, Mrs. Karl. And his pulse is strong. I find no sign of injury to his neck, but I can't be certain that's so when he is unable to respond. However, his other injuries need to be treated. I'll take him back to my shop to do that. That's all I can tell you."

The woman nodded, obviously struggling for control. "Minna, take your sister home and watch over her. I'm going with Mr. Warren."

He looked at the tears streaming down the woman's face. He would need help, and it was obvious Mrs. Karl could not do what would need to be done.

I'm considering becoming a nurse...

The knots in his stomach twisted tighter at the thought of working with Katherine. But this was no time to think about himself. He had a patient who needed immediate care. "With your permission, Mrs. Karl, I would like Minna to go to the Latherops' and ask Ka—my wife to come to my shop immediately. I will need her help." He made his voice kind but stern. "You are, of course, welcome to wait in my shop while I do what I can for Eddie. I will need you to care for our baby."

"But I want to—"

He shook his head. "This is no time for argument, Mrs. Karl. I need dispassionate, steady hands to assist me." He picked up Eddie as gently as possible and started back to the path.

"Yes, of course. I'll do whatever is best for Eddie. And I'll be happy to care for your baby. Minna, do as Mr. Warren asked—and hurry." Mrs. Karl lifted her toddler into her arms and fell into step beside him.

* * *

Katherine burst into Trace's shop, stopping at the sight of Ivy Karl leaning against the counter, her face pale, her eyes swollen and red and shadowed with fear. "Why, Ivy! What— Minna said—"

"Through there." Ivy waved a shaking hand toward the door behind the counter.

Had something happened to Trace? Katherine's heart lurched. She slipped behind the counter and rushed through the door, fearful of what she would find. "Trace? Are you all right? Minna told me you wanted me—" She stopped, stared. Trace was bent over Eddie, who was lying with his eyes closed on a long table. The boy's torso was draped with a cloth that left his legs and arms exposed. *Bloody* legs and arms. Her stomach flopped. "What happened?"

"Eddie fell out of a tree. I need you to help me patch him up."

"Me?" It came out a squeak. She looked at Trace washing blood off Eddie's leg. An ugly gash appeared on the boy's thigh. Fresh blood welled from it. She swallowed hard and leaned back against the door for support.

"You said you wanted to be a nurse."

She closed her eyes. "Yes. But for sick—"

"This is your chance."

"But I don't know anything about—"

He glanced up, fastened his gaze on her. "Eddie doesn't have time for you to learn, Katherine. Just do what I tell you. First, wash your hands in that bowl of carbolic acid."

"But Howard—"

"Mrs. Karl will care for him. And Audrey. Now hurry—and wash thoroughly."

His voice was stern, authoritative. She pulled in a breath, stepped to the table and washed her hands.

"Now dip one of those cloths in this bowl of warm water and carbolic acid and clean the cut on his forehead. Make certain you remove any foreign material like bits of bark or pine needles or moss or dirt. When it's absolutely clean, tell me." He went back to cleansing the gaping wound on Eddie's leg.

Her stomach roiled. Tears sprang to her eyes. She stared down at the rambunctious nine-year-old scamp she'd come to know. "What if I hurt him?"

"There's no need to whisper. Eddie can't hear you. He's unconscious. He won't feel a thing. Now blink those tears from your eyes— No! Don't touch your face. Your hands are clean! Do not touch anything you haven't washed in the carbolic acid. Now hurry and get the work done before he wakes up."

She blinked her vision clear and watched him cleaning the wound on Eddie's leg, his movements quick and sure. *Please help me to do this, Lord! Please don't let Eddie wake up—don't let him feel any pain.* She dipped a cloth in the acid water and dabbed at Eddie's cut. It wasn't as bad as she expected once she washed off the blood. "I'm finished."

Trace looked up from his work, stepped to her side and peered closely at the wound. "Excellent job, Katherine."

It was over! She sagged against the table and looked toward the door, waiting for the strength to come back into her legs so she could leave.

"Now come and hold this wound together so I can stitch it."

Stitch it! Bile surged into her throat. She stared after him as he moved back down the table to Eddie's leg. "Trace, I can't—"

"Yes, you can. I need you to help me if I'm to get this done before he wakes."

She took a breath to settle her stomach, but her hands and knees were shaking beyond her power to control.

"Put your hands here...like this."

His hands closed on hers, moved them into place. Strength flowed into her at his touch. The shaking eased. He looked down at her.

"All right now?"

"Yes."

"Good. Now hold your hands steady so the edges of the wound stay in place."

She watched him prepare the needle, then fixed her gaze on him. His hands brushed against hers as he worked. She closed her eyes and concentrated on the warmth of his touch. His hand touched her shoulder.

"I'm finished. Now we will do the same for the cut on his forehead."

She held her breath and held the wound closed, thought about Howard and how he was trying to make little baby sounds when she talked to him. He waved his arms and kicked his legs and—

"Very good, Katherine. Now we've only to set his arm and—"

His tone had changed. She opened her eyes and looked at him. "And?"

The muscle on his jaw jumped. "Wait for Eddie to wake up." He dumped powder from a bag into a bowl, added some water and stirred.

She looked down at Eddie, so pale and still. She hadn't thought— Fear knotted her stomach, closed her throat. Her thoughts darted to Ivy Karl waiting, praying, while she tended Howard... *Make him wake up, Lord. Please make Eddie wake up.*

"Come over here beside me, Katherine." He took hold of Eddie's arm, ran his fingers along it, twisted it.

The room swayed. She grabbed the edge of the table.

"Katherine, open your eyes! Look at me!"

She forced her eyes open, focused on his face. "Don't give out on me now, Katherine. I need you to hold Eddie's arm in position while I wrap it. Take a deep breath."

She nodded, blinked and took Eddie's arm in her hands, tried not to think about the tension in Trace's voice when he had mentioned waiting for Eddie to wake up. *Almighty Lord, please make Eddie wake up.* Trace's hands blurred. The strips of cloth he dipped into the plaster then wrapped on Eddie's arm became a hard white splotch without form. Water splashed. Something blue waved through the air. Trace's hands touched hers.

"You can let go now."

He wiped plaster from the edge of her hand with a wet cloth, dried it with a blue towel. Tears welled into her eyes, boiled into her throat. She turned her back and buried her face in her hands, tried to stem the flow with pressure from her fingers.

"Katherine…"

She shook her head, tried to speak and choked on a sob. His hands closed on her shoulders, turned her around. She collapsed against him, sobbed against his solid chest. His arms closed around her, held her close.

"Don't cry, Katherine. It's over. It's all over now…"

His deep voice washed over her, quiet and reassuring. But the hand that wiped tears from her cheek trembled. He pulled in a long, deep breath, the sound a whisper beneath her ear, and then there was only the beat of his heart and the strength of his arms holding her while she cried.

The frost on the grasses glistened in the moonlight. Trace yanked his collar tighter around his neck, blew on his hands and stared at the soft golden glow of the kitchen windows. Katherine was waiting for him. His heart thudded.

He clamped down on the longing to march into the house, take her in his arms and kiss her until he'd satisfied the yearning that had been building since the first time he'd looked into her eyes at the train station. Since holding her in his arms this afternoon, he doubted that satisfaction was possible.

He frowned and walked toward his house that was beginning to feel like a home. He couldn't afford that. Even the catch in his breath at the anticipation of her waiting for him was too much.

How had he let this happen? He knew better than

to allow another woman into his life. But Katherine was so— He broke off the thought. It didn't matter what Katherine was. He didn't want her in his heart *or* his head! He'd suffered enough because a woman he'd loved had died. He would not go through that again. He needed to maintain his emotional distance from Katherine until the right woman answered the posting he'd sent out to the newspapers in New York City and Philadelphia. He wanted no more errors.

He firmed the thought in his mind, climbed the porch steps and hung his coat and hat in the entrance. The smell of coffee hit him when he stepped through the kitchen door. But it was the sight of Katherine standing in the center of the room, her shoulders squared, her hand pressed to the base of her throat and her incredible eyes shaded with worry, that slugged him in the gut.

"Eddie's awake. He's going to be all right." Her smile stole what little was left of his breath. "Is that coffee fresh?" He growled the words, frowned and cleared his throat. He didn't want coffee—he wanted Katherine in his arms. He gritted his teeth, turned his back and closed the entrance door. Her long skirts swished. China rattled against china. *Two cups*. He clenched his hands.

"Thank the Lord for His blessing. I'm so happy for Ivy and Pastor Karl. It had to be terrible for them waiting for—" Her soft, husky voice broke. "Well, that doesn't matter now." Liquid flowed. The coffee smell grew stronger. "Thanks to your care, and the Lord's mercy, Eddie will be fine." She set the coffeepot back on the stove, turned and looked at him. "He *will* be fine, won't he?"

He stiffened at her praise. He didn't want her or anyone else to start thinking of him that way. "All I did was patch Eddie up. Waking him was the Lord's doing. His healing is out of my hands." He lifted his cup from the worktable and switched the subject. "I apologize for treating you so harshly this afternoon, Katherine. I'm sorry. I ask your forgiveness."

"You have it, though none is needed. You did exactly the right thing, Trace. If you hadn't, I would have collapsed—much sooner..."

She looked away. But not before he caught a glimpse of the memory of those moments after the surgery in her eyes. "Katherine, I need to—"

Her hand lifted palm out. "Pardon me, Trace, but I think I hear Howard crying. I'll have to forgo my coffee. Good evening." She whirled and hurried from the kitchen.

The baby wasn't crying. He fought down the urge to go after her, stared at the empty doorway and listened to her footsteps fade away as she climbed the stairs. Guilt knifed him in the heart. He resisted it. He had to be brusque with her. It was the only way he would survive.

He drew his gaze from the doorway, spotted a cloth draped over a dish on the table, walked over and lifted the towel. He sucked in a breath. There was a cold beef sandwich, a sliced pickle and two hard-boiled eggs. A piece of chocolate cake rested on a dessert plate. His chest squeezed so tight it hurt.

Ah Key didn't bake cakes.

Chapter Eleven

It was because it had been so long since anyone had held her. Had made her feel…*cared* about. That was all it was. For the last five years *she* had been the strong one. *She* had taken care of others. Katherine took a deep breath and wiped the tears from her eyes. It was time to stop her foolishness. Trace Warren did not care for her. This afternoon had been… had been mere kindness. Why, he could barely tolerate her presence in his house. And it was getting worse. Even the politeness between them was becoming strained.

She yanked off the crocheted snood that held her long hair in a thick roll at her nape, marched to the dressing table and dragged her hairbrush through the dark, wavy mass. Would it have been so difficult for him to be just a little grateful that she had waited for him through the long hours he'd spent with Ivy and Konrad Karl waiting for Eddie to wake up? Or that she had fixed him a light meal and made him coffee? And baked him a cake?

The tears flowed again. Why had he had to hold her this afternoon anyway? It certainly wasn't the first time she had cried with no one to see or hear or comfort her. She didn't need Trace Warren to hold her, to take care of her. It just made everything… worse. She whirled from the mirror, checked to make sure Howard was sleeping, then strode to the closet for her nightgown and dressing robe and carried them to the dressing room. She needed a long, hot bath!

Water splashed against the prow of the boat. She peered into the haze in front of her. Yes. He was there. A shadowy figure standing in front of the ship at the end of the stone jetty. Waves broke over the stone, lapped at his feet. He moved toward the ship.

"Hurry! Hurry!" The plea to the unseen rowers burst from her throat. Katherine flopped onto her side in her bed, tightened her grip on the covers.

"Richard? Richard, wait!" She lifted her hems, climbed from the boat and ran toward the man at the end of the jetty. The hazy figure faded into darkness. She boarded the ship and looked around. Music came from somewhere inside. She stepped through a portal, stopped. Richard stood beside a man playing the piano. Her heart raced. She moved toward them. Richard turned, smiled and faded into the mist.

She watched him disappear. The grief in her heart rose in a cloud and drifted away. A sadness remained. She closed her eyes to hold back her tears.

The music stopped. Strong arms closed about her. She leaned into their embrace, her heart soaring— the chords that were broken vibrating once more.

Lips claimed hers. She sighed and opened her eyes. Trace!

She woke, her heart pounding. Howard was whimpering. She turned over and glanced at the clock on the wall. It was too soon for him to have another bottle. She must have called out because of the dream and wakened him. "Shh…shh…" She stretched out her arm and rocked the cradle, shaken by the dream. Always before it had ended when Richard smiled and disappeared. She must have been more…*comforted* by Trace holding her this afternoon than she realized.

Howard whimpered louder, started to cry.

"What's wrong, little one? Do you need your diaper changed?" She shook off the wistful longings awakened by the dream, rose and shrugged into her dressing gown. She pushed her hair over her shoulders out of her way and bent down to pull back the blankets. His soaker was still dry. He cried harder, the pitiful whimpers touching her heart.

"It's all right, precious boy. I'm here…" She lifted him into her arms, snuggled him close and patted his back. He was trembling. Heat radiated from his tiny body. She turned up the oil lamp and looked down at him. His cheeks were red. His normally bright eyes dull, but glassy. She whirled and ran out of her room and down the hall.

"Trace! *Trace, wake up!*" She jiggled the baby in one arm, fisted her other hand and pounded on Trace's door.

"What is it?"

His door opened. Trace stood in the gap, tying the belt on his dressing gown. His gaze locked on hers.

Reality cleared away all residue of the dream. Even so, seeing him made her feel better—and a little foolish for her panic. She took a breath. "I'm sorry to disturb you, but I think Howard is sick. He's awfully hot. And he's been fretful all day and is more so tonight."

A frown creased his forehead. His hand brushed against her face as he placed it on Howard's tiny cheek. "You're right. He has a fever. And he's trembling." His face took on that frozen look she'd grown to hate. "Take him to your dressing room and undress him, but don't let him get chilled—keep him wrapped in his blanket. I'll be right there."

She swallowed back a dozen questions, hurried to the dressing room and worked quickly, cooing comforting words to Howard as she undressed him beneath the cover of a blanket. His little chin quivered. His small body shuddered. "You're going to be all right, little one…yes, you are. Trace will make you all better…" *Please, Lord…*

She wrapped the baby in his blanket and held him on her shoulder, rubbing his tiny back—at a loss as to what to do next without Trace's guidance. She snatched at that thought to hold back the worry tightening her chest. Why did Trace always seem to know exactly what to do? Where had he learned to treat the sick and help the injured? And how did he know so much about babies?

Footsteps. She sagged with relief and fastened her gaze on the doorway. Trace stepped into the dressing room wearing trousers and a shirt with rolled-up sleeves. Her pulse jumped, steadied. She held her silence and watched him fill the baby's tub and spread a towel on the bottom.

"You're giving him a bath?"

He nodded and reached for Howard. "I'm hoping to bring down his fever. And make him more comfortable." He slipped the baby into the warm water. His forehead creased in another frown. "I don't like his trembling. I'm hoping to prevent any seizure—"

"Seizure!" Her stomach clenched. She looked down at Howard lying in the tub, crying. He usually wiggled and kicked his legs and waved his arms. "What's wrong with him?" She forced the words past the lump of fear in her throat.

"I suspect he's got the flu that is going around."

"But we've been so careful! I use the alcohol and—"

"Sometimes being careful and doing all you know to do isn't enough."

His words were weighted with bitterness. She jerked her gaze to his face. All expression was gone except for some tightness around his mouth and eyes. His eyes! Pain shadowed them like a dark curtain. She bit down on her lower lip and clenched her hands at her sides to keep from offering him comfort.

"He's stopped trembling. A minute more and you can dry and dress him. But again, don't let him get chilled. Is everything ready?" He glanced up at her.

Their gazes met. She nodded, willed her hands to stay steady and held out a towel. He lifted the baby into it and quickly wrapped the excess around him. Her breath caught when his hands touched hers.

He stepped back, rolled down his sleeves. "While you put his nightclothes on him, I'm going to add coal to the fire in his room. I prefer he stay warm without being bundled in blankets."

"He sleeps in his cradle in my bedroom."

"Not while he is sick. I will sit up with him tonight."

His tone was firm. She stiffened. "I'm not going to leave him, Trace. He needs me." She blinked away a rush of tears. "And I need to be with him."

He stared at her. She stood her ground, refused to look away. The muscle in front of his ear twitched. "Very well. We will both stay with him. I will carry the rocker in from your bedroom."

The reluctance in his voice plunged deep. What had she done that he did not want her help with Howard? Was it because she had broken down after helping him tend to Eddie's wounds? Did he think she would collapse instead of caring for the baby? Well, she would prove him wrong.

Trace set the rocker down opposite the one on the other side of the small table, pulled the shutters back and opened the window enough that the air in the room would be freshened, but not chilled.

The whisper of Katherine's silk dressing gown rasped along his nerves when she entered the room. He tensed, waited until she'd had time to walk by then turned back to face the room. His heart jolted. She stood facing him with the baby in her arms, her white silk dressing gown shimmering in the moonlight, her hair, dark as the night, flowing over her shoulders.

"Why did you open the window?" Her eyes, large and dark and beautiful, looked straight into his. "I thought you wanted to keep Howard warm without a lot of blankets."

He motioned toward the end of the room. "The fire in the heating stove will keep the room warm. I opened the window to keep the air in the room fresh."

Her forehead creased. She rocked side to side and rubbed the baby's back. Her long hair swayed with her movement. Moonlight rippled along its dark waves. "I don't understand. I was always told to keep my mother's and father's windows closed because the fresh air was bad for their health."

He nodded, moved to the end of the room and checked on the bottle sitting in a pan of water on top of the stove as an excuse to not look at her. "There are two schools of thought in the medical profession about open windows—according to my old doctor friends." The bottle was warm enough. He moved the pan to the side where it was cooler. "Some of them cling to the old way of keeping the windows tightly closed, and some say the new way of opening the windows is best."

"And you agree with the new way?"

"I do." He turned back to look at her. "Have you ever noticed how when you go outside after being shut up in a closed room, the air outdoors seems easier to breathe—more satisfying and refreshing?"

"I've never thought about it. But now that I do—what you say is true." Howard whimpered and she offered the baby the bottle he handed her. She started walking again, her dressing gown floating around her.

He focused on his explanation. "Well, I believe that is because the fresh outside air has health-giving properties we know nothing about."

She glanced at him over her shoulder. "I'll remember that…when I'm a nurse." Her voice choked off.

"Are you all right, Katherine?"

She shook her head, her hair moving like a deep shadow against her white dressing gown. "No. I'm worried. Howard should have had a bottle over an hour ago. And he won't drink this one. Come on, baby boy, drink your bottle…" She walked across the other end of the bedroom, turned and came toward him again.

"Perhaps he's too contented being held and comforted." He lifted the other pan of warm water holding the bottles of sugar water he'd prepared to one of the shelves hanging on the wall. "Put him in his crib. That might make him fuss for his bottle. But don't use the quilt. It's too warm."

"If you think that's best…" She laid the baby in his crib, leaned over him and whispered words of comfort.

He turned away from the sight of her at the crib, but he couldn't shut out the sound of her voice. Katherine was a natural mother who should have children of her own.

If their marriage was a true marriage…

His traitorous mind whispered the thought to his aching heart. Pain rose. And anger. He was already too involved with the baby left in his charge. He wanted none of his own. Not ever again. He turned from the shelf, wished for something to do. Had he missed anything that could be done for the baby? If Howard didn't take a bottle soon… He scrubbed his hand over the taut muscles at the back of his neck and glanced at the clock, noted the time. "Try this sugar water, Katherine. It will be easier for him to swallow if his throat is sore." He traded bottles with her.

"I didn't think about his having a sore throat." She touched the rubber nipple to Howard's lips, tried again when he turned his head. "Come on, little one, drink the water." She glanced up, tears glistening in her eyes. "I wish he could tell us what is wrong."

He nodded, scrubbed his hand over the back of his neck. "It's one of the things that makes it so difficult to treat a baby—"

Her head lifted.

"I imagine." *Watch your tongue, Warren!* He turned to the stove and placed the baby's bottle back in the pan of water to avoid her gaze.

"You must have had a lot of doctor acquaintances back in New York."

He stiffened. Was she only making conversation? Or did she suspect the truth? "Quite a few, yes. They would discuss their problems with me in the hopes that I could compound a medication that would help." *True—as far as it went.*

"It must have been very rewarding to have them

trust you that way." There was a soft inhalation of breath. "I can understand why."

Had he given himself away? He turned. The softness in her eyes took his breath.

"I trust you to care for Howard."

The words pierced through his lowered defenses and tore open his wounds. *There is no better doctor in all of New York, Trace darling. I trust you to take care of me and our baby.* Guilt flooded him. He clenched his hands. "My skills and knowledge are limited, Katherine. I can only do so much."

"There is only so much any man can do in the face of illness or injury or…or fate." Her soft, husky voice poured balm on his pain. "I meant only that I know you will do everything possible to help Howard get better. After that, it's in God's hands."

He nodded, fought the memory of the day his wife and unborn son had died despite his frantic efforts to save them.

The hours ticked away. Howard's fever climbed again. He brought it down to a safer level with another bath. But no matter how Katherine coaxed, the baby refused the bottle.

He paced the floor, uneasy about the baby's condition and his need to be away from him. He would have to get ready and go and open the shop soon. And check on Eddie. And Asa. And Audrey. The list was getting longer, his deception harder to maintain. At least John Ferndale would let him know about Dora. But it was Howard he was most concerned about. He set his jaw, grabbed one of the bottles of sugar water, strode to crib and lifted the lethargic baby into his arms.

"What are you doing?"

"I'm going to make the baby drink this water."

"But—"

"There's no choice, Katherine. He needs to drink it." The tone of his voice gave weight to his grim words. The muscle along his jaw twitched. "Sit down." He nodded toward the rocker by the open window. She sat. "Now take Howard and place him in a sitting position on your lap with his back leaning against you. Good. Lean him back a little more."

He knelt in front of her, opened Howard's mouth, dribbled a bit of the sugar water on his tongue and let go. The baby's chin quivered, he let out a squall, coughed.

"Did it work?"

He looked up and nodded. "Yes. He didn't like it, but he swallowed most of the water." He opened Howard's little mouth and dribbled in more. Bit by bit he forced the baby to swallow half of the water. "That will do for now. He's getting too tired."

He rose, went to the crib and folded the quilt. "You saw what I did to lower his fever and make him drink." He glanced over at her. She nodded, and he looked down and tucked the folded quilt in the corner. "You're going to have to do the same while I'm gone. When you feed him, prop him here in the corner and lay him back against the quilt. That will keep your hands free. Just be sure he stays propped up and give him only a tiny swallow of the water at a time so he doesn't choke. When he becomes too agitated, stop and soothe him, let him rest a short while then give him more water. If he doesn't drink it, he will become very ill…"

"All right." Her dressing gown rustled. The scent of flowers teased his nose. "Trace, are you…"

He turned his head toward her. Their gazes met.

"Never mind…"

He jerked his gaze away, stepped back from the crib and walked to the stove to add coal to the fire. He was more comfortable with distance between them.

She laid Howard in his crib, walked back and folded the light blanket she put over him when she rocked him by the open window. "I don't know what to do about Audrey, Trace." She glanced his way. "I've tried to think of an answer, but I won't leave Howard. And I—"

He tamped down the guilt rising at the look of worry shadowing her extraordinary eyes. "I will have Ah Key make dinner and supper for the Latherops. Beyond that, Blake should be able to take care of Audrey's needs. He can give her a bell to ring if she needs him when he is downstairs. It's only for another week."

"That's very generous of you, Trace. It is my obligation—"

"*Ours.* I'm the one who put you in this situation in the first place."

She bit down on her lower lip and shook her head. Tears filmed her eyes. She draped the folded blanket over the arm of the rocker and took a deep breath. "You keep saying that. But it's not true. I *chose* to

stay because of Howard. Because he needed someone to care for him." She looked back over at him.
"I'm not sorry, Trace, so you can stop feeling guilty."

The look in her eyes brought a warmth to his heart
he didn't want to feel. He strode back to check on
the baby once more. "I'm late. I have to get ready to
leave. I'll be in my dressing room or in my bedroom
should you need me before I go."

"At least you won't have to spend time hitching
up the runabout."

The slight quiver of her lips when she smiled was
like a punch to his gut. He longed to reassure her, to
tell her Howard would be all right, but he couldn't.
Perhaps if he was a better doctor… He clenched his
hands. "Yes. There is that…" He ignored the aching
desire to stay with the baby, wrenched the knob and
opened his dressing room door. "I have to check on
Eddie and Audrey, but I will close the shop and come
home between trains." The muscle by his ear jumped.
"If you…need me for any reason, send Ah Key. I'll
close the shop and come immediately."

She caught her breath and nodded.

He closed the door. But he couldn't close out
the fear in her eyes—or in his heart. He'd seen too
many infants— He jerked his mind from the thought,
turned on the hot water and reached for the soap.
There was nothing more he could do. And there was
no reason to expect the worst. Howard was a robust,
healthy baby, thanks to Katherine's care. And that
boded well for the baby's recovery. If he would start
to take a bottle again.

He frowned, turned his face toward the lamplight

and took a swipe with the razor down his cheek. He couldn't stay home. He had an obligation to the people of the town and on the trains to open his store and dispense elixirs and medicines to help them feel better. Katherine would care for the baby as well as he could. Perhaps better. She could certainly soothe the fretful baby better than he. But if—

He shook off the thought, splashed the soap from his face, dried off and strode into his bedroom to get a clean shirt. His long, dexterous fingers made short work of fastening the buttons and tucking the tails under his belt. He would have to forgo his breakfast to make it to his shop on time.

He reached for his tie, paused. His jaw clenched. He fought the urge, but his gaze lifted in spite of his effort. His hands followed. He grasped the black leather bag that had been tucked away for two years and lifted it down. His heart thudded. His stomach knotted. What if his instinct was right and Howard had developed pneumonia?

Bile rose in his throat. He looked toward the nursery. What if he lost this battle, too?

I meant only that I know you will do everything possible to help Howard get better. After that, it's in God's hands.

Katherine's words eased the ache in his heart. He had failed to save his wife and child. But no man— no *doctor*—could have done more. The pain would never leave him. But it was time he stopped feeling guilty and went back to helping those who needed his care.

The clock on the wall chimed. The time didn't

matter. He would not be going to his shop today. He would go to check on his patients and then come back home. He shrugged into his suit coat, wrapped his fingers around the familiar handles on his doctor's bag and hurried down the stairs.

Chapter Twelve

Her heart lurched. Had Trace returned? Katherine held her breath and listened, glancing down at Howard lying so still and listless against her shoulder. "Do you hear that, little one? Your papa has come home." She looked toward the door and tried to arrange her features so the fear twisting her insides wouldn't show.

The footsteps stopped. There was a soft tapping. The door swung open and Trace entered the room.

Tears surged. She swallowed hard, but couldn't stop them. He looked so strong, so capable and unshakable. And she was so afraid.

"How is the baby? Has he taken more water?"

"A little. But—I think—" She shook her head, fought the fatigue that clouded her thoughts and stole her strength. "His breathing seems more labored." A shiver slipped beyond her control, coursed through her. She pushed with her feet against the floor and started the chair rocking to hide it. "He seems to breathe easier if I hold him upright against my shoulder while I sit here by the window. I don't know what else to do to help him. I—" Tears welled, slid down her cheeks. "He doesn't even cry."

Trace nodded, set a black leather bag on the table under the window and opened it.

She caught her breath, watched him pull out a stethoscope like the doctor had used to listen to her mother's chest. Her heart thudded. Her suspicions had been right. She ignored the throbbing in her temples and lifted her gaze to his face. "You're a doctor." Oh, what relief those words brought.

"Yes." His mouth closed on the word. His face went taut. He fitted the tubes on the stethoscope to his ears, knelt in front of her, pulled down the blanket and placed the end of the instrument against Howard's tiny back. "Don't move him."

Another shiver shook her. His gaze lifted to her face. "Sorry. The air is chilly here by the window." She leaned back out of the light, wishing she could push back the strands of hair clinging to her moist forehead.

He studied her a moment then bowed his head.

She held her breath and willed her body to still. *Please heal Howard, Lord. He's only a baby...* She looked at Trace's grim face and her heart sank. "What is it?"

He shook his head and tapped the baby's back with his fingertips. Howard coughed, whimpered. Trace rose and put the stethoscope back in his bag.

She grabbed his arm. "What is it, Trace?"

"What I suspected. Howard has pneumonia."

Her hand lost its grip, fell away. Her stomach

clenched. "My father..." Memories engulfed her. She clutched Howard to her heart, fought for control but couldn't stop her tears.

"Katherine, listen to me."

She blinked her vision clear and looked at him.

"You said you trusted me to care for Howard." His face was set, his voice firm. "I will not lie to you. Howard is very ill. But he should be all right if we can bring him through the next few hours. It will be a battle—but it's one I do not intend to lose. Now you hold him and I will get some more sugar water in him."

If we can bring him through... Please, Lord... She put Howard on her lap and glanced up at Trace. There was something so steady and reassuring about him. Her pulse settled. Strength and determination washed over her. She would fight this battle with him. And they would win. She held Howard upright with his back against her chest and watched Trace open the baby's tiny mouth and spoon in the water a bit at a time. Her dressing-gown sleeve became wet from the spills and dribbles. Cold air blew in the window. She shivered, clenched her jaw to keep her teeth from rattling. The chills lasted longer, were closer together—it must be getting colder outside.

"That's enough for now. He's too weak to force him to take more." Trace set the bottle and spoon aside, reached out and lifted Howard into his arms. His gaze caught and held hers. "I'm afraid I've soaked your sleeve. I'll take care of Howard, so you can go and put on a different gown."

She nodded, afraid her teeth would chatter if she

tried to speak. She pushed out of the rocker—the room reeled. She grabbed for the edge of the table to keep from falling. He glanced at her. "I guess I've been sitting too long."

"You need some rest, Katherine. I'm here now. And I'm going to stay. You get some sleep."

As if that was possible. She drew in a breath and willed her trembling legs to carry her to the dressing room, stopped at the wash basin and splashed cold water on her face to try to ease the throbbing in her temples. Chills chased each other up and down her spine. Goose bumps prickled her flesh. She had sat in the cold draft from the window for too long. And the lack of sleep was telling on her. The bedroom looked huge.

She fixed her gaze on the closet door, ignored the fatigue dragging at her and went to get dressed. The row of dresses with their small buttons and fancy sashes were uninviting. She hadn't the energy or time to don one. And what did her appearance matter? Caring for Howard was the important thing.

She went back to the bedroom and pulled a quilted cotton dressing gown and matching nightgown from her dresser. It was cozy and warm. And the cotton was soft and comfortable for Howard to rest against. Tears filmed her eyes. She blinked them away and hurried toward the nursery. Tears would not help. She latched on to the tattered thread of her remaining faith. *Please, Lord, make Howard well. Please give Trace wisdom to care for—*

She stopped in the doorway. Trace had moved the table and pulled one of the rockers directly in front of the window. He sat in the chair holding Howard against his shoulder with the baby's face toward the window opening. A blanket and a knit hat protected the baby from the cold air. Sunlight brightened Trace's wavy blond hair. Worry darkened the blue of his eyes. His hand, strong and protective, covered Howard's small back. The image seared itself into her heart.

Her chest tightened. Her throat swelled. Trace was only her pretend husband. And Howard was only her temporary baby. But not in her heart. Somehow, sometime in the last month their in-name-only family had become real to her. Pain squeezed her heart. *Please, Lord, I know I have to give them up. But not this way. Please not this way. Heal my baby. Please heal my baby...* She didn't correct the words. Howard was her baby. He would always be her baby—in her heart. She slipped to the side and sagged against the wall, held a towel against her mouth to muffle her sobs.

"Fight, little man. I'm doing all I can to help you, but you need to fight to live! Do you hear me, Howard? Fight!"

Trace's voice stopped her sobs. He hid it when she was near, but he was struggling with fear, too. She wiped the tears from her face, took a deep breath and pushed away from the wall.

The brush of her dressing gown against the floor blended with the whisper of the rocker. The everyday sounds gave her a strange sort of comfort—as if nothing bad could happen. She squared her shoulders and straightened her spine when Trace looked her way. "I'm back. Is it time to give Howard more water? I've brought a towel to catch any spills."

"I told you to get some sleep."

She shook her head, bit her lip to hold back a moan at the pain that shot into her temples. "I'll sleep when Howard is better."

"You'll sleep now. You're sick, Katherine. You need rest."

"Sick?" She stared down at him, startled by the idea. "I'm not sick. I'm only tired."

"Being tired doesn't give you chills."

"Sitting in front of an open window in November does."

"So does a fever."

"I don't have a fever."

"You're perspiring."

"The room is overly warm away from the window."

"And the headache and enervating fatigue? What reasons have you for those?"

She stiffened, at a loss for an answer. "How do you know I have a headache?"

"Tension in your face, squinted eyes, pain furrows on your forehead."

She stared at him as he listed her symptoms. *Please, Lord, I can't be sick. Not now.* "I've been two days without sleep."

He rose from the rocker, came and stood in front of her. "Stop making excuses, Katherine. You have the flu. You need to rest. Now give me that towel and go to bed."

What if he was right? Her stomach flopped. Tears

threatened. She gripped the towel with both hands to keep from wiping the moisture from her forehead. "If I *were* sick…would I make Howard worse by taking care of him?"

His gaze, warm with understanding, locked on to hers. "No. You are the one who will get worse."

She almost collapsed from the relief. She touched Howard's back then turned toward the shelf. "I'll get a bottle of sugar water."

"Katherine—"

She spun around, tears flowing down her cheeks. "He's my baby, Trace. And I'm not going to leave him." She swayed from her quick movement, grabbed his arm for support.

"You sit down. I'll get the bottle." He helped her to the rocker and put Howard in her arms.

She cuddled her baby close, shut her eyes and prayed.

"Katherine, you need to stand up for a moment." She opened her eyes and stared at the quilt Trace held in his hands. He helped her to her feet, spread the quilt in the rocker and helped her sit back down. "This should make you feel a little better, keep the chills from getting worse." He pulled the quilt up around her neck and pulled it forward over her shoulders, covered her lap.

It was the concern in his voice, the tender touch of his hands against her cheeks and neck, that made her feel better. Everything in her wanted to lean her head against his shoulder and rest there with his strong arms holding her. But of course, that was unacceptable. "Thank you, Trace. It does help."

* * *

The baby turned his head and whimpered. The water ran out of his mouth and dribbled onto the towel tucked under his tiny chin. "Come on, Howard, swallow the water." Trace frowned and tried to get him to take another spoonful, but the baby refused to swallow it.

"What's wrong?"

He glanced up at Katherine. "He's caught on to the way we are force-feeding him. He's refusing to swallow."

"But he needs the water! What shall we do?"

"Try a different way. Or perhaps the right way." He grasped the bottle of water and touched the rubber tip to Howard's lips. The tiny mouth opened and he slipped the tip inside. Howard suckled for a minute then stopped.

"It worked! Oh, Trace, he took the bottle!"

He looked at Katherine's feverish face. Happy tears glittered in her eyes. He hated to spoil her relief. "Yes, for a minute. I surprised him. Let's hope it works the next time, too. For now, we'll let him rest. And you."

She nodded, lifted the baby to her shoulder so he could breathe the fresh air and closed her eyes.

His fingers twitched to touch her forehead and see how high her fever had climbed. He tugged the quilt back in place that had slipped away from her neck, rose and threw a sour look at the sky outside the window. *Why are you doing this to me? You've already taken one wife and child from me!* Wife? The word jolted him to his toes. When had he started thinking of Katherine as his wife?

He shoved his fingers through his hair and looked down at her sitting and rocking the baby. Her baby. That was what she'd said. *He's my baby, Trace. And I'm not going to leave him.* She was as fiercely protective as any natural mother. What would it do to her if he failed and Howard—

He jerked his mind from the thought. He couldn't fail. Not again. He forced the memory of the two graves in New York from his mind. He needed all of the confidence in his ability as a doctor that he could muster. If he didn't believe he could win this battle, he was already defeated.

He set his jaw, grabbed the bottle of vegetable strength restorer he'd brought home and added a spoonful to the baby's next bottle, then poured a dose into a small glass and carried it to the rocker. "Katherine…"

She opened her eyes—their glassy shine knotted his stomach. He held out the glass. "It's time for more medicine. Drink this." She reached for it, but he pulled it back. "You're shaking too hard, you'll spill it." He frowned and held the glass to her lips. She swallowed the medicine, shuddered. "Now this water." He couldn't resist any longer. He placed his hand on her forehead while she drank. The heat from her flesh seared into his hand. "Katherine—"

"No, Trace. Howard is less fretful when I hold him. I'm staying right here."

The clink of the dishes and flatware against the table was as loud as a clanging gong in her head.

Katherine winced and pressed her lips together to stop from telling Ah Key to go away. She closed her eyes against the pain in her head and rocked Howard back and forth, ignoring the chills that shook her aching body.

"Thank you, Ah Key."

She leaned into the softness of her quilt cocoon and drew comfort from the firmness in Trace's voice. Her "German stubborn" was giving out and she was leaning on his strength more and more as the day wore on.

"I go give soup to Mr. Marsh and Mr. Latherop now. Get dishes when I come back. One hour!"

She leaned her head back against the chair and smiled. Everything the houseman did took one hour.

"I'll set the dishes on the tray outside the door when we finish. You can pick them up there."

The door closed. Trace's footsteps crossed the nursery, stopped. She opened her eyes.

"I'll hold Howard now. I want you to eat your supper while it's hot, Katherine. At least the broth. And drink the water."

"I just had water…"

"Must I force-feed it to you?"

The image tickled her imagination. She smiled then immediately remembered trying to get Howard to take a bottle and sobered. "All right." She hated to move—it made the chills worse. But the worst thing was having to let go of her baby. *Her baby.* She would think of him as hers from now on. No one could take him from her heart.

She shivered her way to the chair by the table and sat so the light from the oil lamp fell on Howard resting in Trace's arms. And on Trace's face. Her heart hurt for him. What had caused that shadow of pain in his eyes? The tension around his mouth? If only she could comfort him. But he wanted nothing from her. She closed her eyes on that painful truth and bowed her head, wished her faith was as strong as it had been before Richard's disappearance. The thought gave her pause.

How distant and long ago that event seemed—as if it had happened to someone else. *Blessed Lord, I know now that Richard is never coming home. And I accept that. But I'm begging You to please heal Howard. Please, please make him well. And please heal Trace's heart. And bless this food, Lord. Use it to make me strong enough to care for my baby, I pray.*

Tears stung her eyes. She forced herself to eat a spoonful of the chicken broth, and then another and another. The fatigue dragged at her. She put down the spoon and fought to stay erect in the chair. It seemed the only time she had strength was when she was holding Howard.

The baby coughed, whimpered—would not be comforted. She forced down half of her water and rose, holding on to the table. "I'll take him."

Trace looked at her bowl and frowned.

"I have no appetite, Trace. I just need to hold Howard." Her tears spilled over. "I just need to hold him."

He nodded, helped her into the rocker, covered her with the quilt and put Howard in her arms.

The evening passed in a blur. Howard grew more fretful, but they no longer had to force sugar water into him. He accepted the bottle from her and drank a little at a time. Every swallow he took brought her hope, but his fretfulness stole it away.

"Shh, little one, shh…" She slid her hand inside the blanket and then inside his drawers out of habit. Her fingertips touched wet cloth. Fear gripped her. What did it mean? He had not wet his diaper since he became so ill. *Please, Lord, let it be something good.* She tried to rise, to take Howard to his crib and change him, but she didn't have the strength. She glanced toward the wardrobe that held clean diapers. It sat at the far end of the nursery. She would never make it that far. She slid her gaze to Trace, who was boiling bottles and preparing more sugar water at the heating stove. "Trace, would you please bring me a diaper? Howard is wet and—"

Trace pivoted. "He's wet his diaper?"

"Yes. Not like he normally does, but I thought it might be bothering him, and—" She stopped, stared as Trace strode across the room and lifted Howard into his arms. Fear closed her throat as he peeled back the blanket and felt the baby's diaper.

"You're right, he's wet himself."

The tone of his voice chased her fear away. She watched him touch his fingers to Howard's tiny forehead. "His fever has dropped." The tension left his face.

"You mean—" Her heart soared at his nod.

"He's passed the crisis, Katherine. He should be all right now."

His words took the last of her strength. She slumped into the quilt. The last thing she saw was Trace's smile.

Chapter Thirteen

"Katherine!" Trace propped Howard on the folded quilt in the corner of his crib and dropped to his knees in front of the rocker. He lifted Katherine's unresisting arm and felt for her pulse. It was steady. He blew out a gust of air, rose and hurried into her bedroom, threw back the covers on her bed, propped her pillows against the headboard and returned. She was struggling to rise. "What are you doing?"

Her gaze slid his way, glassy and unfocused. "Howard's fussing…"

"I know. I'll change his diaper as soon as I get you into bed."

"I'm n-not go—"

"Yes. You are." He scooped her into his arms. Her head dropped against his shoulder, her eyes closed. Chills shook her. He carried her to her bed, laid her on the stacked pillows and pulled the covers up over her. A quick tug moved the bedside table close. He lit the oil lamp, checked her fevered brow, frowned and went back to the nursery.

"Here we go, little man. Let's get this wet diaper changed." The baby whimpered, waved his arms. The tension in his stomach eased. Howard's lethargy was waning. He pinned on the clean diaper then buttoned his soaker in place. The whimpering got louder. "Getting irritated, are you? Are you going to start fighting me? That's good." He smiled, wrapped Howard in his blanket and walked to the shelf to get a bottle of the medicated sugar water.

There was a soft tap on the door. "Come in, Ah Key."

His houseman stepped into the room, a bucket swinging from his hand. "Bring coal for night. Keep baby warm." The houseman's black eyes sharpened. He turned his head, swept the room with a keen gaze. "Where Missy W?"

"She's sick. I've sent her to bed." He cradled Howard in his arm and offered him the bottle. "Take the coal to her room. There is enough here for tonight."

Ah Key nodded, padded toward the connecting door. "If Missy W sick, who take care of baby when you go shop?"

He'd been mulling that over. There was no answer. He frowned and shook his head. "I'll have to stay home and leave the shop closed. There is no woman in town—"

Ah Key stopped, looked back at him. "Missy Zhong much good with baby."

He stiffened, studied his houseman's face. "Who is Mrs. Zhong?"

"Her man work railroad. He die. Missy Zhong old.

She run away, hide in hill. She not want work in… bad place. She clean house. Very much like baby."

"How old is she?"

Ah Key frowned, shrugged. "Old like mother. But she still strong."

The pressure in his chest eased. He looked down at the baby in his arms. It was too…*comfortable* holding him. Even with him fussing. He was becoming too attached to the little man. And Katherine… He straightened, nodded. "All right. You bring Mrs. Zhong to see me tomorrow morning. I'll decide then if she is a suitable nanny for Howard." A thought struck him. "Does she speak English?"

Ah Key smiled and bobbed his head. "She talk English good like me."

He would have laughed had he not been so desperate. He watched his houseman carry the bucket of coal through the door then turned his attention to Howard. The baby turned his head and pushed the rubber tip of the bottle out of his mouth with his tongue. "Come on, little man. You're not out of the woods yet. You need to drink your bottle and get stronger." *His bottle.* He glanced at the regular bottle he'd prepared, took it off the shelf, put it in the pan of hot water sitting on the heating stove and carried it into Katherine's bedroom.

Warmth was pouring into the room from the fire Ah Key had fed. He set the pot of water on the heating stove, laid Howard in his cradle and walked over to open the window enough to let in fresh air. Howard whimpered and Katherine stirred. He grabbed the desk chair and carried it back to sit at her bedside. The dimmed light from the oil lamp touched her delicate features with gold. He brushed an errant strand of hair off her forehead and laid his hand on her hot, moist skin. Her eyelids fluttered. A smile trembled on her lips, faded away. Even in sickness her beauty stole his breath. He frowned, lifted the baby from his cradle and offered him the warmed bottle. Howard fought it, then caught a taste of it on his tongue and began to suckle. He held him close and paced the room while he fed him.

How was he to care for both the baby and Katherine? He thought about Mrs. Zhong, gave her serious consideration. If the Chinese woman understood enough English for him to make his demands for cleanliness to protect Howard's health clear, she could be his answer.

Silence settled around him. The dimmed lamplight gave blurred definition to the furniture in the room, shone on the baby in his arms. But it was Katherine who held his attention. She was getting restless. Her fever had to be climbing. He burped Howard, laid him down to sleep in his cradle and went to the dressing room to fill a basin with cold water. He tossed in a couple of cloths, grabbed a towel and carried it all to Katherine's bedside table. She was muttering. Worry shot through him. If her flu turned into pneumonia…

He threw back the covers, unbuttoned her dressing gown and slipped it off, then undid the three buttons on the high collar of her nightgown and folded it down. He lifted her head and shoulders, placed the folded towel on the pillow, squeezed out one of the cloths in the basin and placed it on top of it. The silky strands of her long hair brushed against his hands and wrists. He moved the long, wavy black cloud aside and lowered her down to rest with the exposed back of her neck against the cold cloth. A shiver shook her. He squeezed the excess water from the other cloth, folded it and placed it on her forehead. A soft moan escaped her. Her hand lifted and grasped his. Her head turned toward him; she sighed and laid her cheek on their joined hands. The throb of the pulse at the base of her throat beat against the heel of his hand.

He tried to pull away, but she frowned and tightened her grip. "D-don't...go... Richard... P-please..." Her words trailed off into a moan.

Richard? Who was Richard? He stared at their joined hands beneath her cheek, fighting back an unwelcome and inappropriate surge of jealousy. He had no right—no *reason*—to feel jealous. Katherine was not his wife. She was nothing but a convenient solution to his nanny-for-Howard problem. And that was about to be solved in a more...advantageous way. For him.

"Baby...m-my baby..." She threw off the blankets, tried to push erect.

He grabbed her shoulders, eased her back down on the pillows. "Howard is sleeping. He's better, Katherine. Remember? He's going to be all right." He picked up the cloth that had slipped off her forehead. It was already warm to his touch. He dipped it in the cold water.

"He's...b-better?"

"Yes." He put the rag back on her forehead. "You are sick."

Her eyelids fluttered, opened. She looked up at him, angry sparks in her eyes. "Stop it, Richard! I'm not sick! And he's my baby!" Her eyes closed; her head slumped to the side.

He rose, put another blanket over Howard and opened the window wider. A gust of the winter air penetrated his shirt and vest and made him shiver. He hurried into the nursery, shrugged into his suit jacket, grabbed the pitcher of water and the bottle of strength restorer and mixed her a dose. He carried it all back to her bedside table then slipped his arm beneath her. "Drink this, Katherine."

"Hmm…"

Heat from her head and shoulders warmed his arm through the wool sleeve of his jacket. Her fever was still climbing. "Katherine, swallow this water!"

Her eyes opened. She smiled. "You're a d-doctor."

"Yes. Now drink this." He tightened his arm around her and pressed the rim of the glass against her lips. She took a few swallows.

"When d-did you c-come home, Richard?" She gave him a smile that dimpled her cheeks. "I have a b-baby now." Her eyelids swept down, her long dark lashes rested against her flushed cheekbones.

The knots in his stomach twisted tighter. She was slipping in and out of consciousness, and there was nothing more he could do. Her fever refused to budge. He lowered her to her pillows, rose and paced the room, trying to hold on to his professional training and manner. What if— No! He wouldn't even think of failing! There had to be something… He jammed his hands in his jacket pockets and his fingers touched a small tin. His heart leaped. It was the fever and headache pills he'd intended to give to Asa Marsh yesterday morning. The stationmaster had no longer needed them. Could Katherine swallow them? She had to!

He whipped around and rushed to the bedside table, dumped three of the pills into the bowl of the spoon and crushed them with the bottom of the glass. He added a small amount of water, leaned down and lifted her head.

She moaned. "Head h-hurts."

The pain on her face ripped at his insides, shredded the professional demeanor he was trying to reconstruct. He slid his arm beneath her shoulders. "I know. I want you to take this. It will make you feel better." Her cheek turned toward his palm, her flesh heating his skin.

"Your h-hand makes it b-better."

His breath caught. She was hallucinating again. "Swallow this, Katherine…please." Her mouth opened. He slid the medicine onto her tongue, dropped the spoon on the table and held her close so she wouldn't choke.

"B-better…"

Her head leaned against his chest. He slid the chair closer to the bed, sat and held her in his arms, telling himself it was only because it was what she needed.

She pressed her lips together and stared at the man at the end of the jetty. The hazy figure faded into darkness. She started after him.

A baby cried, floated out of the darkness and

landed in her arms. She looked down at him, so precious, so sweet. Her baby. She glanced out over the water, watched the man disappear. "Goodbye, Richard."

A woman with no face hurried toward her, reached for the baby in her arms. "No! You c-can't have h-him! He's m-my baby!" *She tried to twist away, but she was too weak; she couldn't move. Strong arms held her. The moon glinted against the dark water, turned into a huge silver spoon and floated toward her.*

"Shh...shh...it's all right. No, don't turn away. Swallow this, Katherine. Please swallow this. It will bring down your fever and make you feel better."

Trace was holding her. She was safe in his arms. No. No, there was something wrong with that. She struggled against the weariness, tried to open her eyes and ask him why she should not want to be in his arms, lost the battle and slumped against his chest. She would remember, if only she could think...

Trace yawned, rolled his head and shoulders and scrubbed his fingers through his hair. The lack of sleep was catching up to him, but he would be able to take a short nap soon. Howard had fallen into a health-restoring normal sleep after drinking half of his last bottle, and Katherine's tossing and turning had finally lessened. The cold cloths and pills were working. Her fever was finally coming down.

He rose and stretched, carried the uncomfortable straight-backed chair he was sitting in back to the desk and walked to the nursery to get the rocker he'd taken there yesterday. The quilt he'd pulled off his bed to cover Katherine was heaped on the seat. He lifted the rocker, quilt and all, and carried it to the empty space between Katherine's bed and the baby's cradle. So much for distancing himself from them. His face drew taut. He had been holding one or the other of them in his arms all night—and it felt too right. All he'd ever wanted was to have a loving family to come home to when his days at the hospital were over. And Katherine was exactly what he wanted. And that was too dangerous to allow to continue. He looked down at her, touched her fevered cheek with his fingers. Fear rushed through him. If he lost her...

He scowled and walked to the window, shoved his hands into his pockets to hold his jacket closed against the cold air flowing in and looked out at the black night. He couldn't deny the feelings he had for Katherine—all he could do was protect himself from them. The baby was different. The child was a part of his life whether he wanted it that way or not. And caring for the helpless infant during this crisis had opened his heart to Howard in a way he had never wanted to happen. He couldn't let the same thing happen with Katherine. He would care for her, but he would not let her into his heart.

He yanked his hands from his pockets and strode to her bedside. He set his heart against any feelings and changed the cold cloth on Katherine's forehead. She muttered something garbled about Audrey and Blake and went back to sleep. Weariness tugged at him. He sat in the rocker, pulled the quilt around him and stared at a piece of paper on the floor by the window. He'd not noticed it before. The breeze must have blown it from the desk. He'd pick it up later, when he got up to feed Howard. He rubbed at the tension in his neck and closed his eyes.

There was a dull ache in her temples. Katherine frowned and eased her eyes open. The area around the bedside table was barely visible and the rest of the room was in darkness. Why had she dimmed the lamp so much? How was she to see to care for Howard?

Howard. Memory rushed back. The baby was sick! Why was she sleeping? She tried to rise, but was too weak to lift her head off her pillow. Her whole body ached. Trace had been right when he told her she had the flu. He had also said Howard was going to be all right. That they had brought him through the crisis.

She took a deep breath and turned her head toward the cradle. *Trace.* He was sleeping in the rocker, his chin resting on his chest. A quilt covered him. Light from the lamp reflected off the water pitcher, glass, spoon and bottle of health restorer on the bedside table. Had he stayed in the chair all night to care for her? Her heart thudded. She stopped the direction her thoughts wanted to travel and glanced at the cradle beside Trace's chair. Of course he would be here to care for Howard. And to care for her. He was a doctor. Even if he did hide the fact. Why would he do that?

She closed her eyes and pondered the question

while she slowly moved her arms and hands and legs and feet. The ache in them brought a moan to her lips. She clamped her jaw closed against it lest she wake the baby or Trace. Both needed sleep. And she needed to go to the dressing room.

She glanced through the darkness toward the door that seemed so far away and gathered her strength and determination. With slow, careful movements she turned onto her side and edged her legs over the side of the bed, bit down on her lip and waited for the trembling to stop and her aching to ease. If she could just make it to her feet…

She pushed back the covers and grabbed on to the corner post. Breath gusted from her. She pressed her forehead against the post and clung there, waiting for the room to stop swaying. A cool breeze drifted across her face and shoulders. A shiver shook her. She took another deep breath, grabbed the post with both hands and pulled, willed her legs to hold her. She stumbled to the dressing room grasping furniture and sliding along the wall.

How was she to make it back to her bed? Her strength was exhausted. She pulled herself to the door and opened it, gasped and pitched forward. Trace's strong arms caught her.

"What do you think you're doing?" There was anger, concern in his harsh whisper.

She tried to straighten her legs but her knees refused to obey her will. "I—" embarrassment stopped her "—wanted to s-see if I could walk."

"You've been very sick. It's too soon for you to walk. The next time nature calls, wake me. I'll carry

you." His arm held her tight against him. He leaned
down, scooped her into his arms and carried her toward the bed.

It was so tempting to rest her head against his
shoulder, to allow herself the pleasure of being in
his arms. But it wasn't her right. She shut her mind
to the thumping of her heart. "How is Howard?"

He glanced down at her and their gazes met. Her
stomach fluttered. His arms tightened. He sucked in
air, laid her down on her bed and pulled the covers
up over her. "Howard is fine. He's taking his regular
bottle and sleeping normally."

He turned to the nightstand, poured a drink of
water, dumped some pills out of a small tin into his
hands and held them out to her. "Take these."

"What a-are they?"

"Pills to help your headache and keep your fever
down."

"I have a f-fever?"

He nodded, slid his arm beneath her shoulders
and held her up while she swallowed the pills and
drank the water.

Warmth spread through her. It was so wonderful being in his arms—even if it was only because
she was weak, and he was taking care of her. His
touch was different than any she'd ever known. It
made her feel…*special.* She looked down lest her
thoughts show in her eyes and handed him the water
glass. "Thank you. I'm s-sorry you had to miss your
n-night's sleep because of me."

He laid her down on the pillows, set the glass on

the table and rubbed his hand over the back of his neck. "Katherine…"

There was an uncertainty, a hesitance, in his voice. What did it mean? Had he found a woman to replace her? She grabbed the covers and held them like a shield. "Yes?"

"Who is Richard?"

"Richard?" She stared at him.

"You were mumbling about him in your delirium."

"Oh." She relaxed into the pillows and eased her grip on the covers. "I'm not c-certain I can explain Richard."

"If you'd rather not, it's really none of my business."

His face had taken on that frozen look. "Yes, it is, Trace. You're m-my husband—even though our marriage isn't a r-real one." She took a breath against the pain that stabbed her heart at that truth. "It's simply that Richard was such a l-large part of my life. He was our neighbor when we were young. And he was k-kind to Judith and very tolerant of me." She smiled at the memories. "We had a playhouse, and, though I know it emb-barrassed him, he would always be our husband and our doll's f-father when we asked…well, *begged* him. And he would take us on adventures in the w-woods. He was our hero and best friend." Her smile faded. "I l-loved him all of my life." She braced herself for the pain that always struck her when she talked about his disappearance. "We were to have been m-married on my eighteenth birthday. A Christmas wedding. But it w-wasn't to be. He was on his way home from a trading t-trip on one of his father's ships in early December when something h-happened and the ship and everyone aboard disappeared at sea."

"I'm sorry, Katherine. I know how painful it is to lose someone you love."

"Your w-wife?"

"Yes." The word was terse, almost angry.

She studied his taut face. Suspicion dawned. "She died from pneumonia."

"She and our unborn son died because I was not a good enough doctor to save them." Pain and bitterness tainted the words.

Anger shot strength through her. She shoved to a sitting position, slipped her legs over the side of the bed, stood and grabbed hold of his shirt to stay erect. "Whoever told you that was *wrong*, Trace. You're a w-wonderful doctor! You saved Howard and—"

"And I don't intend to lose you." His arms tightened around her, pulled her close.

Her heart raced. Could he possibly mean— She tipped her head back and looked up at him. Everything went still. A tremor shook his arms.

Howard whimpered, let out a wail.

Trace sucked in air, looked away. "You need to get back in bed before you take another chill." He helped her to the bed, eased her down and turned toward the cradle.

She pulled the covers over her, blinked tears from her eyes and stared into the darkness, her heart aching. When had she fallen in love with Trace Warren?

Chapter Fourteen

"Katherine…"

Trace's voice wooed her from the darkness. She tried to open her eyes, felt her eyelids flutter then still. Trace's arm slipped under her shoulders, lifted her. She tried to help him, but she had no strength. Her head rolled to the side, came to rest against his shoulder. Something cool and hard touched her lips.

"Swallow this."

It took a moment, but she succeeded. Cool liquid slipped over her parched tongue and down her throat. He lowered her back onto the stacked pillows and pulled the covers up over her. His hand touched her brow; a cold cloth followed. A shiver slid downward, shook her. His hand touched her cheek.

"You have to fight, Katherine. Do you hear me? I'm doing all I know to help you, but it's not enough. You have to fight!"

She and our unborn son died because I was not a good enough doctor to save them.

Did Trace think she was dying? Was she? No.

Trace would blame himself. She tried to reassure him that she would fight, but she couldn't form the words. *Help me, Lord. Give me strength. Give me a way...*

The covers over her arm moved, sent another chill racing through her. Trace's hand gripped hers. His long, strong fingers wrapped around her palm. Warmth and strength flowed into her hand, traveled up her arm. *Thank You, Lord.* She curled her fingers around his and smiled.

The knock jerked him upright in the rocker. Trace scrubbed his finger and thumb over his eyes, yawned and went to the door. "Yes, Ah Key?"

"Churchman come." His houseman stood square in front of the door, staring up at him. "You want he come in?"

"Pastor Karl is here?" *Eddie.* Trace shook his head, scrubbed his hand over his neck. "Yes, of course. Send him in." He ran his fingers through his mussed hair, tugged his vest into place and gathered his thoughts while his houseman hurried back down the hallway. There was a mumble of voices. Pastor Karl came striding down the hall toward him, his hat in his hand.

He stepped out into the hall though Howard was a sound sleeper, and there was little chance of their voices waking Katherine from her exhausted state. "Forgive my appearance, Pastor Karl. How is Eddie?"

"Eddie is fine, thanks to your excellent care, Doctor. I came because I noticed your shop is still closed." The pastor slid his hat brim through his fingers. "Ivy and I have been praying for your baby son. And I came this morning to tell you and your wife if there is anything that Ivy or I can do to help, you've only to ask…"

He held back a frown. He'd asked the Karls not to call him doctor. "No, nothing, Pastor Karl. Howard has passed the crisis and is well on his way to a full recovery."

"Well, thank the Lord! That is good news! Please forgive my intrusion, but when I noticed your shop—" The pastor smiled at him. "Ah, perhaps there *is* something I can do to help. The stove in your shop has gone out. I would be happy to start a fire on my way home so the shop will be warm when you arrive."

"The stove!" He scowled, scrubbed his hand across the stubble on his chin. "I forgot all about it." He glanced toward a window then looked back at Konrad Karl. "Thank you for your offer, Pastor Karl, but I won't be going to the shop today. Katherine has taken ill and I must stay with her. Fortunately, it's not cold enough that any of my supplies will freeze."

"I'm sorry to hear your wife has taken ill, Doctor. But she is in excellent hands. And you can be certain that Ivy and I will be praying for her healing. As for your supplies freezing, don't give it another thought. I will start the fire and tend the stove until you return to your shop. Good day, Doctor Warren. And rest assured, you, too, are in our prayers."

His frustration at the talk of prayers boiled over. "Thank you, Pastor, but—" He looked into the pastor's eyes and halted his words.

"Yes, Doctor?"

"Don't forget Howard. Babies often have re-lapses…"

The pastor nodded, slapped his hat on his head then reached out and rested his hand on his shoulder. "The baby, too. None of you will be forgotten."

Howard whimpered, let out a cry.

Pastor Karl smiled. "Your son is calling you."

He nodded, stepped back and closed the door, puzzled by the odd feeling of comfort that had washed over him at the pastor's touch.

"Katherine!" He rushed over to the cradle, grasped her by her upper arms, lifted her off her knees and carried her back and tucked her under her covers. "I told you to stay in bed."

"Howard was c-crying." Her eyelids slipped closed. "I c-couldn't reach him."

"So you climbed out of bed to go to him?"

"He's my baby."

Guilt shot through him. He didn't mean to, but he had put Katherine in a position that would break her heart. "Go to sleep, Katherine. I'll tend to Howard."

A smile curved her lips. "I know. You're g-going to be a w-wonderful father to him." Her smile faded.

Guardian. Not father. The muscle along his jaw twitched. He looked around the room, stared at the door. He couldn't leave. He was trapped by circumstances of his own making. He walked over and placed a bottle in the pan of hot water, picked up the baby and carried him to the dressing room. The bottle would be warm by the time he had finished changing Howard's diaper and dressed him for the day.

He tried not to, but he couldn't help tickling and playing with the baby who wiggled and squirmed and made soft little noises that seemed to burble their way up from his toes to his tiny mouth. He wrapped the dressed infant in a blanket and carried him back to Katherine's bedroom to feed him. He would give Howard advice and supervision and all that money could provide as he grew to manhood. But he could not give him a father's heart. He didn't have one to give. His was buried in a grave in New York.

He sat in the rocker, started feeding Howard his bottle and glanced up at the clock. When would Ah Key bring Mrs. Zhong to apply for the position of nurse-nanny? She was his only hope until some woman answered the postings he'd placed in the New York and Philadelphia newspapers.

Her head didn't ache. There was no pounding in her temples. No chills shook her body. Katherine opened her eyes to the dim glow of the oil lamp. Trace was asleep in the rocker. Her stomach fluttered at the sight of him. He looked younger with his blond hair mussed and the tension gone from his face.

Thirst drew her gaze toward the pitcher and glass on the nightstand. She braced herself for the consequences and turned onto her side. No aches spread through her. Only that debilitating weakness.

Trace's eyes opened. His gaze met hers. He leaned forward and touched her brow, nodded. "You're better." There was relief in his voice and eyes.

"Yes." The word scraped its way out of her dry throat.

He rose, poured water into the glass then slipped his arm beneath her head and shoulders and held it to her lips. "Drink slowly."

She held the first bit of water in her mouth a moment to let it moisten the dry tissue, then drank a few swallows. It felt wonderful. So did his arm holding her. She had a sudden wish that her hair was brushed.

"Do you want more?"

She nodded and finished the water. "Thank you." Fatigue gripped her. Her eyelids slid closed, refused to open again. He lowered her to her pillows and pulled the covers up. His hand brushed against her face, lingered a moment and then moved away.

Katherine bent over the crib, caught Howard's tiny hands in hers and clapped them together. "Pat-a-cake, pat-a-cake, baker's man…" The baby smiled and kicked his legs, wiggled and cooed his baby talk at her. Her heart ached with love for him. She longed to pick him up and hold him, but it wasn't safe for him in her weakened condition. Howard liked to bounce and to grab fistfuls of her hair. It was Mrs. Zhong who tended to him now. The Chinese nanny had proved very capable over the last few days. Howard no longer needed her to care for him. It was she who needed him.

"Time give baby bottle, him go sleep."

She looked at the Chinese woman and smiled to hide the pain in her heart. Howard had grown too big and too active for his cradle. "Yes, of course." She leaned down and kissed Howard's little hands and his chubby cheek, forced words from her constricted throat. "Sleep well, little one. I'll see you when you wake." She straightened and made her way to her bedroom. Her *borrowed* bedroom. For how long?

The hem of her velvet gown whispered across the floor as she crossed to the writing desk. She picked up the letter from New York she had found on the floor and stared down at the address in feminine handwriting—"Mr. Trace Warren, Whisper Creek, Wyoming Territory." Was this the one? Was this the woman who would replace her as Trace's wife?

Her stomach knotted. She took a deep breath and slipped the unopened letter in her pocket to take downstairs to him. It was time to stop this charade they were playing for all their sakes. And her continued weakness from being ill was the perfect reason. It would be Trace's explanation when she was gone.

The whistle echoed down the valley announcing the train's arrival. *Come and let me take care of you until you get your health and strength back.* Katherine tucked Judith's letter in her purse and looked out the window. Trace would be getting ready to dispense his medications to any sick passengers that came to his shop. Things were back to normal for him—but not for her. They would never again be the same as they were for her. She had fallen in love with her husband.

She leaned against the desk chair and watched the snow falling, the big fluffy flakes clinging to the wood grid that separated the small panes of glass and piling on the sill. Soft sounds came from the nursery. Mrs. Zhong was a quiet woman. Tears filmed her eyes. She blinked them away, buttoned on her coat, tied on her hat and hurried out of her bedroom and down the stairs. She had said her goodbyes to her baby, and if she saw him again she would not have the courage or strength to leave him.

She swallowed back her sobs, pulled on her gloves and went out on the porch to wait for Ah Key to bring the carriage around front—not to the back kitchen entrance where she'd waited every day for Trace to take her to town. She couldn't bear to see the nanny rocker, or the table where she first sat and had coffee with Trace at night.

Trace. He wouldn't be coming to the train station to say goodbye. She had asked him not to, and he had agreed. She opened her purse and looked to be certain she had the ticket to Fort Bridger he had bought for her. Her fingers touched the tin of fever and headache pills he had insisted she take with her in case of a relapse. Tears fell. The *doctor* was concerned about her leaving. The *man* didn't care. She sagged back against the porch wall and fought to keep her knees from giving way.

The train whistle blew its warning signal of imminent departure. The last of the passengers that had come seeking medicine or advice hurried out the door. The bell jangled. Trace tore his apron off, grabbed his coat and hurried out the back door of his shop. The supply road was shorter.

The cold penetrated his shirt and vest, chilled his skin. He shoved his arms into the coat's sleeves and yanked it over his shoulders, his long strides eating up the distance to the railroad station. He had told her he wouldn't come to see her off, but he had to see her aboard that train. She was still so weak—

He broke into a run. A stone rolled beneath his foot, his ankle twisted and he fell to his knees. The train whistle gave its double blast. *No!* He surged to his feet, gritted his teeth against a sharp pain and ran. His ankle gave. He crashed to the ground, grabbed his ankle, felt for any misplaced bone. It was not broken.

Black smoke puffed into the air. The train lurched forward then chugged off down the valley.

She was gone. He had got what he wanted. A safe, *empty* life.

He rolled to his knees, rose and hobbled back toward his shop.

"Katherine! Oh, Katherine, look at you!" Judith's arms wrapped her in a fierce hug. "You're so thin you feel like a stick!"

Tears threatened. She pulled out of her older sister's arms and smiled. "Well, *you* look wonderful, Judith. Oh, it's so good to see you again!" Her words choked off. She walked to the edge of the platform and looked out at the groups of buildings a short distance from the station to gain control. "That is Fort Bridger?"

"It is. That row of buildings on the right side is the officers' quarters." Judith came and slipped her arm through hers. "But you will learn all of that soon enough. For now, let's get you home. You look exhausted." She waved a hand toward a soldier standing by a wagon. "Private Durgan, get my sister's trunk and valise loaded and take us home."

"Yes, ma'am." The soldier hefted her trunk onto his shoulder, carried it to the wagon and set it in the back. "Allow me to help you, miss. It's hard to climb into these supply wagons." Hard hands gripped her thin waist and heaved.

"Oh!" She grabbed for his shoulders. He swung her over the side onto the board seat, turned and helped her sister climb up by using the wheel. She shook out her skirts and made room for Judith to sit beside her.

The private tossed her valise in the back with her trunk and the other crates he had loaded, climbed to the seat, picked up the reins and looked at her sister. "I'll go easy as I can, ma'am."

She held on to the front of the seat as the wagon jolted and jerked along the short stretch of road from the railroad rails to the fort, then stopped in front of a rectangular log building with two windows and two centered doors.

"This is it." Judith backed over the sideboard, put her foot on the wheel hub, hopped down and opened the door on the right. "Welcome, Katherine."

She smiled her thanks to the soldier who lifted her down and followed her sister into the house. It was small and cozy. A warm fire welcomed them. The exhaustion that had plagued her since her sickness washed over her in a wave. She placed her hand on the back of the settee for support.

"In there." Judith waved the soldier carrying her trunk and valise toward a door on the left. She tugged off her gloves, hung her coat on a peg by the front door and hurried over to her. "Let me take your coat and hat." Her sister's fingers undid the ties and buttons, draped her hat and coat over the back of the settee. "Now you are going to bed."

"No, Judith, I'm—"

"Not to argue with your older sister." Judith wrapped her arm about her waist and half carried her to the bed in the small room. "Now you rest while I make us some tea. And then we'll talk while we unpack your trunk."

The log-cabin quilt on the bed stole her protest. She lifted the corner, sat and brushed her hand across the fine stitching. "This is the quilt Mother made for you and Robert."

Judith nodded, bent down. "One of them." There were tugs on her feet and ankles as her sister unlaced and removed her boots. "The wedding-ring quilt is on our bed. It's kept us warm on many a cold night. Now rest. And pay no mind to bugle calls and shouting and horses racing by. That sort of thing goes on all the time at an army post." The door closed, and the room went dim.

She looked toward the door, considered following her sister out into the other room, but the bed was too tempting. She slipped her legs under the quilt, pulled it up over her shoulders and touched it against her cheek. It was almost like having her mother's hand resting there. She sighed, wiped the tears from her cheeks and closed her eyes.

Trace's footsteps lagged. Wind swooped down off the mountains, plastered the wet snow against him. He tucked his chin against his chest, tugged his hat brim down and stared out from under it at the house. The windows glowed with soft golden lamplight, but there was no welcome in them. She wasn't there.

The band of heaviness that had squeezed his chest all day tightened. He firmed his gloved grip on the crutches and tried to close out the image of the train carrying her away. Her going to Fort Bridger to see her sister in the hope that her strength would return with rest and care was the best thing that could have happened. Mrs. Zhong was caring for Howard. Katherine had an opportunity to improve her health. And he had exactly what he wanted. Katherine had removed herself from his life. He was free of her company. He would eat his meals alone. Drink his coffee alone. And he had no reason to feel guilty. It had worked out perfectly. Except for the pain in Katherine's eyes.

He sucked in a breath, coughing when the frigid air burned his lungs. He should have taken her to the station and put her on the train in spite of her request that he let her go alone. Maybe then he wouldn't feel so…troubled. Maybe he wouldn't have this empty feeling gnawing at his gut if he'd taken the opportunity to tell her goodbye. And he wouldn't have this sprained ankle.

He scowled, stomped the snow from his boots as best he could, climbed the steps and crossed the porch. The nanny bench sat against the house wall, abandoned and sprinkled with snow. He closed his mind to the memories of Katherine rocking Howard or sitting with her feet drawn up under her long skirts and sipping her coffee and yanked open the kitchen door. The smell of food turned his stomach sour. The glimpse of the one place set at the dining room table did the same for his disposition. So much for the pleasure of dining alone. Was she dining with her sister? Or being entertained by a group of army officers?

That thought didn't improve his mood. He shrugged out of his coat, jammed it and his hat on a peg, leaned the crutches in the corner and thumped his way through the dining room to go upstairs. He was in no mood for an inquisition from Ah Key about his leg. He strained against the silence to hear any sound. There was no laughter or baby cooing. No soft, husky voice singing a lullaby.

He fought the urge to go to the nursery and check on Howard, opened his bedroom door and flopped on his bed to rest his ankle until it was time to wash up for supper.

Chapter Fifteen

"Ooh, this blue silk is *beautiful*! I love the way this overskirt pulls up at the side."

"It is pretty." Katherine lifted a dark green taffeta dress from the trunk and smoothed out the lace on the bodice. The fabric felt stiff, the lace scratchy, but she didn't have to think about the baby's comfort anymore. She blinked and cleared the lump from her throat. "You take the dress, Judith. It will look wonderful on you with your blond curls and blue eyes."

"Oh, no, I couldn't. But I *will* borrow it for the Officers' Christmas Ball." Judith laughed, held the gown up to her and twirled around in the free space in the small bedroom.

Christmas. She would have to act happy and festive. Katherine forced a smile, hung the green gown on a peg and sat down to rest. "The gown is my gift to you—and Robert. He won't be able to take his eyes off you. Not that he ever does when you two are in the same room." Her voice broke. She looked down at the open trunk to hide her tears. *Thank You,*

Lord, that Judith is so happy with Robert. Thank You, that she has her true love. Please answer the longing of their hearts and give them a child. A baby. Pain ripped through her.

"You're too generous for your own good, Katherine." Judith smoothed out the dress and hung it on a peg. "Tell me about this stranger you married for the sake of his baby."

"I told you most of it in my letters, Judith." *Concentrate on the details, not on your feelings.* "Howard is not Trace's baby. He was born out of wedlock to the woman with whom Trace Warren had entered into an in-name-only marriage agreement."

"I've never heard of such a thing!"

"Nor had I."

"But you signed such a contract…" Judith lifted a ruffled petticoat from the trunk and shook it out.

"Yes. For the baby's sake. Miss Howard had bequeathed custody of her baby to Trace, who had agreed to raise him as his own. But there was no woman in town to…care for an infant." Her throat thickened. *Please, Lord, no more questions.* Judith's arms closed around her, hugged her close.

"I'm sorry, Katydid. I know the way you give away your heart, and—oh, Katydid, I wish I could help you."

She found the strength to drag up a smile. "You can. Stop calling me that horrid childhood name." She forced a semblance of the old childhood threat into her voice. "You don't want the soldiers on this base to call you Puffball, do you?"

"You wouldn't dare!"

"Oh, but I would." They broke into laughter. The painful knots in her stomach eased. Perhaps she would survive after all. She smoothed out her blue quilted nightclothes and slid them into a drawer in a small dresser in the corner. "Is there more tea, Judith?"

"I thought you preferred black coffee."

An image of Trace standing on the back porch, looking at her over top of his coffee cup, flashed before her. Tears welled. "Not anymore." Her sister looked at her. She closed her eyes and rubbed at her temples. "I find I don't want coffee since—" she drew a breath to control the tears "—since I've been ill."

Judith closed the trunk and took hold of her hand. "I think you're working too hard, little sister. Why don't we go and sit in front of the fire and visit?" She followed as Judith led her to the settee. "Robert is leading night patrol and won't be home until late tomorrow afternoon. We can finish your unpacking after supper. Now, you were telling me about Trace Warren."

She sighed. There was no point in trying to change the subject again. Judith would not give up until she knew the whole story. "What do you want to know?"

"When did you fall in love with him?"

She stared. Tears welled into her eyes and flowed down her cheeks. She lifted her hands and wiped them away. "I don't know. I—I think it was when he taught me how to bathe Howard. He was so strong and sure of himself, so…comfortable and tender with the baby and yet somehow…afraid." She looked down at her skirt, smoothed out a wrinkle. "There is this little muscle in front of his ear that twitches when he is upset or angry and it was twitching then. I wondered why and—and—"

"You wanted to help him."

"Yes."

"Oh, Katy."

She sat up straighter. "Don't you tell me that I'm too softhearted for my own good, Judith. It's been five years since Richard disappeared, and no man has...has—" She gave a helpless little wave.

"Made your stomach flutter and your knees go weak? Made you lie awake at night thinking about how it would feel to be in his arms? To have him kiss you?"

All of that and more. "Stop. Please." She covered the hollow ache in her abdomen with her hands.

Her sister studied her a moment, rose, took her hands and tugged her to her feet. "Time to eat. Come into the kitchen." She motioned her to the table, ladled soup into two bowls and set one down in front of her. "What are you going to do about it?"

"Nothing."

"That doesn't sound like the Katy I know." Her sister picked up a knife, sliced two pieces of bread then carried the plate and a crock of butter to the table. "I remember when you ran away from home to follow Richard when the Robinsons moved across town."

"I was eight years old!"

"And 'German stubborn.'"

"And I suppose you aren't?"

"Of course I am, but we're not discussing me." Judith sat and reached for her hand. They bowed their heads. "Dear Gracious Heavenly Father, I thank You for this food and for every blessing You pour out upon us. Thank You, Father, for leading and guiding us through each day. Please protect Robert and his patrol, I pray. Amen.'

Please, Lord, watch over my baby and Trace. She had little appetite, but she picked up her spoon and tasted the broth, swallowed her tears along with her soup. Her sister had always been a good cook and if she didn't eat, Judith would probably force-feed her. Like she and Trace had fed Howard the sugar water.

"Why don't you write your husband a letter?" Judith gave her a measuring look. "There's no harm in reminding him of what he's missing."

Her stomach churned. She regretted eating the soup. "Trace is my husband in name only, Judith. And he's thankful I'm gone from his life." She clenched her hands in her lap and forced out the words. "He is a widower. His wife and unborn child died two years ago. He does not want a wife *or* a child. But Howard is his ward, and I know he loves him—though he would deny it." She drew a breath and rubbed at a nagging pain in her temples. "But your idea of a letter is a good one. Trace thinks I have come only for a visit and will return when my strength comes back. I will write and tell him the truth."

It was a wretched meal. Trace choked down another bite of meat, crossed his knife and fork on his plate and scowled at the empty place at the other end of the table. He knew she was gone, but he kept waiting for Katherine to come and join him, to hear the rustle of her gown as she entered the dining room and the sound of her soft, husky voice and musical laughter. And he kept thinking of things his patrons had said that he wanted to share with her. Most of all, he wanted to know if Katherine was eating well. She would never regain her strength if she didn't eat.

He lunged to his feet, hobbled to the window and looked out. It had started to snow. If he had known the weather was going to turn so cold so fast, he wouldn't have agreed to her going to visit her sister. If she didn't dress warm enough and took a chill, she could have a relapse. Fort Bridger was on the edge of the frontier. Did they even have a doctor? And what of the Indian attacks that had been close to that area?

Don't you ever wonder who or what may be watching you from the shadows of the trees?

He sucked in a breath, stared out at the night. Was she afraid? Was the fort strong? Was there a safe place for her to go if an attack happened? What if she were injured? He wouldn't be there to help her. The doctor in him thought of the grim possibilities. His stomach knotted.

He turned from the window and limped through the dining room into the parlor, seeking distraction from the silence, the emptiness and his thoughts. He opened the cover on the piano and drifted his fingers over the keys. "Beautiful Dreamer, awake unto me..."

His voice echoed off the walls and ceiling, faded away. The memory of Katherine coming downstairs to listen to him play held him in its grip. That was the night he'd almost kissed her, the night he'd truly recognized the danger she was to him, and set himself to hold her at a distance—to fight his attraction to her. He glanced at the books in the secretary to rid himself of the memory. He didn't even know if she liked to read or cared for poetry. He'd never asked her anything personal, beyond what he needed to know to maintain their charade. He should have. Perhaps he would offer to loan her some of his favorites when she returned.

If she returned. The thought he'd been holding at bay surfaced on a tide of fear. His dinner turned to stone, weighted his stomach like a boulder. There'd been something in her eyes when she said goodbye.

He frowned, scrubbed his fingers through his hair but couldn't dislodge the vision. She'd looked so fragile when she had handed him that letter from the woman in New York, wished him well in his search for her replacement, and told him she was going to her sister's to get her strength back. He was well aware that her illness had taken its toll. The feisty young woman ready to fight for the baby she held when she arrived had disappeared. Her eyes— eyes that looked like they'd been made from the petals of violets—had dulled. Her "goodbye" had felt more like "farewell."

He stiffened, blew out a breath. What was he doing? It was good that she was gone. It was what he wanted. Wasn't it? He didn't want her here laughing and singing and drinking black coffee out in the cold with him. It would be best if she never returned. And she'd been right. Her illness was the perfect excuse for her to leave. He'd find a way to keep the house and shop without replacing her. He had to. For Howard. His regret was that Katherine had been hurt by having to give up Howard.

I chose to stay to help you keep your home and shop for Howard's sake. I'm not sorry. I may be hurt by my choice, but I'll never be sorry.

The memory of her words plunged deep, twisted like a knife. He was a coward. All the time he had been protecting his heart, Katherine had opened hers. She didn't deserve to suffer for her goodness. But there was nothing he could do. An image of Pastor Karl, standing in his hallway with his hat in his hand, flashed before him.

"God in Heaven, please heal Katherine, strengthen her and give her the desires of her heart."

The words were out before he could stop them. Not that they mattered. He shook his head, sat on the settee and rested his foot on the cushion beside him to ease the ache in his ankle. It would be good if he could ease the one in his chest as easily. He didn't believe in prayer. Not anymore. But something— probably guilt—had driven him to whisper this one.

The back door closed. Ah Key was gone for the night. He leaned back, closed his eyes and tried not to remember.

The wind howled around the building and rattled the panes of snow-covered glass in the window beside her bed. Katherine pulled her mother's quilt closer around her neck and watched the light from the flames in the fireplace of the main room flicker through her partially open door to dance against the whitewashed logs.

A shadow blacked out the dancing light. There was the crunch of a log being added to the fire followed by a frantic flickering as the flames licked greedily at the new fuel. Water splashed. Iron scraped quietly against iron.

She slipped out from under her covers, shrugged into her dressing gown and pulled on socks and slippers. Her hems whispered against the Oriental runner that ran from beside her bed to the door. Her sister was spooning dried leaves into a ceramic teapot. The scent of peppermint mingled with the smell of burning wood. She frowned. Judith was worried about Robert. Her sister always drank peppermint tea when she was upset. "Am I invited, or were you going to drink that tea all by yourself?"

Her sister glanced over her shoulder. "Did I wake you? The fire needed to be fed. I tried to be quiet."

"As a mouse. I wasn't asleep." She hastened to correct that admission before Judith figured out the real reason. "It's a strange place."

"Umm."

She moved over to stand by the fire. "Is a snowstorm as fierce as this one common in Wyoming Territory?"

"They happen occasionally." Her sister moved to a cupboard and took down two cups and saucers.

"I don't know how soldiers are trained to handle being out in a storm, so I've been praying for Robert and the others."

"Thank you, Katy."

She nodded, glanced at her sister's pale face and forced certainty into her voice. "I don't know those other soldiers, but I know Robert. And he will do the right thing at the right time, training or not. Remember that time when we were walking by the river, and he saved those two young boys by running ahead of them and climbing out on a tree branch to pull them from the water?"

"I do." Judith gave her a hug. "Thanks for encouraging me. I know Robert will do what's right. It's only that the storm came so fast they might not have had time to reach some sort of shelter. And if they can't see…"

"The Lord will guide them."

Judith nodded, lifted the cast-iron teapot off the trivet and poured the steaming water into the ceramic pot. The smell of peppermint filled the air. "That sounded like Mother speaking, Katherine. Her faith was so strong." Her sister rested her hand on her forearm and smiled. "You're like her."

It was no time to tell her sister that her faith had shriveled to a tiny thread that was ready to snap. "So are you, Judith."

Her sister smiled and walked over to stand facing the snow-plastered window. "Tell me about your friend Audrey in Whisper Creek, Katy. Is her baby going to be all right?"

She took a breath at the change of subject. *Please don't start talking about Howard.* "I believe so. Trace is taking care of Audrey and he's a wonderful doctor."

"And his friend, Audrey's husband, owns the general store. What other stores are there in the town?"

So Judith wanted distraction…not information. "Trace's apothecary."

"Only two stores?"

She poured a cup of tea and carried it to her sister. "At present, yes." She searched for a way to keep the conversation going. "And, of course, the railroad station and post office. And there is a sawmill owned by Mr. Todd, who does all of the building. And the church. And a hotel that opened on a limited basis, last week."

"And—"

She poured her tea and went to stand by the fireplace. "And what?"

"Shh. Do you hear that?"

"The wind?"

"No. It's—"

The door burst open. Snow flew into the room. The wind swirled smoke from the fire. She coughed, watched her sister drop her teacup and throw her arms around the snow-covered figure that slumped to the floor. "Robert! Oh, Robert, I was so frightened for you!"

She hurried around Robert and Judith and pushed with all of her strength to close the door, but couldn't manage. Judith jumped up and helped her, then leaned down and grabbed her husband's arm and tugged. "Help me get him by the fire, Katy!"

She grabbed Robert's other arm. Snow crushed against her dressing gown. She shivered and pulled then snatched the snow-covered scarf from around his neck and face. "I'll get a blanket. You get him some socks!" She ran for her bedroom and yanked her mother's quilt off the bed, tossed it on the settee to warm.

Judith draped his socks over a trivet at the side of the fire, sank to her knees, threw back the cape of his overcoat and clawed at the buttons. "They're frozen closed!"

"The tea!" She grabbed her cup off the table and poured hot tea on the metal buttons and surrounding fabric. The ice crackled and melted and fell away. She grabbed Robert's right glove and tugged it free, pulled the jacket sleeve off his arm and turned to his boot. Judith worked on his left side. Together they got him out of his snow-and-ice-caked clothes. She dragged the clothes over by the door while Judith covered her husband with the warmed quilt and tugged on his warmed socks. He shook with chills.

What would Trace do? She glanced down at the warm stone hearth. "Judith, if we can get him onto the stone it will help to warm him."

They knelt side by side and pushed Robert onto the warm stones. She rose and poured more hot tea and handed the cup to her sister. "This should help." She watched while Judith lifted her husband's head onto her lap and held the cup to his trembling lips.

"Robert, drink this." There was no response.

She thought of Trace force-feeding Howard the sugar water and grabbed a spoon, sank to her knees on the cold, wet floor and took the hot tea from Judith. "Hold his head up and I'll spoon in the tea." Her hands shook with the cold, but she got most of the hot tea into Robert. It was all she could think of to do.

Weary to her bones, she placed the teapot on the

trivet to stay warm, pushed to her feet, walked to Judith's bedroom and brought back a blanket to drape around her sister's shoulders.

"Thank you, Katy."

Her sister's smile eased the ache in her heart. She nodded and staggered to her bedroom, changed into warm, dry nightclothes and crawled under the covers. She was cold and tired and aching, but she knew now what she would do. She would go back home and become a nurse. She would never have a husband or children of her own, but she could help to take care of others.

Chapter Sixteen

"Have you medicine for a sore throat?"

Trace took a bottle off the shelf on the wall behind him and held it out to the young woman. "This will help. Take one spoonful every four hours and sip water in between the doses to keep your throat moist. I also have Smith Brothers cough drops. Many of my patrons find them soothing."

She nodded and reached into her purse. "I'll take a bottle of the elixir and a dozen of the cough drops, thank you." The woman glanced toward the windows at the front of his shop, tugged the hood of her coat into place and wrapped a scarf more closely around her neck.

He opened a Smith Brothers cough drop envelope, scooped in a dozen of the round drops from the large glass jar and put them in a bag with the bottle. "Here you are, madam." He handed her the bag and her change. "Be careful walking back to the train. It's easy to fall on ice."

"Indeed. With this weather one might as well be

back in Chicago." She put the change in her purse, picked up the bag and left the store.

The bell on the door jingled a merry goodbye. He cast a sour look in that direction. He was getting tired of that bell.

A man at the counter wiped his forehead with a handkerchief. "May I help you, sir?"

"I'm in need of some sort of tonic for a headache and sore throat. And my chest hurts."

"Do you have aches or pains, fatigue?"

The man frowned and nodded. "I'm pretty tired, but I figure it's the trip."

"I believe you have the flu, sir. How long have you been ill?"

The man wiped his forehead again. "Three days."

"Then you should be feeling better soon, if you rest and drink a lot of water. This tonic will help. And these pills will ease your headache and your aches and pains." He placed them in a bag.

"What do I owe you?"

"One dollar, twelve cents." The train whistle blasted its warning of pending exodus. The man handed him the coins and grabbed the bag. "Thank you for your help, sir."

He nodded, dropped the coins in the cash box and slipped it beneath the counter, grabbed the alcohol and wiped down the counter. He headed for his workroom out back to compound some of his headache and fever pills. His footsteps echoed through the empty store.

He scowled and pulled on his apron. He was getting sick of hearing the sound of his own footsteps at home and here in the shop between trains. But there were too few townspeople— The bell jingled.

"Trace! You here?"

His head jerked toward the door to the store. There was urgency in the hail. "In the back!"

Boots thumped. Garret Stevenson backed into the room supporting a larger man. "Mitch cut his leg. Looks bad."

"I'm all right."

He looked from the blood-soaked towel tied around Mitch's calf to his pale face and grabbed his free arm. "Put him on the table, Garret. Lift him on three. One…two…three!" He took off Mitch's boots and pants, revealing his long underwear. "Can you lift your legs up onto the table?"

"Sure."

He watched Mitch's face, smiled and thumped his shoulder. "You might as well stretch out and rest while you have the chance. How did this happen?"

"One of the men at the mill was chopping off branches. The ax head flew."

"And you were in the way." He reached down to the shelf below the table for a pair of scissors.

"That was pretty much the way of it." Mitch shot him a suspicious look. "What are you going to do with those?"

"Cut the leg off your wool drawers."

"You going to need me, Trace?"

He looked at Garret and nodded. "You can bring his wagon around to take him home."

Mitch lifted his head off the table. "I'm not going home. I plan on finishing—"

"Your plans have been changed, Mitch."

"Now look, Trace—"

"*Doctor.* Doctor Trace Gallager Warren. Trained and accredited in medicine and surgery by New York Medical College and Hospital." He set two bowls on the table, poured some medical alcohol in them then pulled his doctor's bag from the cupboard, selected a suturing needle and thread and placed it in one of the bowls.

Mitch gaped at him.

Garret shifted his weight and leaned against the table. "Some of us thought you might be a doctor, after the way you took care of Eddie. But Pastor Karl wouldn't say."

"I asked him not to tell anyone."

Garret gave him a questioning look. "But now you've changed your mind?"

Best to stop this conversation before it took a turn he didn't want. Not that it hadn't already. He tugged his lips into a grin. "If I'm going to have patients, I might as well charge them."

Mitch snorted and slapped his hands down on his knees. "And I get to be the first one."

He widened his grin and nodded. "You get to be the first. But don't worry. I'll take my fee out in trade. I'm going to need an office." The words shocked him. Telling the townspeople he was a doctor shocked him. He added warm water to one of the bowls and dipped a cloth into the solution, wondering when he had made that decision.

Garret thumped him on the shoulder. "Well, let me be the first to welcome you to Whisper Creek,

Doctor Warren—free of charge." The motel owner grinned at Mitch. "You've got to do what the doctor says, so I'll go get your wagon. But you might want to think about subtracting the cost of your ruined drawers when it comes time to pay your bill."

Mitch picked up the cut-off leg of his woolen underwear and chuckled. "Good idea, Stevenson. I'll keep it in mind."

"So will I." He waved the cloth like a weapon, smirked and began to clean the wound.

The trumpeting of a bugle and the sound of marching startled her awake.

Howard! Katherine jerked upright, reached for the baby's cradle, touched the log wall and remembered. She would never hear Howard crying for her again.

The ache in her heart drove her back beneath the covers. She closed her eyes and hoped for sleep to return and hold her in its grip until the pain of losing Howard was gone, until the memory of his sweetness overcame the pain of his loss.

The clink of china and the soft sound of lowered voices pulled her from her restless tossing and turning. The low rumble of a man's voice took her thoughts where she could not bear for them to go. Trace. The ache turned to an unbearable longing to be with him, to talk with him and laugh with him, to truly be his wife and belong to him. Tears welled. Sobs clogged her throat.

She blinked and set her jaw, threw back the covers. She would *not* cry. And she would *not* stay alone in this room and feel sorry for herself. She drew on her "German stubborn," slid her legs over the side of the bed and felt for her slippers. Her toes touched something cold and wet. She looked down at her nightclothes piled where she had dropped them last night, shoved them aside, gathered her courage and ran on tiptoe across the room to her trunk. The cold floorboards sent chills shooting up her legs. She fumbled the latch open, snatched out a pair of woolen socks and hopped from one foot to the other, pulling them on.

Her door squeaked. "Katherine, come out by the fire and have some coffee. It will warm you up."

"C-coming." She cast a longing glance at her dirty, wet quilted dressing gown, snatched her green cape off a peg by the door, swirled it around her shoulders and hurried into the main room.

"Katy!" Robert pulled her into a hug that squeezed the air from her lungs. "It's good to have you here."

"Especially last night." Judith smiled at her.

"Yes." Robert lowered her to the floor. "I don't remember anything much after I shoved open the door and fell into the house. But Judith tells me you were brilliant."

She shook her head. "Judith exaggerates. I was terribly frightened for you, Robert. How did you ever find your way home in that blinding snowstorm?"

"We were fortunate. The storm came so fast the river and the irrigation ditches were not frozen. We were at the edge of the river when the snow hit, so I had the men dismount and form a human chain with the horses as our pivot point. We kept walking in large circles until a trooper stepped into an irrigation ditch. Those ditches run in a straight line behind the houses here on officer's row. We just walked in the water until we reached home."

"It's a good thing you thought to follow the ditches. And to stay anchored to the river until you found them." She stepped onto the warm hearth and smiled at him. "I must say, you look much better than you did last night." She gave him a teasing grin. "Of course the uniform helps. How do you feel?"

"I'm fine now that I've warmed up and have some coffee in me." He returned her grin. "But I must admit I will have a certain fondness for peppermint tea from now on. Though I'm not certain how Captain Lamont will feel about my greatcoat smelling of it."

She laughed at the memory of pouring the hot tea on his frozen buttons. "It worked."

"It did indeed."

A bugle blew.

"Reveille. Time to go." Robert shrugged into his greatcoat and tugged on his hat and gloves.

She sniffed and grinned. There was definitely a scent of peppermint wafting from the front of his greatcoat. "I hope your horse doesn't eat your buttons."

Robert laughed, kissed Judith, tossed her a salute and hurried out the door.

"He recovered quickly."

"Yes. Thanks, in a large measure, to your help and imaginative ideas." Judith brought her a cup of coffee and swept an assessing gaze over her. "You look exhausted. I'm sorry, Katy. I didn't even think about how sick you've been when you were helping me last night."

"Neither did I." She wrapped her cold hands around the hot cup. "But then we were both just a little preoccupied with trying to keep your husband alive." She blew on the dark brew and took a sip. "Mmm, this is good coffee."

"All the same—"

"Stop, Judith." She reached out and squeezed her sister's hand. "I'm *grateful* for last night. Not for your distress or Robert's danger and discomfort, of course. But for helping to care for him. It helped me to be certain of what I will do with my life." *My empty life.* Her voice broke. She blinked hard and took a steadying breath. "I'm going to go back home and train to become a nurse." She tried for some humor to erase the stricken look from her sister's face. "Perhaps that way, I won't get in t-trouble by h-helping others." Tears gushed. Sobs shook her.

"Oh, Katy!" Judith snatched the cup from her hand and pulled her into her arms, held her close. "Your phony husband had better never come here, Katydid!" Her sister's fierce whisper touched the raw hurting place in her heart and brought another spate of tears gushing forth. "For his sake, he'd better never come here!"

She wished with all her heart that he would. But it was a foolish wish that would remain unfulfilled. She stepped back out of her sister's arms and forced a smile. "This tiredness from being ill makes me very weepy. I don't know how you put up with me, Judith. It will be refreshing for you to see your friends, who do not burst into tears over every little thing. Especially when planning the Christmas festivities." She stepped to the table and picked up her cup of coffee, took a sip. "I'll get ready for the day and then clean up these breakfast dishes while you are at your meeting."

"I wish I could stay home, Katy. But Sylvia Lamont outranks me." Judith lifted her cape from its peg by the door, buttoned it on and tugged her hood into place. She yanked on her gloves.

"I understand, Judith. Don't concern yourself. I'll be fine." She moved a little closer to the fire. "Please thank Mrs. Lamont for her kind invitation and make my excuses. Now calm down before you ruin those gloves."

"I wish they were Trace Warren's neck! I would— well, you know."

"Yes, I know." She swallowed hard and forced a little laugh. "Take a breath and smile, Judith, or you're going to frighten your friends."

Her sister drew in an exaggerated breath and stretched her lips back from her teeth.

She broke into real laughter. "That's lovely."

Judith wrinkled her nose at her, turned and slipped out the door.

A log fell. The fire crackled and threw sparks up the chimney. Katherine added a new log to the fire, poked it into place, then turned and looked around. Judith's living quarters were small and her furniture was a bit damaged from being transported from post to post, but none of that mattered. Judith and Robert were in love. Only being childless marred her sister's happiness.

Howard. Her baby... She would carry him in her heart forever. Her memories might become a bit damaged over time, like Judith's furniture, but she would always have them with her—wherever she might be. She pushed thoughts of her unknown future from her and continued to look around her sister's home. She had thought it would be frightening living on the frontier, but the whitewashed log walls looked sturdy and safe. A sampler between the door and the window caught her attention. Judith did beautiful needlepoint work. She walked over and read the words. "O my God, I trust in thee: let me not be ashamed, let not mine enemies triumph over me. Psalms 25:2."

Her lips curved into a smile. Trust Judith to choose the perfect verse for a soldier's home. *I trust in thee.* She didn't. Not anymore. She wanted to. She missed that strong sense of love and security that filled her when she'd prayed. But her faith had eroded a bit with every unanswered prayer for Richard's safe return. And now—

She blinked, rubbed her constricted throat and walked into her bedroom. Soldiers marched by the house counting cadence as they passed. A train whistle blew. And somewhere a horse whinnied a challenge. Life went on in spite of a broken heart. And so must she.

The hem of her velvet gown whispered against the floor on her way to her trunk. She opened the lid, removed her box of writing supplies and carried them out to the table. She opened the box, set out a blotter, the ink and her pen and lifted out a piece of stationery.

The fire flickered. She turned up the oil lamp hanging from a chain pulley overhead, stared at the blank sheet of paper then sat, folded her hands and closed her eyes.

"I know my faith is small, Lord. But Your Word says if I have faith the size of a mustard seed I can move a mountain. My mountain is pain over losing precious little Howard, the child of my heart, and Trace, the love of my life. Please move this mountain for me, Lord, and give me strength to go on. Help me to find purpose in helping others. I will thank You for it. Amen."

The wind whistled around the window. She wiped tears from her cheeks, opened her eyes and picked up the pen. Pain squeezed the breath from her lungs. How should she open the letter? What should she call him? My Dear Husband? No. She hadn't the right. My Dear Trace? Even that sounded too intimate. He was not hers. And she was not his.

Dear Trace,
I hope this letter finds you and your son well. Howard is in my heart and my thoughts. I pray he continues to gain health and strength. I know that with your care and guidance he will grow into a fine young man.

Tears blinded her. She rose and walked to the fireplace, buried her face in her hands and struggled for control. If she broke down every time she thought of Howard and Trace she would never be able to write the letter. And Trace deserved to know the truth. He had to make a new plan. One that did not include her. He needed to know she would not return.

She took a deep breath, walked back to the table and took up her pen.

I must ask your forgiveness. When I left, I was not honest with you. No, that's not right. I was not honest with myself. I thought I could return, that I could uphold the pledge I made to you in our in-name-only-marriage contract. For very selfish reasons I find I cannot.

Mrs. Zhong is an excellent, kind and caring nanny to Howard. He no longer needs my attention, and you are now receiving replies to your postings in the New York City and Philadelphia newspapers inquiring as to a permanent marriage-in-name-only wife. You will soon find my replacement as your stand-in bride. I wish you well in your search and pray that you will find a suitable, compatible woman who will love Howard and be the comfortable companion you both desire and deserve. I believe that you having your son with you will fulfill your legal obligation to Mr. Ferndale to live with your family in Whisper Creek for five years. Thus, I am left with no reason or purpose to return to Whisper Creek. My promise to Miss Howard has been fulfilled. Howard has his father. And I know you will be a wonderful father to him.

I am sorry for failing you, Trace. But I cannot live a pretend life any longer. Not one without purpose. I told you once that I thought I would like to be a nurse and care for those who are ill or hurting. I have decided that is what I will do.

I will stay here, at Fort Bridger, with my sister until I have regained my strength, and then I will go to New York City and enter a nurse's training program. I will send you my address when I am settled as you may need to be in touch with me for some legal purpose. To that end, I will state here and now that I do not, in any way, oppose your wish for an annulment of our in-name-only marriage.

I wish you all happiness in the future.
With sincere affection,
Katherine

It was done. She folded and sealed the letter, directed it to Mr. Trace Warren, Whisper Creek, Wyoming Territory, and placed it on the little one drawer stand by the door for Robert to send out with the post mail.

Her temples throbbed and her head ached from holding back tears. Fatigue drained her strength. She put her writing supplies back in their box, closed it and carried it to her bedroom. She couldn't make it to her trunk. She put the box on the floor, crawled under the covers and cried.

* * *

He couldn't take the silence in the house any longer. "Shall we go outside, little man?" He fastened Howard's hat and coat, bundled him in his blanket and carried him downstairs. He didn't know what had made him tell Mitch and Garret he was a doctor, but now that he had he was full of plans. And he wanted someone to share them with. No. He wanted Katherine to share them with! She was the one who had encouraged him to believe in himself as a doctor again.

He slapped his hat on his head, buttoned his coat, tugged on his gloves and limped out onto the porch. Large, fluffy snowflakes sparkled and danced to the ground through the glow of the coach light at the bottom of the steps. Was it snowing at Fort Bridger?

"See the snow, Howard? Next year you'll be big enough to play in it. You'll like that. Maybe we'll make a snowman." He cuddled Howard close, leaned against the porch post and watched the snow fall. It would be Christmas in a few days. Would Katherine be well enough to return by then? Did they have any sort of entertainments at the fort? Most likely a church service. And an officers' ball. His mind froze on that thought. Katherine's sister was married to a lieutenant. They'd attend the ball with Katherine as their guest. What if she met someone?

He stiffened, shoved away from the post and stared out into the night. Most of the soldiers at the frontier posts were single. He scowled, tried to remember if any officers from Fort Bridger had come into his shop. None came to mind.

A gust of wind blew the snow against him. "Are you warm enough, little man?" He laughed at Howard's baby babble answer and turned to protect him from the wind. He looked toward the mountain behind the house, picturing the long slope at the bottom. Maybe he'd order a toboggan. It could be here before she returned. Katherine was an adventurous woman. She would probably like a toboggan ride. He could teach her how to guide it by leaning the right way at the right time.

A smile curved his lips. He leaned back against the post and thought about toboggan rides for two. And skating on the pond. He would order a push sled for Howard so they could take him with them.

If she came back.

He shoved the thought from his mind. She loved Howard. She'd be back. He lifted the baby into the air and smiled up at him. "It won't be long until your mama comes home. Maybe Christmas..."

Chapter Seventeen

"I don't think you should have written your husband that letter yet, Katy."

Katherine reached for another dish on the draining rack, pulled her hand back and stared at her sister. "*You're* the one who told me to write it."

"That was before I knew how much you love him."

Pain stabbed into her heart. She took a breath and picked up a bowl to dry. "How I feel doesn't matter. And stop calling him my husband."

"That's what he is."

She swiped the towel around the inside of the bowl and shot her sister a look. Judith was on a campaign. "Only in name. You know the truth of my situation. Now stop—or you will finish these dishes by yourself." She stacked the bowl with the others, tossed the towel over her shoulder and carried them to the cupboard.

"'German stubborn…'"

"What was that?"

"Very well. But you still shouldn't have sent that

letter." A dish clinked against one already on the draining board. "You can't go to New York City until you get your strength back. And who knows what might happen meantime?"

"There is nothing that can happen that will make me change my mind." Katherine finished drying a plate and looked at her sister. "You haven't done something foolish I should know about, have you?"

"Of course not! But there is the Christmas ball in a few days and—"

"*And* I told you I'm not going."

"I know. But I hope you will help me decorate for it. I volunteered us."

Her stomach clenched. She had been decorating for their Christmas wedding when Richard disappeared. And now— "Why would you do that, Judith?"

"Because the ball is going to be held in the empty quarters in the other half of this building and you will be able to come home and rest when you tire. And because Mrs. Colonel Lamont asked."

"And she outranks you."

"Exactly."

"All right. I'll do it for you and Robert."

"Good. Because the decorations are here and I need your creative touch. Leave the rest of the dishes to drain and come along. And leave your apron on."

She took a deep breath, set her mind to do what was needed and followed her sister into the main room. At least the sun was shining. And the stone walk in front of the house had been cleared of snow.

She lifted her hems and ran out their door and dashed in the other.

A fire roared in the fireplace. The scent of pine filled the room. She skirted the huge pile of green boughs and stopped at a makeshift table of thick planks on top of two sawhorses. A pile of twine hung from a long spike driven at the center of the edge of the table. Two small hatchets and two pair of scissors waited beside two wicker baskets. A pile of long strands of thicker rope divided the table.

She looked askance at the tools. "I've never used an ax, Judith."

"It's a hatchet. Axes are much bigger. Watch me." Judith laid one of the large boughs on the table, picked up a hatchet and brought it down sharply at the base of each smaller branch severing them from the bough. "That's all there is to it. Why don't I chop and you start making swags for the window and doors?"

"Thank you, Asa." Trace clutched the letter in his gloved hand and hurried across the platform and down the steps, his heart thudding. Perhaps she was coming home. No more lonely meals or silent, empty house. And what a surprise he had for her.

His long strides ate up the distance to his shop. He stomped the snow from his boots and went inside, the bell jingling its greeting.

"That you, Trace?"

"Mitch?" He shoved Katherine's letter into his pocket, hurried through his shop to the back room and hung his jacket on a peg beside the door. "I didn't expect you today. Is there a problem?"

"The opposite." Mitch tugged off his knit hat and scrubbed his hand through his hair. "I had a talk with a couple of men on their way to help build a depot in Utah. I told them about how we're building a whole town here and they decided to stay. That gives me enough of a crew to start on your building before I finish the hotel."

He laughed and thumped Mitch's hard shoulder. "That's good news for me. But the owners of the Union Pacific are going to ban you from their property if you don't stop hiring their builders away from them."

"I only hire the good ones." The construction boss chuckled, shoved his hat in his pocket and pulled the rolled up paper from under his arm. "I have a couple of questions before we get started."

"All right." He grabbed a couple of bottles and set them on the corners to hold the paper down. "What's your first question?"

"It's more of a suggestion. You want your office facing on the road on your new lot next door, here—" Mitch's thick, callused finger pointed out the spot. "And the examining rooms, here toward the back. Right?"

"That's correct." His stomach tensed. "And a roofed passage between the buildings into this back room that I can use in inclement weather. And living quarters above the new building."

"So my suggestion is, why not deepen your new building to match this one and then build all the way across the rear of both buildings and join them to this back room? You'd have more rooms if you need a place for patients to stay overnight, and you could use the attic space above this shop as part of the living quarters."

"I like that, Mitch. It gives me twice as much building on the same amount of land. Let's do it."

"I'll get the men started tomorrow. See you then."

He was going to be a doctor again. With his own clinic! And it was all thanks to Katherine. He couldn't wait to tell her. When was she coming home? He hurried to his jacket, pulled her letter from his pocket and opened it. His heart thudded as he scanned the words, jolted to a stop, then read them again.

She wasn't coming home.

It took him like a fist to the gut. He folded the letter, put it in his pocket and walked out of the back room. Snow was falling again. He pulled up his collar, jammed his hands into his pockets, walked to the back of Blake's general store and crossed the supply road.

The ground was frozen. He followed the path that wound through the pines to the pond, leaned against one of the boulders and stared at the patterns in the ice. He'd been so excited, so eager to share his plans. And now—now his life was empty again.

She wasn't coming back. And why should she? What had he ever given her except the promise of a broken heart?

He stiffened, caught his breath. That was what he'd seen in her eyes when she told him goodbye— the shadow of her broken heart. And fool that he was, he'd let her go. What an imbecile he was to deny his feelings for her out of fear of losing her to death. He was losing her now—to life.

Unless—

A train whistle echoed down the valley. He listened to it fade into the distance then shoved away from the boulder and ran.

Katherine ran an assessing glance over the room. It was looking very festive.

"The garland needs to hang down a little more on the left, Robert. Do you agree, Katy?" Judith turned and looked at her.

"Yes. It's hanging almost a foot lower on the right side. So…pull it over six inches." She grinned and held her forefingers six inches apart when Robert glanced at her.

"I'll get even, you know." He growled the words and stepped off the chair he was using to gain height. "I don't know how yet, but I will get even." He moved the chair back to the other side of the window, climbed on it, adjusted the garland as directed and then repeated the process on the left side. "Is that all right, Judith?"

"Yes, dear."

"Katy?"

"Well…"

He growled.

"It's perfect." She laughed, pulled another branch from the basket at her feet and placed it on the fireplace mantel, added another pinecone and some walnuts.

"That's really pretty, Katy." Judith picked up one of the wreaths they'd made yesterday and tied it to the center of the window shutters with a piece of twine.

"I think it will look nice when the oil lamps are lit. But it would be prettier if we had some apples or berries for the light to shine on."

"I can get you some cranberries from the mess, if you would like them, Katherine."

"That would be wonderful, Robert. Can you get at least a pound of them?"

"I can manage that. I'll be right back."

She nodded and moved the second oil lamp into place at the opposite end of the mantel, bent to the basket and grabbed a handful of branches to place around the base. "When do you think the soldiers Robert sent to cut down a tree will be back, Judith?"

"I don't know. He expected them earlier. And I've seen him casting concerned glances at the window. I think that's probably what is behind his offer to bring you cranberries. He will try to find out if anything has gone awry. There, that's the last wreath we need hung!" Judith arched and rubbed her back. "Would you like me to make some coffee?"

"Coffee would be wonderful."

"All right. Just let me throw out the rest of these branches. Oh, good. The patrol is back." Judith stilled, tilted her head and listened.

"Judith, Katherine, come out here!"

Her stomach clenched. She jerked her gaze to her sister.

"Something is wrong." Judith frowned and ran out the door.

She tossed the pinecones she held back in the basket and hurried after her sister.

"They're too young to put in the infirmary, Robert. Bring them in the house."

She stopped, stared at two small, dirty and bloodied children wrapped in soldiers' coats being lifted from a wagon. The poor things were crying and shaking with cold and fright. "I'll get things ready, Judith." She ran to spread a blanket on the warm hearth, then raced to the dressing room, filled a bowl with warm water, snatched up soap and towels and washcloths and hurried back to the main room. Judith was kneeling on the floor talking and soothing the children lying on the blanket while she stripped their torn and dirty clothes off them.

"Thank you." Her sister dipped a washcloth in the warm water and talked softly while she washed off the blood on the child closest to her.

She wet a cloth and knelt by the other child. The toddler let out a cry when she touched her arm.

"Judith, I think her arm is broken." Her stomach churned. "Where is Robert? We need him to get the post doctor."

"I'm here." Boots pounded across the floor. "There's no doctor on post at present. Only an untrained orderly. But this gentleman has offered his services."

She looked up. Her heart leaped. "Trace!"

Judith darted a glance at her, caught her lower lip in her teeth, and went back to washing and soothing the child.

"I'm happy to help, Lieutenant." Trace's calm and

confident voice filled the room. "I'll need a doctor's field kit. And splints suitable for a small child."

Robert strode to the door and issued his orders.

Trace removed his coat, rolled up his sleeves, squatted and washed his hands. He smiled and ran his fingers gently over the toddler. "You're right, Katherine. Her arm is broken, and her leg, also. She'll need to be watched for any signs of internal injury. As will her sister." He looked down at the other toddler who was staring up at him and smiled. "I'm Doctor Warren. What's your name?"

"J-Jen-ny." Her little jaw quivered. She held up her hand, her middle fingers extended. "I'm f-free. Betsy's a baby. She g-gotted hurt." The toddler fisted her hand and wiped at her eyes.

"We'll make Betsy better." Trace touched a lump on the toddler's forehead, slid his fingers through her brown curls. "It looks like you've had quite an adventure, Jenny. Did you fall down?" His hands moved gently over the small body as he talked.

"Papa's w-wagon falled down th-the hill." Tears rolled down the toddler's cheeks. "Him and Mama w-won't get up."

Trace nodded to Judith, who pulled Jenny onto her lap and cuddled her close while she finished washing her.

The orderly hurried into the room. "I couldn't find anything for a small splint, sir."

Robert nodded and handed Trace the kit. There was nothing of use.

"Would the cover of a book do, if it were cut into wide strips?"

"An excellent idea, Lieutenant."

Robert pivoted, grabbed a book off the mantel and pulled out his knife.

Trace's gaze caught and held hers. "I'll need your help with the little one, Katherine."

She nodded, fought to control her breathing.

Trace opened jars, handed one to Judith and smiled. "That salve will treat Jenny's bruises. Why don't you wrap her in a blanket and take her to the kitchen for something to eat. She looks hungry to me." Judith's face paled. Her sister rose and carried the toddler to the kitchen. Robert took Judith's place on the hearth and slit the book covers into four pieces.

"The little one is all clean, Trace." He looked at her and nodded. *His eyes...* Her heart fluttered.

He lifted a roll of bandage from the kit and placed it beside the makeshift splints. "Are you ready?"

She took a breath and nodded.

He pulled a small rag out of the kit, opened a bottle and put a few drops of liquid on it. "Hold this under her nose and take it away immediately when she closes her eyes. If she begins to wake, do it again. Do you understand?"

"Yes."

"Don't take your eyes off the child."

"I won't." She wanted to look at him. To drink in the sight of him kneeling beside her, but she did as he directed. From the corner of her eye she saw him place two splints on the toddler's small arm and wrap them with the bandage. His shoulder brushed hers when he moved on to splint the toddler's leg. Warmth washed through her.

"I'm finished. She should wake up in a few minutes. Give me the rag, Katherine." He tossed it in the fire and closed the medical kit.

Robert handed it to the orderly. "Dismissed." He looked at Trace. "Well done, sir. I should like to have you on my post at any time."

"Thank you, Lieutenant. But I have other plans." Trace's smile took her breath away. She wrapped the little toddler in a blanket and cuddled her in her arms as close as the injuries would allow.

"Will she be all right?" Judith's voice was full of tears.

Trace rose and pulled on his coat. "I believe so, Mrs...."

"Judith, please."

Her sister's smile was radiant.

"Robert, if you will take Jenny—" Judith handed the toddler she held to her husband and extended her arms "—I will take Betsy. And free our guest to talk with the person he came to see. Perhaps over in the ballroom, Katy..."

Warmth crawled into her cheeks. She nodded, took the hand Trace offered her, rose and walked to the door. What did he want? Why was he— A spasm hit her stomach. "Howard! Is—"

"He's fine, Katherine." Trace leaned forward and opened the door.

"In here." She took a breath and led the way into the house they'd been decorating. The fire crackled. The pine scented the room. He must have come because of their contract. Hadn't she made it clear she wouldn't oppose an annulment? She clenched her hands down to her sides, dug her nails into her palms to keep from crying and turned to face him.

"Why have you come, Trace? I wrote you—"

"Yes. Your letter is why I'm here." He came farther into the room, sniffed. "It smells good in here. Looks pretty, too."

"Thank you. But—"

"Thank you? Did you do all of this?" He waved his hand to include the whole room, stepped closer to the fireplace.

"Judith and I, yes. But about the letter. I don't understand. If I didn't make it clear—"

"All that you said was very clear." He picked up a small log and placed it on the fire, pushed it into place with his foot.

He was too close. Her heart fluttered. She took a step backward. "Then what brought you here?"

"I came to offer you a job. And after what I've just seen, I'm more certain than ever it's the right thing to do." He reached for a walnut she had dropped when she ran out the door. "Is this supposed to be here with the other ones?" He moved to the hearth, looked at her.

Her knees threatened to give way. She reached behind her and braced her hand against the stone. "A *job*?" She stared at him. Was he insane? Didn't he understand anything she had written?

"Yes. You see, I've made a few changes since you've gone. And so, when your letter came—"

It was too much. She snatched the walnut he was

fiddling with from his hand and slapped it down on the mantel. "It goes here! As for a job—"

"As a nurse."

"What?" She turned back to face him.

"Yes. You see one of those changes I mentioned was to tell the people in Whisper Creek that I'm a doctor."

Joy flooded her. "Oh, Trace, that's wonderful! I'm so happy for you. And for everyone in Whisper Creek. They need a doctor."

"They have one now. And it's because of you. You're the one who encouraged me to trust in my skills and become a doctor again."

His voice was quiet, deep. His eyes dark. She swallowed hard and stepped back to where she had been to let the stone support her.

"And a doctor needs an office. That's another change I made. You see, when John Ferndale learned that I am a trained and certified doctor from New York Hospital he was overjoyed. He offered me the lot next to my apothecary shop and free lumber to build my doctor's office and a clinic." His gaze captured hers. "And when I explained our unusual agreement, he told me because the need for a doctor at Whisper Creek is so dire I could stay on with no contract. Do you realize what that means, Katherine? I no longer have to be married—not even in name only."

Her throat closed. She held back tears. "I—I'm happy for you. I know you didn't want to be forced to marry."

"Exactly."

Don't look at him. Think about the details. Don't cry. "So there will be no problem for you in obtaining an annulment."

"I hope that won't be necessary." He took a step closer. The reserve, the caution, was gone from his eyes. "I love you, Katherine Warren, and I want to be married to you and no other." He slid his arms around her, pulled her close against him. "I was a fool and a coward to deny my feelings for you. I've loved you from the moment at the train when I looked into your eyes." He lifted his hand and cupped her neck. His thumb brushed against her cheek. "Will you come home and be my wife in truth and in love forever?"

His eyes took her breath; his words took her strength. She leaned against him and nodded. "Forever."

His lips touched hers, warm, soft, caressing. He slid his hand into his pocket, then grasped hers and slipped a gold band on her finger. "Now and always, my love." His arms tightened, and his lips covered hers, asked... She slid her arms around his neck and gave him her promise. He lifted his head and gave her a look that made her pulse race. "Let's go home to our son, Mrs. Warren."

Chapter Eighteen

"Here is your Christmas present, Judith." Katherine handed the gown to her sister. "You look so beautiful in that blue silk gown I'm going to be sorry I will not be here to see Robert whirling you across the floor in it. Of course, no present can equal the one you and Robert received today." She placed her slippers on top of her packed gowns and smiled at the toddlers resting on the bed they would share. "Everything has happened so quickly. I can't believe the girls are to be yours! I'm surprised Colonel Lamont has that power."

Judith's eyes filled with tears. "He is the law at the fort. That's the way it is out here on the frontier. And he was relieved when Robert told him we wanted to have the girls for our own. His only other choice was to have a soldier take them back east to an orphanage." Her sister stroked her new daughters' hair. "There is no one to claim them, and no way to know where they came from or where they were going. They're too young to tell us. And there was nothing left in the wagon. The soldiers don't even have a name to put on their mother's and father's graves."

"I know. Such sad things happen to people. And so quickly out here on the frontier. But the toddlers will have a wonderful life with you and Robert. You must write and tell us how the youngest one mends."

"I will, Katy. And you must write about your new profession as nurse to your doctor husband." Her sister's eyes sparkled at her. "And thank you again for helping to save Robert."

She laughed at the memory and buttoned on her coat. "Whoever would have thought peppermint tea could save someone? When correctly applied, of course."

There was a rap of knuckles on the door. "Judith. We need to load Katy's trunk if they're to catch the train."

Katherine opened the door and motioned her brother-in-law into the room. "It's ready to go, Robert. And so am I." She gave her sister a hug and followed the soldier who shouldered her trunk and headed for the door. Her heart fluttered at the sight of her husband waiting for her. Her *husband*! When she had given up all hope. She glanced at the sampler on the wall and smiled. *I trust in thee, Lord. I trust in thee.*

The snow crunched beneath her boots as Trace helped her to the wagon. He lifted her in, his gaze holding hers, his hands lingering at her small waist. Her pulse raced. She settled herself on the seat and turned for one more wave as the soldier climbed to his place and took up the reins. Robert and Judith stood in the doorway of their home, holding their new daughters and beaming with happiness. *Lord, I pray You will bless them with health and happiness.* All that had happened in her short visit popped into her head. There were so many dangers on the frontier. *And please keep them safe.*

The train whistle blew.

The soldier snapped the reins and the horses broke into a trot. The buildings of Fort Bridger grew smaller in the distance. The train was at the station, the conductor waiting by the steps when they arrived. Trace helped her down from the wagon and they hurried to board. The doors closed. "Ready, Mrs. Warren?" She looked at her husband and nodded, her heart too full to speak.

The train lurched, rolled forward. She sat on the seat beside Trace, their shoulders rubbing with the sway of the train. His hand held hers, his thumb making little circles on the inside of her wrist. Strength flowed into her at his touch. Her heart soared with happiness. She and Trace were going home to their baby.

"Tell me about Howard, Trace. How much has he grown?"

"In the time you've been at your sister's—perhaps a quarter of an inch."

"I'm serious!"

"So am I. Babies don't grow that fast." He smiled and touched the tip of her nose. "But they do change quickly. Howard is trying to talk. I think he will learn to make sounds much quicker when he has his mother talking and playing with him again."

His mother. How wonderful those words sounded.

She clutched Trace's arm and leaned her head against his shoulder.

The wheels clacked over the cold steel tracks. The train swayed its way along the miles. She fought to stay awake, to hold the fatigue at bay. She was improved, but with all that had happened, she was not fully recovered.

"So much has happened so fast I haven't had a chance to ask you, Trace. Have you injured your foot?" Concern darkened her eyes. "I thought I saw you favoring it once or twice."

"You see, I'm right to hire you. You have the natural instincts of a nurse." He smiled down at her. "You were almost correct. I sprained my ankle."

"How did it happen?"

"I was running to catch your train when you left."

She stared at him, tears shining in her eyes. "You were running after *me*?" Her voice was soft, husky.

He gazed down at her, brushed a tendril of hair back off her forehead. "I was. And I will be for the rest of my life."

The car quieted. They glanced at the other passengers and lowered their voices to a whisper. He chuckled, his eyes twinkling with amusement when she told him about trying to save Robert the night of the snowstorm. "Peppermint tea! Ingenious! And rolling him onto the warm hearthstones was the best thing you could have done for him. You will make a fine nurse, Katherine."

She smiled and wrinkled her nose at him. "Well, the credit is yours. We rolled Robert onto the hearth because I kept wondering what you would do if you were there." She cuddled closer against him and closed her eyes. His arm tightened around her.

"Sleep, dearest. We have a few hours until we reach home."

The whistle blew. The train slowed, chugged to a stop. The conductor opened the door and leaned in.

"Whisper Creek Station. You have twenty minutes, folks."

Her pulse quickened. Trace rose and held out his hand. They made their way to the front of the car, stepped out onto the little platform and walked down the steps. A door opened and her trunk was hefted to a broad shoulder and carried to the platform. Her valise rested on top.

"Evenin', Doctor. Mrs. Warren."

Doctor. How wonderful to hear Trace addressed that way. She brushed snow from her collar and smiled at the station manager. "Good evening, Asa."

Trace threaded her arm through his and walked her to the runabout. A door on the station opened and closed and Mrs. Zhong walked toward them, a bundle in her arms.

"Howard! My baby…" Her heart jolted. Tears flowed down her cheeks. She took her baby in her arms, lifted the blanket over his face and covered his chubby little cheeks with kisses. She laughed at his soft, cooing sounds and choked on tears at the touch of his tiny hand on her face.

"Ah Key wait for you. Me go home to hill three days."

"Thank you, Mrs. Zhong."

"You had her bring the baby to surprise me?" She couldn't stop her happy tears.

"I knew you wouldn't want to wait to reach home to see him. Ah Key brought them in the buggy. Now let's take our baby home."

"Our baby…"

Trace kissed the tears from her cheeks, handed her into the buggy, loaded her trunk and valise, then climbed to his seat and started the horse for home. It was the same and yet so very different from that first night.

Lights shone from the windows on the first floor of the hotel. They warmed the windows of Blake and Audrey's home above their general store. And they glowed at the church and parsonage. She cuddled Howard and snuggled against Trace and watched for the Ferndales' house. The large Victorian-style home loomed out of the dark, its paint gleaming in the snow-streaked moonlight. And now *their* home. Her pulse quickened. She sat forward and peered ahead, remembering how strange it had looked when she first saw its octagon shape.

Trace stopped the horse by the front entrance and Ah Key stepped out of the shadows and took hold of the cheek strap. He smiled and gave a short bow. "Glad see Missy W home."

She cleared her throat and smiled. "It's good to be home, Ah Key."

Trace helped her down and Ah Key led the horse away, her hoofs thudding against the packed snow.

She held Howard close and walked with Trace up

the steps and across the porch, stopped and waited for him to open the door.

"Not this time, Katherine. This time I'm going to do it right." She held Howard tight as her husband lifted them in his arms. He pressed his warm lips to hers then carried them across the threshold.

Trace's strong arm supported her up the stairs. She unwrapped Howard from his blanket cocoon, changed his diaper and put on his nightclothes Trace handed her. The baby's eyelids slid downward, fluttered and closed.

"Looks like the fresh air made him tired."

"Isn't he beautiful, Trace?"

"He is indeed. And healthy and strong."

"Thanks to your skill, and the blessing of the Lord." She tucked the covers close around their baby, leaned down and kissed his soft, rosy cheek. He wiggled and squirmed. His little hand sneaked out from under the blanket and found his mouth. He closed his lips around his thumb and made tiny sucking sounds.

Happiness overwhelmed her. She turned and stepped into her husband's arms, leaned her head against his shoulder and sighed. He raised his hand and touched her cheek; warmth flowed through her. "I love your hands." She turned her head and kissed his palm, caught her breath when he tipped her chin up and their lips met.

"I love you, Katherine." Her heart skipped. He lifted her into his arms and gazed into her eyes. "The thought of spending all the rest of my days with you takes my breath away. It will never be long enough." He claimed her lips again. She slipped her arms around his neck and returned his kiss as he carried her to their room.

* * * * *

Don't miss the first book in the
STAND-IN BRIDES *series by Dorothy Clark:*

HIS SUBSTITUTE WIFE

And enjoy these other historical romances from Dorothy Clark:

*HIS PRECIOUS INHERITANCE
AN UNLIKELY LOVE*

Available now from Love Inspired!

Find more great reads at www.LoveInspired.com

Dear Reader,

My second trip to Whisper Creek is over. When Katherine boarded the train in Albany she was simply on her way to visit her sister at Fort Bridger in Wyoming Territory. And Trace, well, he had turned his back on love and medicine forever—he thought. But that was before they met baby Howard, and compassion for the orphaned infant forced them to follow paths they never expected. I *love* doing that!

I enjoyed writing Trace and Katherine's story, but it's time to move on. Confirmed bachelor Garret Stevenson has a hotel to open. How will he deal with the revision clause in his contract with the town's founder? And with— But that's for the next story. I'm excited to find out what this next journey to Whisper Creek holds in store. How about you, dear Reader? Would you like to come along on my third journey to Whisper Creek? We're underway.

Thank you, dear Reader, for choosing to read *Wedded for the Baby*. I hope you enjoyed Katherine, Trace and little Howard's story. I truly appreciate hearing from my readers. If you care to share your thoughts about this story, I may be reached at *dorothyjclark@hotmail.com* or *www.dorothyclark books.com*

I hope I see you in Whisper Creek,

Dorothy Clark

*Maggie Fillmore's late husband had one final wish—
that their unborn son would inherit their ranch. But when a
greedy relative threatens to take the ranch, there's only one
way Maggie can keep it: a marriage of convenience to the
new Pony Express manager, Clayton Young.*

Read on for a sneak preview of
PONY EXPRESS SPECIAL DELIVERY
by Rhonda Gibson,
available September 2017 from Love Inspired!

"Have you come up with a name for the little tyke?" Clayton Young asked.

Her gaze moved to the infant. He needed a name, but Maggie didn't know what to call him.

Dinah looked to Maggie. "I like the name James."

Maggie looked down on her newborn's sweet face. "What do you think of the name James, baby?" His eyes opened and he yawned.

Her little sister, Dinah, clapped her hands. "He likes it."

Maggie looked up with a grin that quickly faded. Mr. Young looked as if he'd swallowed a bug. "What's the matter, Mr. Young? Do you not like the name James?" She didn't know why it mattered to her if he liked the name or not, but it did.

"I like it just fine. It's just that my full name is Clayton James Young."

Maggie didn't know what to think when the baby kicked his legs and made what to every new mother sounded like a happy noise. "If you don't want me to name him…"

"No, it seems the little man likes his new name. If you want to call him James, that's all right with me." He stood and collected his and Dinah's plates. "Now, if you ladies will excuse me, I have a kitchen to clean up and a stew to get on the stove. Then I'm going into town to get the doctor so he can look over baby James." He nodded once and then left the room.

Maggie looked to Dinah, who stood by the door watching him leave. "Dinah, I'm curious. You seem to like Mr. Young."

Dinah nodded. "He's a nice man."

"What makes you say that?"

"He saved baby James and rocked me to sleep last night."

"He did?"

"Uh-huh. I was scared and Mr. Young picked me up and rocked me while I cried. I went to sleep and he put me in bed with you." Dinah smiled. "He told me everything was going to be all right. And it is."

Maggie rocked the baby. Not only had Mr. Young saved James, but he'd also soothed Dinah's fears. He'd made them all breakfast and was already planning a trip to town to bring back the doctor. What kind of man was Clayton James Young? Unfamiliar words whispered through her heart: the kind who took care of the people around him.

Don't miss
PONY EXPRESS SPECIAL DELIVERY by Rhonda Gibson,
available September 2017 wherever
Love Inspired® Historical books and ebooks are sold.

www.LoveInspired.com

Reward the book lover in you!

Earn points from all your Harlequin book purchases from wherever you shop.

Turn your points into *FREE BOOKS* of your choice
OR
EXCLUSIVE GIFTS from your favorite authors or series.

Join for FREE today at
www.HarlequinMyRewards.com.

Harlequin My Rewards is a free program (no fees) without any commitments or obligations.

MYR17